Christopher Hill

OFF THE ROPES

AUSTIN MACAULEY
PUBLISHERS LTD.

A CIP catalogue record for this title is available from the British Library.

ISBN:
9781784554514 (Paperback)
9781784554538 (Hardback)
9781784554521 (E-Book)

www.austinmacauley.com

First Published (2016)
Austin Macauley Publishers Ltd.
25 Canada Square
Canary Wharf
London
E14 5LB

CHAPTER ONE

The youth popped his head out of the shop doorway and peered down the street. It was clear that he was waiting for someone or something to appear.

Disappointed at not seeing what he had hoped to see, he ducked back inside.

Even though his outfit was almost thirty years out of fashion, he still wore it with a misguided sense of pride.

High-topped Doctor Martens, rolled up Levis, a white button down Ben Sherman and a black Harrington jacket. With a shaven head that made his ears stick out like Plug from the Bash street kids and the obligatory Nazi swastikas, etched into his neck in Indian ink, this unsavoury looking character been christened Martin by his parents, but now liked to be known as Johnny, after Johnny Quango, a black T.V. wrestler from the Kent Walton era, whose speciality was the head butt.

The difference between the two techniques, was that when Johnny Quango head-butted an opponent, his fellow wrestler would stagger around the ring, holding his head, pretending to be in pain. When Johnny the Skinhead head butted someone however, there was none of that playacting stuff. As Johnny was fond of saying, 'when he nutted someone, they stayed nutted'.

The other youth in the doorway with him was nowhere near as colourful. With shoulder length hair and dressed simply in jeans and a sweater, his name, if the letters tattooed on his fingers were in the right order, was Mike.

The two had been standing in the doorway for the best part of half an hour and Mike was beginning to get bored.

"How much longer is this going to take?" he asked, a whining tone to his voice. A few inches taller than Mike, Johnny looked down at him. "Not long now, so stop your whingeing. If you're bored, you can roll me a fag."

Mike tutted and thrusting his hand into his jeans pocket, pulled out a pouch of tobacco along with some papers and proceeded to make a cigarette.

Johnny put his head out of the doorway once more and did a double take, his eyes widening.

"Here he comes now," he said, over his shoulder.

Lighting the cigarette and blowing out a stream of smoke, Mike stood on tiptoe to look over the Skinhead's shoulder. His eyes opened even wider than Johnny's, but not for the same reason.

"Blimey! That's not him, is it?" he asked, sounding shocked.

"Sure is."

"I thought you said he was a pushover," said Mike, sounding even more anxious.

"He is," replied Johnny, not taking his eyes off of the figure walking down the road towards them.

"Yeah, but look at the size of him. He's bigger than both of us."

Reluctantly, Johnny turned away and glared back at Mike.

Are you done?" he snapped.

They stared at each other for a couple of seconds and then a wicked grin began to creep across the Skinhead's face. Reaching out, he patted Mike's cheek. He took his cigarette off of him, and took a long drag and blew the smoke out.

"Don't panic, he's a wuss."

6

It was an accurate if not eloquent description of Robert Kershaw. At a fraction under five feet eleven and with broad shoulders, it was true, at first glance, it did look as though he could be a bit of a handful, but the truth of the matter was that he wasn't.

At school, he had been taller than most of the kids in the school. Consequently, he was never picked on, never bullied, which also meant that he had never learnt how to defend himself.

This realisation hit him, in every sense of the word, when one of the boys from the rougher part of town decided to have a pop at him.

In front of what had seemed to Kershaw to be half the school, he wrestled ineptly, while the nasty boy beat ten bells out of him with his fists.

The fight, if it could be called that, ended with Kershaw running to the protection of the nearest teacher.

On returning home from school that afternoon, Kershaw's mother fussed over his black eye and swollen jaw, but getting home from work that evening, Kershaw's father, a lanky, bespectacled accountant, was less compassionate. As far as he was concerned, fights in the school playground were all part of growing up and his advice to Kershaw was to take a trip to the local boxing club and learn how to defend himself, should he ever get into another scrape.

He spent one evening, or to be more precise, one round, at the boxing club.

The coach there had a hard and fast rule. Anyone who came through his doors had come to fight.

He treated every potential new member the same - that is, he slapped a head guard on them, gave them a pair of gloves and shoved them into the ring.

It wasn't to see if they could box, but whether they had any fighting spirit. He could instruct them in the noble art, but the heart they had to find for themselves. He couldn't help but feel slightly dismayed, as he watched Kershaw's opponent, who was by no means the best fighter in the club, but a fighter nonetheless, systematically take Kershaw apart, whose only answer was to try and grab hold of the boxer, in an effort to stop himself from being used as a punch bag.

In all the time that he was in the ring, which had seemed to Kershaw to be an eternity, he never threw a single punch, whilst his opponent bobbed and weaved, hooked and jabbed.

Even before the allotted three minutes were up, the coach had no option but to pull Kershaw out, take him to one side and diplomatically suggest that he take up a sport more suited to his temperament, like ping pong maybe. Battered and disillusioned, Kershaw decided that rather than learn how to defend himself, the simplest solution was to just avoid all confrontations that came his way. For the most part it worked and when it didn't, well, he was a fast runner. This was due to the fact that he had taken up athletics as a sport.

After seeing all the members at the boxing club working out, he felt that he would like to take up a sport of some kind, but not ping pong, as the coach had so cruelly suggested. As athletics was a non-contact sport, he went for that.

The two disciplines that he excelled at were the one hundred metres on the track and on the field, the javelin.

It was almost as if, now that his body had stopped growing upwards, it was in need of something to start it growing outwards. Athletics proved to be the catalyst. As both events were power sports, the more he trained, the more his body developed.

Not only was Kershaw tall and well built, but he had also been blessed with good looks. Sadly, this had its drawbacks.

When he walked into a pub or club, he knew that the girls were checking him out, even if they were with someone at the time. Naturally, this tended to cause a certain amount of friction, not to mention ill feeling, but Kershaw knew which girls could be approached and which ones he should leave alone, a lesson he'd learnt a while back, the hard way.

He was in a disco one night, when he spotted an attractive girl, standing at the bar. As he liked the look of her, he walked on over and struck up a conversation. She seemed quite friendly, which was hardly surprising as Kershaw wasn't the kind of man a girl gave the cold shoulder to.

He thought that they were getting on quite nicely, but when her boyfriend returned from the toilet, he didn't see it that way. In fact, when he found a tall, much better looking man than himself, chatting to his girl, he found it so distressing that he chinned Kershaw, there on the spot.

Kershaw's initial impact on the girl, as it was on most girls, was such that she instantly switched her affections, calling her soon to be ex-boyfriend a mindless thug. Grabbing hold of a chair, in an effort to keep himself upright, although flattered, Kershaw wished that she hadn't done that. Judging by the expression on the man's face, things were about to get a whole lot worse, for him, at least.

Just then, two doorman appeared on the scene and when the girl told them that the little ugly one had thrown the first punch, they promptly showed her now ex boyfriend the door. After fussing over his bruised cheek for more than was really necessary, they spent the rest of the evening together.

When she finally decided to call it a night, the girl, whose name turned out to be Sandra, wrote her phone number on the back of a coaster, asking Kershaw to call her sometime, soon.

Shortly after that, he himself decided that he'd had enough. When he got outside, he found the ex-boyfriend waiting for him, hellbent on revenge for having had his girlfriend stolen off of him.

The moment Kershaw caught sight of him, he turned and fled. The boyfriend gave chase, but it was a non-event, ending up with Kershaw sprinting off into the distance, his would be aggressor up against a wall, gasping for breath.

So it went and then entered Johnny the Skinhead.

Kershaw was coming out of the local fish and chip shop with what was to be his supper. He was feeling extra hungry and had already unwrapped the parcel before he'd reached the door.

As he stepped out into the cold night air, the steam from the hot food rose up in front of him and his nostrils were assailed with the smell of hot grease and vinegar.

"Give us a chip, then," he heard someone say and out of the corner of his eye he could just make out a figure standing in the shadows. Not wanting to give away any precious supper, he carried on walking.

After spending countless hours brawling in gutters outside of pubs, or scrapping on the terraces at football matches, you learn to read the signs, to be able to tell who should be avoided and who could be exploited.

It was mostly to do with body language and Johnny could tell by the way Kershaw nervously glanced in his direction and by the way in which he walked with his eyes down, that he wasn't dangerous.

It was this, plus the fact that he was hungry, broke and didn't take kindly to being ignored, that Kershaw suddenly found the Skinhead blocking his path.

"I hope you haven't put salt and vinegar on those," said Johnny. "I hate salt and vinegar."

Illuminated by the light from the shop window, Johnny could tell by the look in Kershaw's eyes that he had read the signs right.

By the same token, even though he was taller than the Skinhead, Kershaw knew that it was still a gross mismatch.

Looking down at his fish supper, Kershaw decided that it would be a wise move to offer this nasty piece of work some of his meal, if he didn't want any more trouble. Looking back up, he caught the movement, but was too slow to react. Suddenly, there was a myriad of bright lights, a sharp searing pain above his left eye and he felt himself toppling backwards.

His backside thumped down onto the pavement and as he used his hands to prevent himself from falling any further backwards, the fish and chips spilled out of the wrapping, some onto his lap, some out onto the pavement.

"I can't eat those now, can I?" said Johnny. "You'd better go and get me some more."

Kershaw put his hand up to where his forehead was throbbing. He could feel a swelling, but at least there wasn't any blood, although it still hurt like hell.

He felt pretty certain that if he didn't do as he had been told, he was going to be in a lot more pain than he was at that moment.

Just then, a very fat, very sweaty chip shop owner walked out onto the pavement.

"If you two want to fight, piss off somewhere else and do it, not outside my shop." Johnny whirled round, all ready to redirect his violent nature on the Chip man, when he caught sight of ten customers, who could just as easily become ten witnesses to an A.B.H., watching through the large shop window.

Deciding to cut his losses, he turned back to Kershaw, still sitting on the ground. "I'll see you later, wanker," he threatened and kicking Kershaw's outstretched leg, he stormed off into the night.

Clambering awkwardly to his feet, the rest of his fish supper spilling all over the pavement, Kershaw was about to walk off in the opposite direction.

"And you can clear that lot up before you go, as well," ordered the Chip man, indicating the food on the floor and showing Kershaw precious little sympathy.

In front of the ten customers, who were still being entertained by this impromptu piece of street theatre, Kershaw picked up the fish and chips and along with the wrapping threw it all in the bin by the door.

Even though his head was splitting, his stomach was telling him that he still hadn't been fed. He toyed with the idea of going back into the shop and ordering some more fish and chips, but thought better of it.

He'd go for a Chinese instead.

That was a fortnight ago. Walking down the street at seven thirty in the morning, on his way to work, the bruise over his eye, much like the memory of the Skinhead had all but faded away.

Being Friday, he was deep in contemplation, trying to decide whether he should go in on overtime tomorrow morning.

Suddenly, a youth with long hair darted out from a shop doorway, bringing Kershaw out of his reverie and startling him.

Their eyes met for the briefest of moments and Kershaw got the impression that the short kid knew him, even though, to the best of his knowledge, they'd never set eyes on each other before this morning.

Turning back, Kershaw literally bumped into the Skinhead, who was blocking path just as he had been that night, outside the chip shop.

"Said I'd see you again, didn't l, wanker?" greeted Johnny, sounding pleased as punch.

"In fact, I've seen you a couple of times, walking down this road, same time each morning, in your own little dream world. So this morning, I thought I'd say hello."

Realising that the Skinhead must have materialised from the same doorway as the little guy a second ago, Kershaw glanced over his shoulder, to find Mike standing behind him, his arms hanging by his side.

As Kershaw turned back, Johnny nodded at Mike.

"I brought him along in case you tried to leg it."

As if one wasn't bad enough, there were two of them now. Kershaw knew that he was in double trouble.

CHAPTER TWO

"What do you want?" asked Kershaw, no more able to hide the tremor in his voice than he could the fear in his eyes.

"Well, the thing is, er...what's your name?" asked Johnny, sounding almost chummy.

"Robert," replied Kershaw, not sure where this was heading, but certain he wasn't going to like it when it got there.

"Well, the thing is, Robert, Bob, er, Bobby, I need some fags, but I ain't got no money, so I was wondering if you could lend me a fiver."

Kershaw glanced over his shoulder once more, to make sure that the little one was still there, which he was.

Kershaw turned back. "Lend? What, are you planning to give it back then?"

He regretted the words the instant they'd left his mouth.

The Skinhead's face turned as black as thunder and he peered over Kershaw's shoulder at Mike.

"You see what happens when you try to be nice?" said Johnny, his voice louder now. He looked back at Kershaw, the furious expression still on his face. "Let's put it another way. Give me a fiver, or I'll break your fucking nose!"

Kershaw couldn't help noticing that the Skinhead wasn't sounding quite so chummy as he had a couple of seconds ago.

He considered his options, which didn't take him that long. If he couldn't handle one, what chance did he have against two?

He knew what he should do, but instead he thrust his hand in his trouser pocket and pulled out a couple of five pound notes. He held one out to the Skinhead. Johnny snatched it out of his fingers and held it aloft, like a trophy, for Mike to see.

"Time for a smoke break," he said and laughed.

His eyes returned to Kershaw, who was still looking fearful, not sure whether this was over, or if the Skinhead had something else planned for him.

Johnny reached out his hand, causing Kershaw to flinch, then he patted his cheek, as he'd done to Mike.

"Cheer up, it's only money."

Kershaw imagined that this was meant to make him feel better. It didn't.

Johnny nodded at Mike to indicate that it was time to leave. As the pair of them walked away, Johnny said something to Mike. They both looked back at Kershaw and laughed.

As they turned the corner and disappeared from view, Kershaw was left standing alone on the pavement feeling, well, he wasn't sure what he was feeling, there were so many conflicting emotions running through his head. Anger, shame, relief that he was still standing.

One thing he was sure about though. He was going to have to find a new route to work.

Work was a large cash and carry warehouse on an industrial estate on the outskirts of Brentford.

Although there were a number of people employed to work inside the warehouse, there were only three who worked outside on the bay, unloading the articulated lorry that arrived every morning.

When Kershaw walked into the yard, one of the other two was sitting on the edge of the loading bay, his legs dangling down.

At twenty-seven, Andy Parkin was five years older than Kershaw and a good five inches shorter. An unruly mop of mousy coloured hair sat on top of a chubby face that matched his chubby body.

In the three years that Kershaw had known Andy, he had always been the joker, clowning around, keeping everybody amused and at times, irritated. He always had a cheery smile on his face, even when things weren't going his way.

Kershaw hoisted himself up onto the cold concrete next to him.

Andy smiled. "Hello mate, how are you, alright?"

Having just had five pounds taken off of him by what he could only describe as modern day highwaymen, Kershaw was feeling far from all right but he decided to keep the holdup to himself.

"Yeah, I'm fine, thanks," he replied, putting on a brave face.

It looked as though Andy was about to say something else, when the thick polythene strips that separated the warehouse from the bay, parted and the third member of the trio walked out.

Not to put too fine a point on it, Eddie Barker was a giant.

Not content with standing six feet five, he was also a bodybuilder. With a chest like the back of a Transit van, arms as thick as rugby posts and sporting a military style crew cut, he bore a striking resemblance to the comic book hero, Sergeant Rock.

Kershaw hopped to his feet as the huge man approached.

"Eddie."

"Bob," replied the big man, his deep booming voice seemingly adding to his stature, if that was possible.

Eddie wasn't what one would call a garrulous person, using one word where most people would use half a dozen, allowing his body to do the rest of his talking for him.

Scrambling up, Andy faced the giant, his head coming level with Eddie's chest.

The big man looked down at him and nodded.

"Squirt," he greeted.

Taking an enormous breath and puffing out what little chest he had, Andy imitated Eddie's baritone voice.

"Pussy," he replied.

Kershaw smiled to himself. The intellectual cut and thrust that went on between these two never failed to amuse him and he needed it more than ever this morning, to help rid his memory of that thieving Skinhead. Just then, the lorry began reversing into the yard. It contained yorks, metal cages on wheels, full up with everything from toilet rolls to tins of salmon.

By the time the three of them had unloaded the lorry, wheeled the yorks into the warehouse, unpacked them and wheeled them back onto the lorry, it was time for the first tea break of the day.

Being Friday, they picked up their wage slips on route to the canteen.

Upstairs, they were all sitting at the same table, Andy studying his wage slip, Eddie reading his copy of Flex and Kershaw staring out of the window at the road down below.

"Good job I did that spot of overtime last week," said Andy, to anyone who happened to be listening.

"It'll pay for me to get up to Nottingham this weekend."

Kershaw turned away from the window.

"Are you going up this weekend?"

""'Fraid so," replied Andy, detecting a note of sadness in Kershaw's voice. Over the past three years the pair had become close pals and they usually went out on a Saturday night to a club somewhere or other. These days' girls very rarely went out on their own, preferring to go around in pairs and in Kershaw's experience, they were harder to split than the atom.

One guy on his own didn't stand a chance, but two were much more likely to strike it lucky, especially if one of those was Kershaw, but it looked as though this weekend was going to be a non-starter

"Sorry mate," apologised Andy, "but this should be the last time I have to pay a visit to the wicked witch of the north."

This was a caustic reference to Andy's soon to be ex-wife, Carol. They had been married for almost six years and then she'd started seeing someone else, eventually moving up to Nottingham to live with him. This would be Andy's third trip and Kershaw knew just how much he hated going up there.

Their split had been far from amicable, in fact, if it had been any more acrimonious, they could well have ended up killing each other.

The man Carol had chosen over Andy was the director of his own successful company. They lived in a large house and Carol had since found herself a job up there. They wanted for nothing, whereas all Andy wanted was to be allowed to keep the house, but Carol wasn't playing.

"Ah, don't worry about it," said Kershaw, accepting the inevitable. "I'll find something to do. You never know, Eddie might want to come out for a drink tomorrow night."

Andy let out a short laugh. "Hah! Don't be silly. He'll be too busy down the gym, getting ripped."

He irreverently and in Kershaw's opinion, somewhat imprudently, tapped the cover of Eddie's magazine.

The giant lowered his periodical and stared at Andy blankly.

"Isn't that right, big guy? You wouldn't want to go out for a drink with Bobby tomorrow night, you'll be too busy, down the gym, pumping iron."

He comically made a classic bodybuilder's pose.

"NNNNGGG!" he grunted. "That's how it goes, isn't it?"

Eddie continued to stare at him for a few moments more.

"Don't talk like a twat," he growled and went back to reading his magazine.

Andy grinned at Kershaw and winked.

"He's got a way with words, hasn't he?"

"So what time are you going up?" asked Kershaw.

It was five thirty and he and Andy were standing at the gates in the yard.

Andy checked his watch.

"I'll give the traffic time to die down and get going about seven. Once I'm up there, I'll find myself a place to stay and get round first thing in the morning."

Kershaw could see that he wasn't looking too happy about it.

"This is a last ditch effort. Hopefully, if I spend all weekend working on her, not in the Biblical sense, you understand," said Andy, giving an involuntary shudder at the thought of becoming intimate with the woman whom he'd once loved, but now couldn't stand to be in the same room with.

"I could come back victorious." He made it sound as if he were going into battle, which didn't surprise Kershaw. He'd met Carol on more than one occasion and knew what she what she could be like.

"Well, good luck," said Kershaw, with feeling.

"Yeah, I'll see you Monday," replied Andy and turned to walk to his red Mazda.

After one step, he turned back.

"If this turns out okay, I'm going to be looking for a lodger. Do you fancy it? I mean, it's got to be better than that Wendy house you're living in at the moment, surely?"

Kershaw stroked his chin, thoughtfully.

"I dunno. It could cramp my style."

"What, all that shagging, you mean?"

Kershaw grinned. "Well, you know how it is."

"No, I don't, as it happens," replied Andy, wistfully.

"Let me have a think about it," said Kershaw.

"If you let me watch, you can live there for free. Let me join in and I'll pay you rent."

Kershaw laughed.

"Yeah, right. I'll see you Monday."

They said their goodbyes for a second time and Andy walked to his car, while Kershaw just walked.

He had owned a car once, a right old banger, that had eventually given up on him. What he really wanted was a place of his own, so rather than shell out for car tax, car insurance and the ever rising price of petrol, not to mention the cost of keeping the thing on the road, he used public transport.

If he went anywhere, he either took the bus, the train, or he walked. He never really went that far afield anyway and when he did, it was usually in Andy's car.

His precious little nest egg was growing all the time and unless house prices seriously went through the roof, he estimated that by this time next year, he'd have the deposit he wanted.

He was well aware that whatever property he bought, it wasn't going to be that grand, but at least it would be his.

The Wendy house that Andy had so disparagingly referred to, was a studio apartment in a large Victorian house that had been renovated.

The property developers had left the outside of the house the same, but had refurbished the interior, putting two apartments on each of the three floors, Kershaw's being on the second.

As studio flats went, it was nothing out of the ordinary. A kitchen area, shower and toilet and a sofa bed. The furniture wasn't up to much, either.

A dining table with two chairs that didn't match, a scratched coffee table and a very battered, but nonetheless, very comfortable armchair.

Apart from some videos, cd's and a couple of posters on the wall, the only thing that really said anything about the person who lived there was a statuette of an athlete, throwing the javelin.

Kershaw had won this in his last year at school. When he'd left, his games master had put him in touch with the coach of the local athletics club. After being put through his paces, the coach had told Kershaw, that as a sprinter he was mediocre, but with the javelin, however, he had potential. If he trained hard and listened to what the coach had to tell him, he could end up throwing for the county, maybe even higher than that. Kershaw trained hard and listened well, but then sex had raised its ugly head.

Every week the coach would ring Kershaw up to find out why he hadn't been training and every week Kershaw would come up with a reason, when all the time he was out chasing anything in a skirt.

Eventually, the phone calls stopped and since then, athletics had taken a back seat, or to be more precise, no seat at all. However, Kershaw still kept up the training regimen that the coach had set up for him when he'd first joined the club.

He had a very powerful body, but it wasn't huge. If the truth were known, Kershaw found people like Eddie grotesque, even ludicrous, although he hadn't mentioned this to the big man, for obvious reasons!

21

Kershaw had strength and power, he simply lacked the courage to use it. The first thing he did when he got in, was to change into a track suit and go for his run. It wasn't far, about a mile and a half, but it was enough to get his body properly warmed up, ready for the weights.

For this he needed two other things. One was a full-length mirror and the other was music, the louder the better.

He strapped on his cd player and slipped in a copy of AC/DC's Ballbreaker. With Brian Johnson and his mates screaming out Hard as a Rock, Kershaw picked up the weights and started on his triceps.

CHAPTER THREE

Forty minutes later, Kershaw stood in front of the full-length mirror, his body covered in a sheen of perspiration. He liked what he saw, although his stomach could do with more definition. That was something he was going to have to work on.

After a hot shower and a cold drink, he checked the television page in the newspaper. There was nothing on, or at least, nothing he wanted to watch.

There was an off license a few minutes walk away where he rented films, when the television was as dire as it was this evening.

He had to be up at seven tomorrow morning, so he didn't fancy a late night.

He'd pop down there and see if they had anything worth watching. Putting on a pair of jeans and a polo shirt and taking his leather jacket as it was getting chilly out there, he left the flat.

When he reached the off license, he looked over at the pub opposite. He'd never been in there, it didn't look up to much, not from the outside, at any rate. He made his mind up. He'd go in and have one pint.

If after half an hour, he was still on his own, he'd go across to the off license and rent himself a film.

Walking into the pub, he could see that the inside wasn't up to much, either. Decorated in black and brown, even with the lights on and the curtains pulled, the place still looked dingy. It had definitely seen better days, which in Kershaw's estimation must have been sometime during the war, although which war, he couldn't say for certain.

Two youths were playing on the pool table, one of the pub's concessions to the twentieth century. The other being a jukebox that hadn't been switched on.

An elderly couple sat in one of the corners, talking quietly to themselves.

Kershaw was about to forget about the pint and just get himself a film, when he spotted the girl on the other side of the room.

From where he was standing, she looked to be quite attractive.

All that was on her table were a handbag and half a glass of what looked to be white wine.

Maybe he would have that drink after all.

When he reached the bar, there was no one serving, which didn't surprise him.

It was hardly happy hour in here.

There was an open door behind the bar and he could hear someone moving around. That was okay. Waiting to be served would give any errant boyfriend, if in fact there was one, the time to show himself.

If by the time Kershaw had gotten his drink, the girl was still on her own, he'd go across and check her out.

He glanced across the room. She was studying a pink notebook of some kind. Kershaw turned back to face the bar. He heard the main door open and looked over his shoulder to see who had just come in.

He quickly turned back. The two men who had just walked in were not the sort of people you wanted to be caught staring at.

The first one through the door was about Kershaw's height, but not as broad. He had long, black, greasy hair tied back in a ponytail. He was wearing jeans and a white tee shirt, under a full-length leather coat.

Following him through the door, the second was a lot shorter, but much stockier. He too was wearing jeans and a white tee shirt, but underneath a green puffer jacket. He had cropped, ginger hair and the couple of days worth of stubble on his face still wasn't enough to mask the livid scar than ran from the corner of his left eye to just below his jaw.

The pair of them stood next to Kershaw at the bar, and he was again having second thoughts about that drink, but for a different reason.

These two were making him nervous.

Just then, a middle-aged man, who Kershaw assumed was the landlord, stepped through the open doorway, and took his rightful place behind the bar. "Right, who's first?" he asked.

"Two pints of Guinness," said the man with the ponytail, abruptly.

As the Landlord began pulling, Kershaw could feel Ponytail's eyes burning into the side of his head.

He was obviously waiting for him to speak out, to say that he should have been served first, but Kershaw wasn't saying a word.

He was keeping his mouth firmly shut and he certainly wasn't about to return the man's stare. He knew what eye contact could lead to and he didn't want any of that, not with these two.

He kept staring straight ahead at the optics in front of him, looking neither left nor right.

When the other two had been given their drinks, Kershaw asked for a pint of lager and moved away from the bar the second he'd been served.

He walked over to where the girl was sitting, still studying her pink notebook.

"Hi, my name's Bob. You look lonely. Mind if I sit down?"

As the girl slowly raised her head to look at him, Kershaw realised that he had made a mistake. She wasn't attractive, she was extremely attractive.

She was every portrait artist's dream, with perfect bone structure and a near flawless complexion.

The only make up that she appeared to be wearing was lipstick and a hint of green eye shadow, which helped to highlight her liquid brown eyes.

Her dark hair was cut short and brushed back behind pixie like ears.

Kershaw thought for a second that he detected a spark of interest in her eyes, but then it was gone, replaced by cold indifference. "No, I'm not lonely and yes, I do mind if you sit down," she replied brusquely, to both his questions.

Returning to her notebook was clearly her way of saying that the conversation, such as it was, was over.

It wasn't the first time that he had been knocked back and he doubted that it would be the last, although, when it did happen, which wasn't that often, it had to be said, he just moved onto another.

This was different. She was one of the prettiest girls Kershaw had ever set eyes on and with her hands in the position that they were, he could see that her ring finger was bare.

This girl was unattached, in the permanent sense.

The spark of interest that he'd seen in her eyes when she had first looked at him was an ember, which if blown on hard enough, would ignite.

He couldn't let her get away after just one attempt. He'd go back across to the other side of the room and if she was still there, on her own, after five minutes, he'd go back and try again and again, if that's what it took. As he turned to walk away, one of the lads on the pool table made a cracking shot, the sound of the ivory balls smashing together, echoing around the room.

Watching them play as he walked, Kershaw had only taken a couple of steps, when he bumped into something.

Looking around, he found to his horror that it was Ponytail.

"You blind fucker!" he swore at Kershaw. "Why don't you look where you're going?"

Some of the man's drink had spilled onto the floor, but more importantly, some had splashed onto the sleeve of his leather coat.

"I... I'm sorry," stammered Kershaw, realising that he could be in serious trouble here.

"I'll get you another drink."

"I think you'd better," said Ponytail, angrily shaking the beer off of his sleeve.

Kershaw knew that after he'd bought the man a drink, it was time for him to leave, girl or no girl.

He had taken one step towards the bar when Ponytail's pal, the one with the scar, placed an open hand on Kershaw's chest, stopping him in his tracks.

"You can get me one, as well."

He spoke with a Scottish accent and his voice was little more than a hoarse whisper, which had the effect of making him appear even more menacing than he undoubtedly already was.

Kershaw could see this for what it was, an out and out challenge.

Either he bought both of them a drink, for no other reason than that they were in the same pub at the same time, or they were going to punch his lights out.

Anyone walking in on this situation, with no knowledge of the three involved, would have thought it a pretty safe bet that Kershaw could have taken these two, or at least have given them a good run for their money, but that person would have been going on first impressions.

Kershaw's first impression was that he was about to throw up.

If he had been on Blackpool pleasure beach and had just passed the point of no return on the big one, his stomach couldn't have felt any worse that it did right then.

Standing there, facing these two, who were glaring at him, waiting for him to make a move of some kind, Kershaw could feel the fear spreading from his stomach down to his legs, which were beginning to tremble.

Being who and what he was, there was only one course of action for him to take. He put his hand in his pocket and for the second time that day, handed over money to save himself from a beating.

"That should cover it," he said and as he held out a ten-pound note, he could see that his hand was shaking.

All he wanted to do was to get out of there before these two decided that mere money wasn't enough to quench their thirst for violence.

As he turned to head for the door, Ponytail grabbed him by the arm.

"I see you in here again, I'll stop your fucking breath," he threatened.

Looking deep into his eyes, Kershaw didn't doubt it for a second.

Pulling away, he started for the door again at a brisk pace, which was why he failed to notice that the girl, who only moments ago had given him the cold shoulder, was now regarding him with more than a passing interest.

As the door closed behind him, he took a lungful of the cold night air.

He would have loved to have been able to lean up against the wall and allow his stomach time to come back down to Earth, but he wanted to get as far away from there as possible, just in case those two morons decided to come out and finish what they had tried to start.

He wasn't going to run, he wanted to leave himself with some vestige of dignity, but if they did come out, they wouldn't see him for dust. He was fifty yards down the road, when he heard the unmistakable clacking of stiletto heels behind him.

Guessing that it wasn't one of those two from back in the pub, he looked over his shoulder and was surprised to see the gorgeous girl who had shot him down in flames, running down the street towards him.

Assuming that she must be late for an appointment of some kind, he turned back and carried on walking.

So he was amazed when she fell in alongside him. Her breath was a little ragged, after her short jog in shoes that had been designed for anything but running.

"I'm sorry...I was so... rude to you back...there. I'm not usually like that.

Kershaw smiled at her. "That's okay, we all have off days."

He slowed down slightly, so that she didn't have to stride out like a soldier to keep up with him.

Her breath was beginning to settle down now.

"There's a nice place down the next street, or is it this street? No, it's the next one," she said, answering her own question.

"Why don't we go in there and start again? I promise that I won't be horrible to you again."

Kershaw told her that he thought that was a great idea and they crossed over the road. With her leading, he could tell, thanks to the tight skirt she was wearing, that she had a very shapely behind. This evening might not be a total disaster after all.

If she was talking about the place that he thought she was talking about, he'd been in there before and it wasn't bad, which made him wonder why he'd gone into that shithole of a pub back there in the first place.

Synchronicity, or whatever the Hell the word was, he thought to himself.

If he hadn't popped out for a film, he would never have gone into that pub and if he hadn't gone into that pub, she wouldn't be walking by his side now.

Things had a way of working out.

It wasn't a pub and it wasn't a wine bar, it was simply a place where people went for a drink and a good time.

It was beginning to get cold now and when Kershaw opened the door, he could feel the warmth from inside and not just from the temperature.

The place was crowded with people enjoying themselves and he was looking forward to joining them.

The combination of loud music and the cacophony of people shouting to be heard above it, meant that Kershaw had to lean close to the girl so that she could hear what he was saying.

"See if you can find us a seat and I'll get the drinks," he shouted.

"What would you like?"

She leant in and told him that she wanted a white wine and they went their separate ways.

It took him a while to be served, as it was so busy, but he wasn't bothered.

He felt comfortable in here; unintimidated.

The place was horseshoe shaped with a three sided bar at its centre. When he did finally get served, he seemed to spend ages wandering around with a bottle of lager in one hand and a glass of white wine in the other, until he found her, tucked away in a corner.

It was quieter here, for which Kershaw was thankful. It meant that they would be able to hold a conversation without having to shout at each other.

She smiled sweetly at him as he placed her drink down in front of her and sat on the opposite side of the table.

"My name's Penny, Penny Marshall," she said, holding out a delicate, perfectly manicured hand. Kershaw accepted it.

"Bob Kershaw. It's nice to meet you, Penny."

"It was very sensible, what you did back in the pub, not fighting with those two.

Walking away was the right thing to do."

Kershaw didn't have the heart to tell her that for him, there was no other choice but to walk away, except run, maybe. He simply nodded and left it at that.

"You live around here, do you Bob?" she asked, after taking a sip of her wine.

"Yeah, I've got a flat, a few minutes' walk away."

"That must be nice."

"Well, the furniture's a bit manky, but..."

"No, I meant that it must be nice to have a place of your own, your own independence."

There was a touch of sadness in her voice, mixed with what sounded to Kershaw like jealousy.

"You don't, I take it?"

Penny shook her head. "No, I still live with my parents. That's the reason why I was having a bad day, why I was so short with you. Parents can be awfully tiresome, don't you think?"

Kershaw smiled. Awfully tiresome. The majority of girls that he hung around with, when something annoyed them, it got on their tits, rather than being awfully tiresome.

Everything about Penny, the way she walked, talked, dressed, every move she made, pointed to her coming from a well to do background.

It wouldn't have surprised him to find that she had attended a public school.

She took another well-mannered sip of her wine, while he swigged from his bottle, trying not to dribble it all down his chin.

He didn't want her thinking that he was some kind of slob. This girl was going to require some subtle handling.

CHAPTER FOUR

"You don't have that problem, do you? Parents ruling your life."

The moment Penny had spoken, she put her hand to her mouth, a mortified expression on her face.

"I haven't said something terrible, have I? Your parents aren't dead, are they?"

Kershaw laughed.

"Very nearly, they live in Eastbourne. They moved down there a couple of years ago. They did ask me if I wanted to go down with them, but I had my job and I didn't fancy all that upheaval."

"Where do you work?"

"Do you know the cash and carry, down on the industrial estate?

Penny shook her head. Kershaw hadn't thought for one minute that she would. She didn't strike him as the sort of girl who would have a great deal to do with places like that. "What do you do there?"

"Nothing very exciting, I'm afraid," replied Kershaw, not wanting to bore the poor girl to death, with stories about baked beans and packets of washing powder. "What about you?" he asked. "What do you do for a living?"

"I'm a temp you know, working at different offices, covering for people who are ill or on holiday. I enjoy it, working with different people all the time, but Daddy says that I should find myself a proper job.

We're always arguing about it. We had another one this evening, before I came out. That's why I wasn't in a very good mood when you spoke to me."

The conversation fell silent as they both took a drink.

"I think it's only fair to tell you, I'm not looking for a man at the moment."

"Me neither," said Kershaw, seriously.

Penny looked at him, reproachfully.

"You know what I mean. I'm not looking for a serious relationship at the moment and I don't want you thinking that us being here together could lead to something."

Kershaw's conquest meter went on to red alert.

Whenever a girl he'd taken a fancy to, told him that she wasn't looking for a man, he knew it was time to begin his campaign, his war of attrition, to wear them down, until they finally gave in to him.

He hadn't lost one yet and he certainly wasn't going to lose this one.

Penny wanted to have a relationship with him, she just didn't know it yet, but she soon would.

They chatted about one thing and another, until looking at her watch, Penny told him that she had to leave.

Opening her handbag, she took out the mysterious pink notebook.

"Why don't you give me your phone number?" she said, taking a small pen out of the spine of the book.

"I thought you said that you weren't looking for a man at the moment?" he asked.

He knew she would cave in eventually, but this was ridiculous. "Just because I'm not looking for a relationship at the moment, doesn't mean that I can't enjoy some meaningless, gratuitous sex, does it?"

Kershaw grinned.

"Certainly not," he replied.

He reeled off his number and she wrote it down, shut up the notebook and replaced it in her bag."

"Thank you for the drink, Bob, I've enjoyed this evening," she said, standing up.

"You can't stay a little longer?" asked Kershaw, sounding disappointed.

"No, I've got a train to catch."

She patted her handbag. "Maybe I'll call you sometime."

Kershaw got to his feet." Maybe I'll answer it," he came back.

Penny smiled, stood on tiptoe and kissed him gently on the lips.

"I'll see you soon," she said, making it sound as if she'd already made plans.

He watched her leave, hoping that she wouldn't leave it too long.

Penny shivered slightly as she walked out into the cold night air and pulling her jacket closer around her body, she started walking. After about twenty yards, she looked back. Seeing no one behind her, one person in particular, she took a mobile phone out of her bag and dialled a number, walking as she was waiting for the connection. When she heard the voice on the other end of the line, she glanced behind her once more.

"Hello? Yes, I'll be at the train station if you want to come and pick me up."

She listened to the person on the other end.

"Okay, oh and by the way, I think I've found what we're looking for." Kershaw worked until one the following morning and all the while, he had Penny on his mind. She was gorgeous and she was available, despite what she had told him. He just wished he'd gotten her number, but he got the feeling that she wouldn't have given it to him even if he'd asked.

She was obviously playing the game by her rules. He fell asleep in front of the television in the afternoon and was woken by the phone ringing.

He was surprised to her Penny's voice on the other end.

"Hello Bob? It's Penny, from last night?" there was a question in her voice, as if she thought that he might have forgotten her. Not much chance of that!

"Hi, how are you?" he asked.

"I'm fine, thank you. I was wondering if you had any plans for tomorrow evening?"

Kershaw couldn't help but feel a little disappointed. He had been looking forward to the thrill of the chase, hunting down his prey, so to speak, but it looked as though she wasn't going to provide him with any sport, or maybe she just wanted to string him along for a while longer.

He made out he was trying to remember if he had any plans.

"Er, nothing, l don't think. Why?"

"My parents are going out for the evening and was wondering if you'd like to come round for a drink."

He didn't want to come across as too enthusiastic, but an image of them engaged in an act of meaningless, gratuitous sex, was causing his heart rate to rise.

He tried to sound offhand.

"Um, yeah, okay. Where do you live?"

"Do you know the Silvermere estate?" asked Penny.

Kershaw was expecting something like that.

Every city and almost every town has an area that you don't wander into, unless you have a big dog with you, better still, two big dogs and failing that, a baseball bat stuffed up your jumper. By the same token, most places have an area that is slightly more upmarket.

Kershaw knew, from time spent checking out estate agent's windows, wondering what property he was going to buy, when he'd eventually raised the deposit, that you couldn't purchase a place on the Silvermere for less than five hundred thousand, but it was rumoured that if you wanted to be considered as a true Silvermere resident, it would cost you a damn sight more than that!

Situated midway between Twickenham and Richmond, he had passed it on the bus a few times and had always wondered what sort of people lived there.

It looked as if he was going to find out.

"You live there, do you?" he asked. He had tried to mask the inflection in his voice, but Penny picked up on it.

"That's not a problem, is it?"

"Not at all," he replied, shaking his head as if she were there with him.

"It's just that it tends to put people off, when I tell them where I live."

"Not me, I'll go anywhere."

Penny laughed.

"Okay then, if you go in the main entrance, the first road on your left is Robin Hill Drive and the first house on the right is mine, Whispering Pines."

"And does it?" he asked.

The line went silent as Penny pondered his seemingly unanswerable question.

"Does it what?" she asked, after a couple of seconds.

"Have whispering pines?"

Penny laughed again.

"I really couldn't say. Is eight o'clock alright?"

Kershaw told her that eight would be fine and that he was looking forward to seeing her. They said their goodbyes and he put the phone down.

So, all he had to do now, was to keep himself occupied until tomorrow evening. He wasn't going to go out, so he ordered himself a pizza over the phone and settled down for an evening's television.

Kershaw looked on Sunday as his day of rest. He normally rolled out of bed around ten, had a shower and went for the Sunday papers.

This was, of course, subject to him having spent the night in his own bed.

Sometimes, even he had trouble keeping track of whose bed he was sleeping in on any given weekend.

His relationships never seemed to last very long. When it came to women, he was like a child with a new toy. Once he'd unwrapped it, seen how it worked and played with it for a while, he became bored and wanted to play with something else. His capricious attitude had broken many a poor girl's heart, but it had never seemed to bother him.

After he had read the papers from cover to cover, it was time for lunch.

He couldn't see the point of slaving over his two-ringed hob, only to produce something totally inedible, when it seemed that almost every pub these days, served up tasty, home cooked Sunday roasts, for less than it cost him to buy the ingredients from a supermarket and then incinerate them. He went to the same pub every Sunday, not just for the food, but also for the company.

Kershaw only knew him as Clive. They had shared a table there, one Sunday, got chatting and now had their lunch together regularly, when they were both there, that was.

After a ten minute walk, Kershaw had worked up an appetite and was looking forward to his grub.

Even though the pub was busy, as it was most weekends, Clive wasn't hard to spot, his snow white hair standing out like a beacon in a sea of black and brown.

Clive was reading a newspaper when Kershaw walked up to his table, pulled out a chair and plonked himself down.

Clive looked up and seeing who it was, smiled.

"Hello Boy, how are you?"

His white hair seemed to make his tanned, weather beaten face appear even darker, so much so, that it almost matched the hue of his intelligent, hazel eyes.

Kershaw wasn't sure exactly how old Clive was, but he estimated him to be in his late forties, even his early fifties, maybe.

At a fraction over six foot and with a large chest and wide shoulders, Kershaw imagined that in his prime, Clive must have been quite a handful, not that he still wasn't.

It wasn't just the man's physique that led Kershaw to this conclusion.

When Clive wore a short-sleeved shirt, as he was now, his arms kind of gave it away.

On his right bicep was tattooed the wings of the Parachute regiment and on his left, the insignia of the Special Air Service.

Because of how old Kershaw imagined Clive to be, he guessed that he could possibly have served in the Falklands, probably the Gulf and almost certainly Northern Ireland.

Kershaw knew that not every S.A.S. operation made it into the newspapers, or onto the television. As Clive tended to be tight lipped concerning his military career, not shouting about it from the rooftops, for all he knew, he could have even been one of the team that stormed the Iranian embassy.

The bottom line was that Clive only allowed people to know what he wanted them to know, making him a bit of a mystery man. "Yeah, I'm fine, thanks," replied Kershaw.

"Are you eating?"

"You bet," said Clive, enthusiastically. "I've already ordered."

"I'd better go and get myself some as well," said Kershaw, his stomach rumbling so loudly, he was sure the people on the next table could hear it.

Getting to his feet, he picked up Clive's empty glass.

"You want a refill?"

"Yeah, I'll have a pint of lager, thanks."

Up at the bar, Kershaw ordered a roast lunch and two pints to take away.

Their meals arrived a couple of minutes apart from each other and they both tucked in, hungrily.

"Are you watching the match this afternoon?" asked Kershaw.

"What's that, football?"

Kershaw nodded.

Clive pushed his empty plate to one side and snorted.

"Nah! That's a poof's game. One crack on the shins and they're rolling around on the floor crying their eyes out. Rugby Union, that's the game."

Kershaw wasn't too surprised that Clive liked that game. He'd always maintained that to be any good at that sport, you had to be a cross between a masochist and a homicidal maniac. He felt sure that Clive fitted the bill.

"You used to play, I take it?"

"Yeah! Used to play for the Army. We had a pretty good team, as it happens."

He gave a wry smile.

"Although, to be honest, more blood was spilt off the field than on it," he said, adding credence to Kershaw's homespun philosophy on the psychological makeup of the average rugby player.

"We were in Cyprus one time, I'll never forget it. A few of us were having a drink in this bar, when a Turk comes over and spits on the floor in front of us. Well, we're all entitled to our opinion, but then he pulls out this knife and starts waving it about. So Dingo gets up..." Kershaw felt that he had to interrupt.

"Dingo? What, was he Australian?"

Clive shook his head and smiled.

"No, we called him that because he was like a wild dog."

Kershaw nodded. Seemed fair enough.

"Anyway, Dingo gets up and instead of trying to get the knife off of him, he grabs hold of the blade."

Kershaw looked suitable amazed.

"This threw the Turk and while he was trying to figure out what his next move should be, Dingo broke his nose with his other hand. Then he took the knife off of him."

"Didn't he cut his hand?" asked Kershaw.

Clive shook his head and held out one of his own large hands and drew an imaginary line across his palm.

"He had the imprint of the blade on his hand, but if he had gone off half cocked, if he hadn't have held that knife as tightly as he did, then yes, he probably would have been sliced. I'd never seen anyone do that before, but then Dingo was one crazy individual."

Crazy or not, it still took a lot of guts to do something like that. I wouldn't advise you to try it," Clive said it in a matter of fact sort of way, rather than an insult.

Either way, it was academic as far as Kershaw was concerned.

If anyone ever pulled a knife on him, he'd be down the road faster than a gazelle with a rocket up its ass!

CHAPTER FIVE

With his stomach full, when Kershaw returned to his flat, he tried to stay awake, watching the football, but nodded off halfway through.

When he awoke, it had just gone six o'clock. Being the expert he was on the local public transport, he knew that the bus would get him there too early, making him appear too keen, whereas, with a five minute walk from the station, the train would get him there almost on the dot.

After tidying up, he took a shower and tried to work out what to wear. In the end, he went for the smart, but casual look, black trousers, red checked shirt and his beloved leather jacket.

Ten minutes later, he was on the platform, studying a poster advertising the major tourist attractions London had to offer, most of which he had never seen. He heard laughing and shouting and glancing down the platform, his heart missed a beat.

The Skinhead and his short assed little sidekick had just run onto the platform. The fact that he was near the end of the platform and that they were looking in the opposite direction, meant that they hadn't spotted him, yet.

He knew that if they did, he might not make it to Penny's house, or if he did, his face probably wouldn't be looking the same as it was right now. Realising that he was standing directly outside the door to the gent's toilets, he dived inside. Leaning up against the cold, tiled wall, he could feel his heart thumping within his chest. He was suddenly struck with an awful thought. The train was due in very shortly. What if they were still on the platform when it arrived?

Not a problem. He'd hear the train when it arrived. As soon as it stopped, he'd run from one door to the other. It would be so quick that they wouldn't have time to recognise him.

Just as he believed he could relax, he was hit by another thought.

What if they were here to get on the same train as him?

He was only going to be on for two stops. He'd find a way to avoid them.

His heart was beginning to return to something like its normal rate, when he heard the Skinhead's voice, getting louder and closer.

"I need a slash!" shouted Johnny.

Kershaw looked about him, frantically.

Taking three large strides, he reached one of the two empty cubicles. He stepped inside, closing and bolting the door behind him.

He wasn't a moment too soon. As he snapped the bolt across, he heard the main door open and footsteps on the floor.

"Christ! I need this!"

"What are we doing here?" Kershaw heard someone say. The voice made him jump, as it came from right outside the door. As he had never heard him speak, Kershaw assumed that it must be the little one.

"Well, l don't know about you, but I'm having a piss," replied Johnny.

Kershaw remembered seeing the other cubicle door slightly ajar. If the Skinhead's pal leant on his door, he'd know that someone was in there. He wouldn't put it past these two to have some fun with whoever was in the toilet.

When they discovered that it was him…

"Let's go down the café," said Mike. "You can tilt his pinball, he always gets the asshole when you do that." It sounded as though he was desperate for something that would relieve the boredom of this quiet Sunday evening. If they found him in here, they'd think that Christmas had come early.

Kershaw leant his head against the wall and with his eyes closed, said a silent prayer for them to leave.

Someone up there must have been listening.

"Yeah, why not," he heard the Skinhead say.

There was the sound of a zipper and then footsteps. The door opened and closed, leaving the room silent. Kershaw held his breath for a few moments longer, then let out a heavy sigh.

He unbolted the door and looked out on an empty room. As he walked to the door, he caught his reflection in the mirror on the wall.

What he had done back there was a true act of cowardice. He knew that, but what else could he have done?

Looking at the reflection staring back at him, he couldn't help thinking what Clive would have made of it, him cowering in the toilets from those two. Ah, bollocks! he thought to himself. We can't all be heroes and he walked to the door.

Peering out, he saw that the platform was deserted. As he walked out, he still had Clive on his mind.

As much as he admired the man, he knew that he could never be like him. We are what we are and that's the end of it, he thought to himself. The important thing now was to get on that train and show this Penny sort that there's more to being a man than having nerves of steel.

Craning out over the platform, he spotted a yellow dot in the distance. Standing back up, he remembered what the little shit had said about the cafe. Kershaw knew which one they were talking about: It was the only place in town, outside of the amusement arcade, where a pinball machine could be found.

He made a mental note to avoid the place at all costs!

When he got on the train, the carriage was empty. A couple of moments later, two girls walked through the adjoining door from the next carriage. They hadn't been on the platform when the train had pulled in, so he guessed that they must be walking up and down the length of the train in search of a seat that they liked the look of.

That seat was across the aisle from him.

He glanced over at them. Dressed in their best glad rags, they were attractive, in a tarty sort of way. One had straight blonde hair, the other curly brown.

Kershaw guessed they were about his age, possibly slightly younger.

The one sitting nearest him, with the blonde hair, returned his glance and there was a mischievous twinkle in her eye. She leant over and whispered something in her friend's ear and she too looked over at him and smiled.

Most men would say that Kershaw was one lucky son of a gun, looking the way he did, but there were times when he found it a curse; like now.

He knew that all he had to do was to go over and sit next to them and he would end up going where they were going and in the morning, he would still be with one or the other, or even both!

The train pulled into the next station, along another deserted platform. He looked across at the two girls again. It was Penny that he had come out to see and even though neither of them could hold a candle to her, they were still an awful temptation.

The train pulled out and Kershaw tried to keep looking out of the window in an effort to keep them out of his mind, but it didn't work. Glancing quickly over, the blonde one was still looking at him, the unspoken invitation still there.

Just then he felt the tell-tale jerk, as the train's brakes were applied, coming to his rescue. Getting up out of his seat, he began walking to the end of the carriage. As he passed the two sirens, they both said goodbye.

He smiled and said goodbye back.

Out in the vestibule, as the train pulled into the station, his hand hovered over the door handle.

They would be a lot less work than Penny, he was sure about that. Steeling himself as the train came to a halt, he opened the door and stepped out. As the train pulled away, leaving him alone on yet another empty station platform, he checked his watch. A slow walk from here to the Silvermere estate would get him to Penny's door almost dead on eight o'clock. It was dark now and the two monolithic pillars on either side of the road leading into the estate, were lit up, as if marking the boundary between the haves and the have-nots.

As Kershaw walked between them, a white van pulled in off of the main road. It carried the logo of a private security company on the side. There were two security officers in the front and as the van passed Kershaw, the guard in the passenger seat stared hard at him.

"It's all right, mate," Kershaw muttered under his breath. "I'm expected."

Turning into Robin hill drive, he walked alongside a line of what he guessed were very tall, whispering pines. The line was broken by a sturdy five bar gate.

Opening it, he let himself in, turned and closed it behind him.

The streetlights helped him to see a very impressive looking house, as he crunched his way down the gravel drive.

Suddenly, he was blinded by two incredibly strong security lights, one at either end of the house. He was unable to see a thing in front of him, but he heard a door open.

"I'm sorry about the lights," shouted Penny. "Daddy had them put in. They're a bit of a nuisance. Hello? Can you see me?"

Kershaw couldn't see a damn thing.

"No, but I can hear you," he told her.

His eyes began to adjust to the brightness and as he got closer to the house, he was able to make out Penny, standing on the porch.

The fireflies had stopped dancing before his eyes and he could see her clearly now. She was wearing a tight red sweater, the porch light overhead, casting a shadow underneath her more than ample bosom.

As he got closer, Kershaw could see that she was wearing what appeared to be spray on jeans, they were that tight.

He stepped up onto the porch.

Penny stretched up and kissed him on the cheek.

"Hello. How are you?"

"Better, now that I've got my sight back," he replied.

"Yes, they are rather intense, aren't they?"

"Just a little."

"Come in," invited Penny, standing to one side.

He walked past her and she peered out into the darkness before following him inside and closing the door behind her.

"Where have you parked your car?" she asked.

"I haven't got one."

Penny seemed a little surprised.

"You haven't got one? What, not at all?"

He shook his head. "Nope."

"How did you get here tonight?"

"By train. That's how I get around, train, bus, or I walk."

"How quaint," said Penny.

Kershaw wasn't sure whether she was being sarcastic or polite, so he just nodded.

"This is very nice," he said, looking around him.

He was standing in a large, semi-circular hall, with white marble beneath his feet and a large chandelier above. Directly in front of him stood a stone plinth, on which rested the bust of someone he was sure he had seen somewhere before, but couldn't put a name to.

The hall had four panel doors leading off of it, all magnolia with crimson piping.

A large staircase ran up the left side of the hall and all the way across and he could see another four doors leading off of the landing. "Thank you," said Penny, walking towards the second door from the right.

"Let's go in here," she said and opened the door, again standing aside to allow him to enter.

"Daddy calls this the blue room," she told him. "As you can see, he's somewhat lacking in imagination."

The room was roughly about the size of Kershaw's flat, with sky-blue walls and white coving.

Looking down, he saw that he was walking on a deep blue carpet that was about the same thickness as his duvet.

The furniture consisted of a two seat, leather sofa with a matching armchair. There was a much less scratched and much more expensive looking coffee than his, standing between the two seats and underneath were what appeared to be copies of Country Life.

The smell of freshly polished leather filled the room.

"Would you like a drink?" Penny asked him. "As you're not driving, how about a beer?" He told her that a beer would be fine and she left the room, telling him that she wouldn't be long.

There were a couple of etchings scattered about and on the wall facing him, a painting, which like the bust in the hall, he knew he'd seen somewhere before, but as art wasn't one of his specialist subjects, he blanked it.

He squeaked himself into the double sofa. If, when Penny came back, she sat in the armchair, then it could be a slow night, but if she sat next to him on the sofa, the sofa made for two, then things could start popping.

Penny came back into the room a few minutes later, carrying a glass of beer in one hand and a tall glass containing something creamy with a froth on top in the other.

Kershaw got a warm feeling in his groin, when she sat next to him on the sofa, their shoulders touching. She handed him his beer.

"Thanks. What's that?" he asked, nodding at her drink.

"It's a snowball. I love these, but I can't have too many, because they make me go all squiddly."

He tried to conjure up an image of Penny, losing her inhibitions and getting squiddly, as she put it. That would be something to see, he thought to himself.

"Cheers," said Kershaw and took a mouthful of beer.

"So, do you have a car?"

"Yes, I've got a Mini," she replied.

"Mm, nice cars in their day," said Kershaw, trying to sound as if he knew what he what he was talking about.

"No, one of the new ones," she corrected him. "Daddy bought it for me for my birthday."

Kershaw almost choked on his beer.

"Your father bought you a car for your birthday?" he asked, incredulously.

Penny nodded, as if it were nothing out of the ordinary.

"Blimey! He must be a great bloke to have as a Dad."

Penny didn't look as if she agreed.

"He can be, sometimes and in other ways, he can be very annoying. He hates the way I dress for example. Take this jumper," she said, pulling it down tight, making her breasts appear to be even larger than they already were.

"He hates this jumper. Can you see anything wrong with it?" she asked, thrusting herself out at him.

Kershaw wanted to say that the only thing wrong with it was that she still had it on, but managed to bite his tongue. Instead, he shook his head.

"Looks fine to me," he told her.

"He says that I dress like a tart. He thinks that the proper length for a woman's skirt is around the knee. I told him once, that most nights, my dress is around my knees. Mummy thought it was quite funny, but he went ballistic. It's always best to bring a man around when he's not here. He likes to check them out. It can be quite embarrassing."

"Just sounds like Daddy looking out for his little girl," said Kershaw.

There was a short pause while they both took a drink.

"Do you remember how our conversation ended, last night?" asked Penny, putting her drink down on the coffee table in front of them.

He was hardly likely to forget it!

"Didn't it have something to do with meaningless sex?" he asked.

Nodding, she reached underneath the sofa and brought out a book. Kershaw managed to catch the title; The A to Z of loving.

Penny opened the book at a page that had the corner turned down and held it out for him to see.

"I thought we might try this," she suggested, sounding for all the world as if she were choosing wallpaper.

Kershaw found himself looking at a photograph of a naked couple engaged in what he could only describe as something bordering on an unnatural act.

"Yes, I can see that could be a, urm, challenge," he said, searching for the right word.

"Good." Penny snapped the book shut and standing up, held out her hand to him.

"Let's go upstairs and see if we can't do it better than them."

CHAPTER SIX

An hour later, Kershaw lay on a king-size bed, with just a sheet over him.

He was exhausted.

He had thought Penny would be fit, judging by her figure and the way she moved generally, but it turned out that he had misjudged her.

Her level of stamina was almost as high as his and at one stage, he actually thought that she was going to overtake him.

Her lovemaking had been ferocious in its intensity and lying there now, for the first time in his life, he hoped it was over.

Penny padded barefoot out of the en suite, wearing his shirt, which came midway up her thighs.

She sat on the edge of the bed next to him and crossed her legs. The movement caused his shirt to ride up, revealing a tiny tattoo of a butterfly at the top of her thigh.

Kershaw touched it with his finger.

"That's nice," he told her.

She glanced down at it. "Yes, l like it, but Daddy hasn't seen it yet. He will, in the summer and when he does, he'll probably order me down to the hospital to have it removed. He's covered in tattoos, but I know he'll be horrified to see that I've got one as well. At one stage, I was considering having a stud in my mouth."

Kershaw grinned at her. "You just have."

It took a moment or two for his comment to register and when it did, she slapped him on the shoulder.

"Don't be so disgusting!" she rebuked.

She pulled the sheet down to reveal his abdominal muscles.

"Mmm, I like these, though," she purred and patted his hard stomach, as if she were patting a horse.

"It takes a lot of hard work to get those," he told her," And even more to keep them, but I'm sure I don't need to tell you that, do I? You must do some kind of exercise to be as fit as you are."

She nodded. "I go to a gym two or three times week."

"What do you do there?"

"Oh, all kinds of things."

She pushed herself up off the bed. "Have a shower, if you want one. I'll go down and make us some coffee," she said, giving Kershaw the impression that she was eager to change the subject.

Fifteen minutes and a shower later, Kershaw came downstairs and the aroma of freshly brewed coffee led him into the kitchen.

If he had thought that the blue room and the bedroom that he had just come out of were large, then the kitchen was enormous.

Penny was wearing a dressing gown and his shirt was draped over one of six chairs placed around a large oak table.

Putting it on, he couldn't help wondering what sort of work could afford someone all of this.

"What did you say your Father does for a living?"

Penny handed him a steaming hot cup of coffee.

"I didn't. There's sugar and milk on the table," she told him.

"He sells things," she said, pouring herself a cup.

"Things?"

"Well, diamonds, actually."

Kershaw nodded. Makes sense, he thought to himself.

"So there's a living to be made out of it, then?" he asked jokingly.

Penny smiled. "Oh, we get by," she came back.

She looked up at the clock on the wall. It had just gone ten o'clock.

"What time is your train? I'd give you a lift to the station, but my car's in having a service."

Kershaw's shower hadn't revitalised him as much as he'd hoped. He was still feeling tired. He guessed that he must be out of practice. He didn't want to ask Penny if she felt tired, she might well take it the wrong way, or the right way, depending on how you looked at it.

"I don't feel like taking the train back," he confessed. "I think I'll get a taxi. Can I use your phone?"

"It's over there," she told him, pointing to the wall. "There should be a number for a taxi firm on the board."

The phone on the wall was next to a large pin board, which was covered in business cards, everything from accountants to window cleaners. Casting an eye over it, Kershaw found what he was looking for.

"Five minutes," he told her, replacing the phone in its cradle.

They finished their coffee and Kershaw put on his jacket which Penny had brought into the kitchen.

He walked over to her and put his arms around her waist, pulling her towards him.

"I really enjoyed myself tonight," he told her.

"So did I."

"Perhaps we could do it again. Not right now, I mean, but soon."

"Well, I'm usually quite busy during the week, what with one thing and another. I'll call you, okay?"

It wasn't the response he was hoping for, but he guessed that it was the best he was going to get. He was about to tell her that he hoped she did call him, when there was the sound of a car crunching its way down the drive.

Penny turned to look out of the kitchen window.

"It's your taxi," she told him and taking his hands away from her waist, she made her way out into the hall, Kershaw following behind.

"I'll see you soon, I promise," she said and kissed him tenderly on the lips.

Kershaw felt that this was a little surreal. Normally, it was the other way around, the girl wondering when she was going to see him again.

He was getting a taste of his own medicine, and he wasn't enjoying it.

He didn't want to appear clinging, so he decided to leave it at that.

"Yeah, I'll see you soon," he told her and walked out of the house and into the waiting taxi.

It wasn't until he was off the estate that he realised that he had used her phone and that the house number had been printed on the cradle on a small piece of card.

He should have memorised it and then he could have called her. Damn!

Back in the kitchen, Penny watched the taxi pull out of the drive, its tail lights disappearing behind the row of trees.

She took the phone off of the wall and dialled a number.

"Hello? Yes, he's just left. Well, he's okay. I told you, I'm not doing this with someone who's ugly and has bad breath."

She listened to the voice on the other end of the line.

"What, now? Well, I am feeling a little tired."

She let out a short laugh. "I expect you could. Alright, give me twenty minutes, okay?"

Replacing the receiver, she hurried upstairs.

Five minutes later, one of the twin garage doors hummed open and a red Mini Cooper shot out, scattering gravel in all directions.

The garage door closed as the car shot out of the drive and disappeared into the night.

Sitting in the back of the taxi, Kershaw was relieved that he hadn't made a note of Penny's number, after all. He'd never made a fool of himself over a woman before and he wasn't about to start now. If he had her number, he'd call her.

He wouldn't be able to help himself.

He decided to take the philosophical approach. If she called, she called and if she didn't, she didn't. He just hoped she would.

He was almost asleep when the taxi reached his flat and after paying the fare, he had to use the bannister to haul himself up the stairs. The evening's activity had definitely taken it out of him. Sex was obviously a lot more demanding than the weights, or at least it was the way Penny went at it!

After cleaning his teeth, he didn't even have the energy to undress. He just lay down on the bed and went straight to sleep. The following morning, sitting on the edge of the loading bay, he still felt a little drained, but he was sure he'd pick up as the day wore on.

Andy walked into the yard, whistling a happy tune. Scrambling up next to him, he looked at Kershaw.

"Blimey, mate! You've got eyes like bulldog's bollocks! Heavy night, was it?"

Kershaw thought about the previous evening.

"You could say that," he mumbled. "What about you? How was your weekend?"

A smile spread across Andy's chubby face that was big enough for both of them.

"I got it," he proclaimed, triumphantly.

"You did? How did you manage that?" asked Kershaw, remembering how negative Andy had sounded, when they had parted on the Friday.

"Well, it was down to Colin, really."

"Oh, it's Colin now, is it? What is it you normally call him 'the ferret'?"

"Yeah, I know," admitted Andy. "But as it turns out, he's not such a bad bloke, after all.

Alright, he's shagging my wife, but he's only got himself to blame for that, but I got the impression that he's been in the position I was in, sometime in the past.

Anyway, he talked to Carol and eventually, she caved in. All I have to do now is sign the paperwork and the house is mine. Great, eh?"

"I'm pleased for you," said Kershaw, sounding genuine, although he couldn't help feeling a little bit jealous.

Andy now had what he wanted, a place of his own. Kershaw knew that he'd get one, he just wished he didn't have so long to wait.

"So what about last night? What were you up to?" asked Andy, eagerly.

Eddie walked out onto the bay at the same time as the lorry began reversing into the yard.

"I'll tell you upstairs," said Kershaw and hopped down. Up in the canteen, Kershaw hardly had time to take a mouthful of his tea, before Andy was all over him, like a rash.

"Come on, then. What happened?"

"I met this girl..."

Andy clapped his hands, gleefully. "I knew it! No one turns up looking like you did, without it having something to do with sex."

"I met this girl on Friday night. We had a chat and a drink and then she phoned me up Saturday, said that her parents were going out for the evening on Sunday and would I like to go round there for a drink."

"Where does she live, then?"

"On the Silvermere," said Kershaw.

Andy let out a short whistle. "Lots of money, eh?"

"And the rest."

Just then, the pair of them thought that they were witnessing a total eclipse, but it was Eddie passing the window to get to his seat.

"Here Eddie, Bobby's pulled himself a rich sort off the Silvermere estate."

Eddie placed a massive hand on Kershaw's shoulder, inadvertently causing him to dip to one side.

"I'm very happy for you, Bob," said the giant and taking his seat, proceeded to read his magazine, the conversation over, as far as he was concerned.

Not so Andy.

"Well, what happened?"

"We went into this study, reception room, call it what you like and we were just chatting and then she brings out this book."

Andy looked as though his world had just fallen apart.

"A book?" he said, sounding disgusted. "What, a War and Peace sort of book?"

Kershaw shook his head. "No, a men and women shagging sort of book."

Andy's lascivious interest was rekindled in an instant.

"What, with pictures and things?"

Kershaw nodded again. "Yeah, with pictures and things."

"Cor!" was all Andy could manage.

"Then she opens it at this page and there's a photograph of this couple going at it and I mean, really going at it."

Andy's jaw was almost on the table and if his eyes opened any wider, Kershaw felt certain they would drop out.

"Then she says, let's go upstairs and see if we can do it better than them."

It was obvious that Andy couldn't believe what he was hearing.

"You jammy bastard."

"I'll say," said Kershaw, feeling very pleased with himself. "Not only is she rich and good looking, but she's a sexual athlete into the bargain."

"Never mind about her," said Andy, dismissing Kershaw's eulogy of Penny Marshall with a wave of his hand. I want to hear more about this book!"

The week passed uneventfully, a little too uneventfully as far as Kershaw was concerned.

Every evening, he hoped that Penny would call, but his phone remained stubbornly silent.

On Saturday, he and Andy went to a nightclub in Twickenham. They'd been there a couple of times in the past and had decided to pay it a return visit.

When they got there about ten thirty, it was quiet, the pubs still hanging on to the majority of their customers.

They were at the bar, having a pint.

"That rich sort hasn't called you then, since last Sunday?"

"What makes you say that?"

Andy snorted. "Well if she had, you wouldn't be here with me, would you?"

Kershaw didn't reply.

"You know what I think?" asked Andy.

Kershaw looked across at him.

"What do you think?"

"I think that she was just using you as a rich girl's plaything. A sort of…dildo with muscles."

Kershaw had to smile, even though, deep down, he had to admit that Andy was probably right.

"Forget about her. You never know, we could meet a couple of librarians here tonight. Think how many books they could come up with."

Kershaw laughed and Andy gave him a playful punch on the shoulder.

"Attaboy! You know it makes sense. I'm going for a wizz. Be back in a jiffy."

Kershaw was still smiling to himself after Andy had walked off to the toilet. The chubby little twat was right again, he should forget about her.

She did to him what he'd been doing to women for as long as he could remember and that was all there was to it.

He looked around him. The place was beginning to fill up. There would be plenty of girls here tonight for him to chase after. Penny Marshall was history. When Andy returned from the toilet, he seemed to be bubbling over with excitement.

"I just got a smile from a bird over there," he said, pointing vaguely over his shoulder.

"She's with a mate. Let's go over there."

Kershaw had to grab him before he disappeared.

"Whoa there, Kimosabe! What does her mate look like?"

Andy looked at him, sheepishly.

"Well… I only saw her from the back, but she seemed alright."

"Quasimodo probably seemed alright from the back," said Kershaw, not relishing the thought of spending the evening with an ugly girl, no matter how nice a personality she had.

Andy looked terribly disappointed and Kershaw found himself feeling sorry for him.

"Okay, here's the deal. We go over there, but if she turns out to be one butt ugly bow wow, you buy the drinks for the rest of the evening, yeah?"

Andy looked at him, suspiciously.

"You're drinking lager, yeah?"

Kershaw nodded.

"You're not going to switch to treble scotches, all of a sudden, are you?"

Kershaw laughed.

"No I'll stay on the lager," he assured him.

Andy considered it for a second or two.

"Okay, let's go," he said, suddenly and he was off.

CHAPTER SEVEN

The club was spread out over two levels, each level having a dance floor, a seating area and two bars. The girl Andy had his eye on was on the upper level.

After having climbed the half a dozen or so carpeted steps, Andy stopped and looked back at Kershaw. The music was a lot louder up here and Andy had to shout to make himself heard "She's over there, next to the pillar."

Kershaw looked to where Andy was directing him. The girl sitting alone at the table was a little on the plump side. Andy probably saw her as some kind of soul mate, he thought to himself. She had a pleasant face, with dark hair, cut in a straight line all the way around.

It made her look a little frumpy, as did the long frock she wore, which rather than lessen her fuller figure, seemed to accentuate it. If he had to choose a word that would best describe her, it would have to be plain. But Andy was smitten with her.

"Shall I go over and ask her if she wants to dance?"

"Unless you're thinking of using telepathy, that would be the best thing to do."

Andy made a face, as if he were telling Kershaw that he was a little rusty at this sort of thing and for him to stop taking the mickey.

Just as Andy began to make his move, the other girl returned to the table and Kershaw was pleasantly surprised to see that she looked quite attractive.

She was tall, but not skinny. Wearing black trousers and a white, sleeveless blouse, he could see that she had a very healthy figure. She had a thinnish face and long, dark curly hair.

She was the sort of girl that he could quite easily spend the evening with.

Damn! He was going to have to buy his own drinks!

He watched as Andy walked up to the table, leant down and spoke to the girl.

She smiled, nodded and stood up. As they walked towards the dance floor, Kershaw approached the table, patting Andy on the shoulder as he passed, to let the other girl know that they were together.

She shot Kershaw a quick glance, as if to let him know that she was expecting him to come over.

He came around behind and stood by the side of her chair. He could tell that she knew he was there. He leant down.

"They make a lovely couple, don't you think?"

She looked up at him. It wasn't very well lit where they were, but even so, when she turned her face towards him, he could see that she was quite pretty.

"Shall we join them?" he asked.

She nodded and they walked onto the floor, next to Andy and his partner, all four of them unaware that they were being watched.

They spent about ten minutes dancing, until the D.J. played a tune that none of them liked and they all trooped off, back to the girl's table.

The introductions had been made on the dance floor, above the noise of the music.

The plump one was called Clare, the tall one, Angela.

The boys asked them if they would like a drink and after taking their order, made their way to the bar.

They found themselves a space and were waiting to be served.

"Her name's Clare," said Andy. "What do you think?" He wanted Kershaw's approval.

He nodded.

"Yeah, she looks nice."

Andy seemed quite proud and was about to speak, when a man barged in between them, gave Kershaw a withering glance and then turned to Andy.

"You're dancing with our birds," he said, angrily.

Andy looked confused.

"Excuse me?" he asked.

"I said, you're dancing with our birds," repeated the man, sounding more indignant than before.

"You come swanning in here, like you own the fucking place, we go for a piss and when we get back, you're dancing with our birds."

Kershaw looked over his shoulder. Standing a few yards away was another man and Kershaw got the feeling that he was waiting for the action to start and then he'd come wading in.

Kershaw could see what was happening, even if Andy couldn't. These two were looking for a fight, the two girls being an excuse. They might have tried it on with them and been told to get lost, he didn't know, but that wasn't the issue here.

For these two morons, a good night out meant a few beers too many and a scrap and he and Andy had been selected for this evening's entertainment.

These two couldn't be reasoned with, they couldn't be bargained with and it was no use apologising. They hadn't done anything wrong.

Even if he and Andy walked off, that wouldn't be the end of it. They'd follow them around the club, dog them all night, if need be, until they thought that the time was right, then they'd start the fight themselves if he and Andy refused to be provoked.

He could feel the anger welling up inside of him. He'd come here for an enjoyable night out and these two were determined to spoil it for him.

That pissed him off.

If he was going to be thumped, and it was definitely looking that way, it should at least be for a reason. So Kershaw decided to give him one.

"I think you're making a mistake," he said, to the back of the man's head.

He whipped round to confront Kershaw.

"Do what?" he snapped.

His face was covered in acne scars. Even though Kershaw was taller, he still felt afraid, facing up to him.

He recalled a Sunday morning, when he had been having lunch with Clive.

The ex-soldier had just finished recounting a story that had left Kershaw slack jawed, as did most of his tales. Kershaw asked him if he ever got scared.

"Course I do," Clive had replied, surprising Kershaw, as he didn't think Clive had a scared bone in his body.

"Everybody does," he continued. "It's what you do with that fear that counts. If you allow take you over, it'll turn you into a blubbering heap and then you're no good to anyone.

But if you control it," he said, making a grasping action with his fist, as if the fear he was talking about were a tangible entity. "Harness it, make it work for you, it can turn you into a different person. You can do things you never imagined."

Kershaw hadn't been quite sure that he'd understood, but standing here, now, he did.

He could feel the fear and knew that it could take him over in the blink of an eye, if he let it.

He didn't want to give this spotty faced wanker the satisfaction. He had to be brave.

"I said, I think you're making a mistake."

"How the fuck do you work that out?"

"They can't be your birds, as you put it."

"Why not?" snapped Spotty.

Kershaw shrugged.

"Because I can't imagine any girl wanting to be around an ugly looking asshole like you."

Staring at the man, Kershaw suddenly saw the anger in his eyes disappear, to be replaced with what appeared to be uncertainty, almost as if he thought he'd bitten off more than he could chew.

No one had ever looked at him that way before, as if he were a threat.

The man's uncertainty only served to fire his confidence, so much so, that Kershaw found himself imagining that he could take him on.

He was about to give him another mouthful of abuse, to bolster his self assurance and to make sure he wasn't reading it wrong, when an enormous hand appeared between them, clasped itself around Spotty's jaw and slowly turned his head away from the bar.

Both he and Andy followed suit, to find Eddie standing behind them, dressed in a black tuxedo and bow tie.

Eddie shot a glance over his shoulder, at Spotty's pal, who, quite wisely, had taken a couple of steps backward, either in an attempt to disassociate himself from what was happening, or more likely, to give himself a better chance of getting away, if the giant suddenly turned on him.

Eddie turned back to Spotty and leant down, so that their noses were almost touching.

"If I thought for one moment, that you two were causing trouble," he rumbled, "I'd have no option but to ask you to leave. That is, of course, after I've taken you into the bog and kicked the living shit out of you."

Kershaw was impressed. For most people, that would have been a sentence, but for Eddie it was a monologue.

Andy, who a couple of seconds ago, had been looking understandably nervous, rested his chin on Eddie's massive forearm and gazed up at him.

"I think you'd better let him go, big guy, he looks like he wants to go to the toilet."

It was true, Spotty was looking somewhat peaky, but finding himself under threat from the Incredible Hulk's big brother probably had something to do with it.

Eddie released his crushing grip, leaving two large white areas on either side of Spotty's jaw, where the blood had run for cover.

"Get out, both of you," he ordered.

Neither Spotty nor his pal had to be told twice. They were gone in an instant.

Eddie looked at his two workmates.

"So, you two having a good time, or what?" he boomed.

"Yeah, it's a hoot," replied Andy.

Kershaw didn't speak right away. Just for a second or two, he couldn't help feeling that he'd been somehow cheated, but then the reality of it hit him and he knew that if he had have tried it on with Spotty, he probably would have received a hammering.

"I didn't know you did this sort of thing," said Kershaw. "I didn't see you when we came in."

Eddie looked skyward.

"I was upstairs. The boss likes to have someone with him when he's doing the wages."

"Do a lot of this stuff?" asked Kershaw.

Eddie shrugged his huge shoulders.

"Now and then," he replied, reverting to his normal taciturn self.

Turning away from the bar, he looked around the club.

"Better circulate."

"Yeah, skulls to crush, ribs to crack, eh?" said Andy, grinning.

Eddie turned on him.

"I'm not a violent person, got that dipshit?" he growled.

Andy shrank back.

"Okay, Big guy just joking."

Eddie shot a quick glance at Kershaw, who saw his top lip twitch, which he knew for Eddie passed as a smile.

"I'll see you on Monday," he said and wandered off.

Standing at the bar, Kershaw could tell that Andy was staring at him. He looked across.

"What?"

"I thought you were going to stick one on that bloke," said Andy.

"That's not like you."

Kershaw realised that Andy was right, it wasn't like him, but for one fleeting moment back then, he had imagined that it could be.

"I guess he just pissed me off," said Kershaw, an explanation that seemed to satisfy Andy.

Just at that moment, Clare and Angela walked up.

"Was there some kind of trouble with those two men?" asked Clare.

"Why, do you know them?" Kershaw asked her.

"No," replied Clare, indignantly, clearly shocked that he could even have thought that they would have anything to do with a pair like that.

"They came up to us earlier, before you arrived," said Clare "They were very rude."

"Well, you don't have to worry about them now, they're gone," piped up Andy.

Clare slipped her arm inside his. "My hero," she crooned.

Kershaw couldn't be certain, not in this light, but it looked as though Andy was blushing.

After they had been served, rather than returning to the table in the dark, with the music blaring out next to them, they moved to a quieter, better lit area, where they could hold a conversation without having to scream at each other.

In the light, Kershaw saw that Angela's hair was chestnut brown, rather than black.

She had green eyes and just the hint of some freckles across the bridge of her nose.

It turned out that the two girls were nurses, currently working at the local A & E department. They had a lot of stories to tell, mostly humorous and nearly all to do with dead bodies.

Their black humour was a release valve, they told the two boys. When you deal with death or serious injury on a day-to-day basis, you can't dwell on it. Their way of dealing with the trauma of it all was to make light of it. Kershaw couldn't fail to notice that as the evening wore on, Andy and Clare were getting closer and closer, in every sense.

In fact, if they sat any closer together, she would have been on his lap.

Angela, on the other hand, although she seemed friendly enough, gave Kershaw the impression that she was keeping her distance, almost as if she didn't trust him.

Outside, at the end of the evening, they were saying their goodbyes.

Angela and Kershaw were standing together next to Andy's car, while Andy and Clare were draped over the bonnet of hers.

"Is that the kiss of life he's giving her?" asked Kershaw, finding it difficult to keep his eyes off of the pair of them.

"It's certainly the kiss of something," replied Angela.

"They seemed to have hit it off alright, don't they?" he asked.

"I'm glad," said Angela.

"She's had a hard time of it, these last few months. Her mother died not long ago and then she got involved with a man who started knocking her about. She deserves some TLC."

Andy seems really nice."

"He is."

Angela looked at Kershaw. "What about you?"

"What about me?"

"Are you nice, as well."

He thought about it for a moment.

"I'd like to think so, yes."

Turning to face him, Angela draped her arms around his neck.

"You'd better be," she warned. "My mother's Irish and I've inherited her temper.

I've got one Hell of a right hook."

"I'll remember that."

"Make sure you do," said Angela and then she kissed him, passionately.

Not as passionately as Clare was kissing Andy mind, the pair now almost engaged in full blown sex, over the bonnet of her car.

"Angela seems alright," said Andy.

He and Kershaw were in the car, on their way home, only after he had managed to prise Andy and Clare apart, before they got themselves arrested for public indecency.

"Yeah, she is."

"Are you going to see her again?"

Kershaw realised that he hadn't thought about Penny once, since meeting Angela.

"Yeah, probably," he said.

Andy grinned." I was hoping you'd say that."

"Why?"

"Because Clare's going to fix up a date for the four of us. Should be good, huh?"

"Yeah, sounds like it could be fun."

CHAPTER EIGHT

Kershaw had just returned with the Sunday papers and as he was closing the door, the phone began ringing. He smiled to himself. Andy had arranged to take Clare out for the day. It was probably him, ringing up for some advice.

It had been a long time since he'd taken a woman out.

Picking up the receiver, he got a surprise.

"Hello, Bob? It's Penny. How are you?"

"Er, I'm fine thanks," he replied, momentarily lost for words.

Then his surprise turned to truculence.

"I thought you might have called me during the week," he said, unable to hide the resentment in his voice.

"I told you that I was going to be busy. You're not angry with me, are you?" she asked, sweetly.

There was a voice in Kershaw's head, screaming at him to tell her that it was over, that he was seeing someone else, which as it happened, was very nearly true, but that wasn't what came out of his mouth.

"No, not really. I was just hoping that you'd call."

"Well, never mind, I'm calling now. Have you got any plans for today?"

That voice was there again, telling him to say yes.

"No," he replied.

"It's going to be a lovely day, I thought we could visit Hampton Court."

"Hampton Court?"

"Yes. Have you ever been there?" she asked.

He had never visited a stately home in his life, although he had stood outside Buckingham Palace once. In all honesty, if had to compile a list of places to visit, Hampton Court would not have been at the top, in fact, it probably wouldn't have been on the list at all.

"No, l can't say that I have," he told her.

"You'll enjoy it," she said, with a great deal more enthusiasm than he had right at that moment. His idea of old houses with gardens meant pubs with hanging baskets, but if that's what it was going to take to spend the day with her, then Hampton bloody Court it was.

"How are we getting there?" he asked.

"Well, if you tell me where you live, I'll come and pick you up."

Kershaw told her his address and how to get there.

"It's ten thirty now, shall we say an hour? Is that okay?"

He told her that an hour would be fine and that he would see her then.

If he'd had a big stick, he would have beaten himself up with it, he thought, after putting the phone down. Why didn't he just tell her that he didn't want to see her? Because he would have been lying, that's why. He put the newspapers down. He'd read them when he got back. He made himself some breakfast and took a shower.

Deciding that he ought to try and smarten himself a bit, rather than jeans, he put on a pair of beige Chinos and a green polo shirt. Wearing a pair of brown shoes, he checked himself out in the mirror. Did he need a jumper? It was quite warm out there, so he left it at that.

He checked the time. It was only eleven fifteen and he was already to go.

As it was such a pleasant day, he thought he'd wait outside.

By the time eleven thirty had come and gone, Kershaw was becoming anxious.

Anxious and annoyed.

There was no way he was going to be left standing in the street by a girl, no matter who she was.

Just then, a red Mini Cooper pulled into the road. Penny waved at him through the windscreen as she pulled up.

He jumped in and she turned the car around.

"Sorry I'm late," she apologised. "I got held up. I did try phoning, but there was no answer."

"It's such a nice day, I thought I'd wait outside," he told her.

"You probably don't own a mobile either, do you?"

"I've never felt the need for one," he told her.

"I don't think I could survive without mine," she said, glancing across at him and then back to the road ahead.

Kershaw tried to imagine someone not being able to survive without a mobile phone, but couldn't.

"We'll have to get you one," she told him.

"We will?"

"Yes and then we'll never be out of touch."

Kershaw liked the sound of that.

He stole a quick glance at her, while she was concentrating on the road.

She was wearing stilettos that matched her short red skirt that had become even shorter, now that she was sitting down, showing off nearly all of her shapely legs.

As usual, she was wearing little or no makeup. Being in the car with her now, he no longer wondered why he had agreed to see her. The answer was obvious.

When they crossed the Richmond Bridge and turned into the entrance to the Court, Kershaw was surprised to see how busy it was.

There were a few large, fluffy clouds in the sky that had the affront to block out the sun from time to time, but for the most part, it was a lovely warm day.

After spending the best part of an hour, wandering around inside the Palace, Kershaw had to grudgingly admit to himself, and to Penny, when she asked, that he had found it quite interesting.

Gazing at paintings that were bigger than the wall of his flat, furniture that was even more distressed than his coffee table, but obviously worth a damn sight more, as were most of the things and of course, the bed, used by the great man himself.

Kershaw guessed that it must have been at least twelve feet high, with plush velvet drapes that reached down to the floor.

"Imagine the fun you could have in there, with the curtains drawn," said Kershaw as they stood there, admiring the enormous piece of furniture.

"And no one would know who you had in there with you," said Penny, adding to the fantasy.

"Or how many," tacked on Kershaw.

"Trust you," said Penny, reproachfully.

Outside, they bought themselves a sandwich each and a can of drink to share.

They sat on the grass, in the warm autumn sunshine.

After they'd finished, Penny got up and taking the sandwich wrappers and the empty can, she walked over to the waste bin.

Returning, she stood in front of him, her legs appearing even more attractive to him, from his vantage point down on the grass.

"Come on," she said, holding out her hand to him. "Let's go in the maze."

After wandering around aimlessly for fifteen minutes, Kershaw was becoming increasingly more frustrated and he noticed that he wasn't the only one.

He seemed to be constantly passing people he had seen only a few minutes previously, heading in the opposite direction.

One person in particular, a woman in a tight blue tee shirt, with enormous breasts and nipples that were standing out like J.C.B. valve caps. She smiled at him every time they passed and he couldn't help feeling that he had come to know those nipples intimately, at least, he would have liked to.

Penny, on the other hand, rather than becoming frustrated, seemed to be thoroughly enjoying herself, giggling every time they came to a dead end. "That was fun," she said, when they eventually found the exit.

"Fun? I don't call wandering lost in a giant bush, fun," said Kershaw.

He leant over and whispered in her ear. Penny looked shocked.

"Now that's what I call fun," he said, grinning.

"I couldn't do that, not in there!"

"Course you could. You could pretend that you were kneeling down, tying your shoelaces."

Penny looked down at her stilettos.

"But I haven't got any shoelaces."

Kershaw considered this for a moment.

"Yes, that would be a bit of a giveaway, wouldn't it?"

"Do you want to come up for a coffee?" asked Kershaw, after Penny had pulled up outside his flat.

"That would be nice," she replied. "I'd like to see where you live.

"It's not quite what you're used to, but its home," he told her as they got out of the car.

Climbing the stairs, he couldn't remember whether he had tidied up or not, before he left that morning, but he was relieved to find, when he opened the door, that the place wasn't looking too bad.

He stood aside to allow her to enter.

"Welcome to Chez Bob," he announced.

"Oh, this is quite nice," said Penny, looking around her.

Having visited her house, Kershaw knew that she was just being polite, but he didn't want to embarrass her by asking want she really thought.

"Take a seat," he invited, pointing to the armchair. "It's tatty, but it's comfortable.

He filled the kettle and switched it on.

"So how long have you lived here?" she asked, sinking into the chair.

"A couple of years. It's got everything I need, it's close to work..." He gave a little shrug.

"It suits me fine."

Penny was looking confused. She'd never seen the inside of a studio apartment.

"You haven't got a bed."

He walked across to the sofa. Thanks to a couple of years practice, with one deft movement, it became a bed.

"Ooh, magic," Penny cooed.

Getting up out of the armchair, she walked over, sat on the edge of the bed and putting a hand into each of his trouser pockets, pulled him towards her.

She looked up at him, seductively.

"Is there anything else here that's likely to spring out?"

When Kershaw arrived at work the following morning, Andy was already there, standing on the loading bay, his hands in his pockets, looking very pleased with himself.

Kershaw climbed up onto the bay, next to him.

"So how did it go yesterday?" he asked, although, judging by Andy's chubby, beaming face, he guessed he already knew the answer.

"Great!" confirmed Andy.

"Did you take her back to your place and show her your collection of Razzle mags, you know, the ones with all the pages stuck together?"

Andy made a face.

"Very funny," he said, testily. "I bet I had a better time than you. What did you do? Go down the pub I suppose?"

"Actually I went to Hampton Court."

Andy looked bewildered, knowing Kershaw as well as he did.

"Hampton Court," he repeated, just as Kershaw had done, when Penny had suggested that they pay it a visit.

Just then, the lorry began reversing into the yard.

"Yeah, I went there with Penny" said Kershaw and jumped down off of the bay.

"You went to Hampton Court with that posh bird?" asked Andy, when they got up to the canteen.

"Yes, she rang up yesterday morning and away we went."

Andy had been full of the joys of spring, first thing that morning, but he wasn't sounding quite so perky now and Kershaw knew why.

He knew that Andy had been hoping that they would go on regular dates with Clare and Angela, as a foursome, but now with Penny still on the scene, he knew that wasn't going to happen.

"What, didn't she have anything better to do?" asked Andy, his voice spiked with malice for a girl he'd never met.

Kershaw desperately wanted to explain to Andy what it was about Penny that made her so special, but he knew that he wouldn't want to hear it.

"She said that she had been busy" he told Andy in her defence.

"What about Angela? Are you going to see her again?"

Kershaw shrugged. "Don't know. We're not going to fall out over this, are we?" he asked.

Andy's shoulders sagged ever so slightly and the harshness left his face.

"Na, I just think you're a fucking idiot that's all." Penny had made some flattering comments about his body, the previous day, so when Kershaw got home that evening, he was feeling inspired.

He wanted to look good for her, if he ever saw her again, that is.

After his run, he put on a ZZ Top album; Eliminator. With Dusty Hill and the boys, sounding like four flat tyres on a muddy road, grinding out 'Gimme all your lovin', he put even more effort into his workout than usual. He ached slightly the following morning, but he knew that it was for a good cause.

When he got up to the canteen for the first break of the day, he found that Andy had beaten him to it and was sitting at their usual table, reading a pamphlet.

"What are you reading?" he asked, after waiting a few seconds for an acknowledgement of his presence that never came.

Without taking his eyes off of the booklet, Andy raised it up, so that Kershaw could see the front cover. It was a pamphlet on courses at the local technical college.

"What, are you thinking about going back to school to get an education?" asked Kershaw.

Still without taking his eyes off of the book, Andy raised his middle finger in an obscene gesture.

"Oh, that's nice," said Kershaw. "Not the sort of thing I'd expect from a mature student."

Unable to concentrate with him babbling away, Andy put the book down.

"They're running evening classes on DIY."

"What do you want with that stuff?" asked Kershaw.

"The Viper chose most of the wallpaper in the house and it's crap. There's even some of that furry stuff."

"Flock."

"Whatever, Anyway, I can't wallpaper for toffee, so these people," said Andy, waving the booklet at Kershaw," Are going to teach me. It'll be cheaper than getting somebody in."

"Blimey! I didn't think you were allowed sharp objects."

"You can laugh, mate," said Andy, ignoring Kershaw's taunt.

"In a couple of weeks, I'll be papering like an expert."

Kershaw laughed. "You're joking, aren't you? It'll be like Norman Wisdom meets Mr. Bean."

"You wait. By the time I've finished, you'll be begging me to let you move in."

Andy allowed his statement to hang in the air expectantly, waiting for Kershaw to say something about lodging with him. It never came. After training hard for two evenings, on

Wednesday, Kershaw was struck down with a severe case of apathy.

He didn't feel like doing much, which was exactly what he did.

By seven thirty, he was bored with the television and decided to give Andy a ring to see if he wanted to go out for a quick pint.

"Sorry mate, I can't," he apologised. "I've got my first class tonight. If I don't turn up, I'll get the cane."

Kershaw laughed. "Ah well, never mind. I'll see you tomorrow." After he put the phone down, he remembered that Clive had told him that the pub where they had their lunch on Sundays was his local.

He'd pop down there. If he wasn't in there, he would just come back and if he was, well, it had to be better than sitting around here.

CHAPTER NINE

Twenty minutes later, Kershaw walked into the pub where he had his Sunday lunch.

He'd never been in there during the week and was surprised to find that it was every bit as busy as on a weekend.

Even though it was crowded, Clive wasn't difficult to spot, as he was right in front of him, sitting on a stool, facing the bar, his brown leather jacket spread tightly across his broad shoulders.

As he walked towards him, for some inexplicable reason, he looked over to his right and received a shock.

Sitting at a table in one of the corners, were the two he'd had the run in with the night he'd met Penny, the one with the ponytail and his scar faced ginger pal.

Kershaw's first thought was to turn around and walk back out.

Judging on the looks on their faces, they would probably follow him, but that wouldn't be any problem. The moment he got out of the door he'd be off and there was no way they would be able to catch him.

Just then, Clive happened to turn around and spot him.

"Hello boy, how are you?"

Kershaw knew that there was no way he could walk out now, but if there was going to be any trouble, he couldn't think of anywhere he'd rather be standing, than next to Clive.

As he walked over, he had another look to his right. They were still watching him.

He knew that they were there and now they knew that he knew.

Standing beside the ex-soldier, Kershaw felt a little more secure, but now that he knew that those two were there, he found it difficult to keep his eyes off of them.

Every time he glanced over, they were both staring at him.

He felt someone poke his shoulder.

"I said, what do you want to drink?" asked Clive. He looked at Kershaw curiously.

"Are you alright? You seem a bit out of sorts."

Kershaw knew that the situation couldn't go on as it was.

There's a couple of guys over there that I had a bit of an argument with a while back," he said nodding his head in the direction of the table.

"You think they might want to have another go?" asked Clive.

Kershaw nodded.

"Well, why don't we go ask them" he said, with a gleam in his eye.

Kershaw wasn't sure that this was such a good idea, but Clive was off before he had a chance to voice his concerns.

He followed on behind, his heart beginning to flutter.

Clive stood in front of the table and looked down at Ponytail.

"You got a problem," he asked, calmly.

Smiling, Ponytail looked over Clive's shoulder at Kershaw.

"Who's this, your Grandad?"

Clive laughed.

"Grandad? If I was going to be a Grandad, I'd rather it was to him," he said, jerking his thumb behind him at Kershaw, "Than to a worthless piece of shit like you."

The smile was wiped off of Ponytail's face in an instant and he lunged up out of his seat, aiming a punch at Clive.

The ex-soldier was ready for him. He blocked the punch with his left arm, grabbing hold of the man's wrist as he did so. At the same time, he brought up his left hand and put it around Ponytails throat. He moved it up a fraction and placed his thumb and forefinger up underneath the man's jawline.

The effect was instantaneous. Ponytail stopped dead in his tracks and the fury that had been in his eyes was replaced by a combination of pain and terror.

Pain because Clive's thumb and index finger were putting pressure on nerves that were situated under the jaw and terror, because at the same time as Clive pushed up, he also squeezed in, closing the man's windpipe, stopping his breath.

Watching this, Kershaw thought it quite ironic, as that was exactly what Ponytail had threatened to do to him.

Clive began to move forward and Ponytail had no option but to move with him, the pain so intense, it destroyed his will to struggle. Clive kept on moving until he backed Ponytail up against the wall.

It was at this point, that Ginger began to get up out of his seat, his hand inside his jacket pocket. Watching, Kershaw just knew that he was going to pull out a weapon of some kind.

Clive had his hands full, literally and Kershaw knew he couldn't just stand by and watch him try and handle both of them, especially now one of them was armed.

He had to do something.

Kershaw stepped forward and as Ginger was standing upright, he thrust the heels of both his hands into the man's chest.

Kershaw had always known that he was powerful, he just didn't know how powerful until now. It was as if Ginger were taking part in a horizontal bungee jump.

He shot backwards, tripped over a chair and then slammed into the wall, the impact knocking the wind out of him, forcing him to drop the Stanley knife he had just pulled from inside his jacket. It clattered to the floor and span away underneath the next table.

When the couple sitting there saw this, they scrambled out of their seats and moved back out of the way, not wanting to get caught up in what was happening.

With little or no breath left in his body, Ginger slid down onto the floor and stayed there.

Kershaw looked to his right just in time to see Clive release his grip on Ponytail's jaw and smash his huge fist into the man's face.

The punch split both his lips and knocked his head against the wall. Dazed, he too slid to the floor, next to his pal and Kershaw thought that the two of them looked quite comical down there.

Kershaw could feel himself trembling, but he wasn't sure whether it was from fear or excitement, being unable to differentiate between the two emotions.

He was just relieved that it was all over.

Not so Clive, though. Standing over the pair, with his fists clenched, Kershaw got the impression that he was willing them to get back on their feet, so that he could knock them to the floor again.

"What's going on?" said a voice from behind him.

Turning around, Kershaw found the man he knew to be the landlord, standing behind them.

He was a big man, almost as big as Clive, but rather than having white hair, he had no hair at all, his head a shiny, bald dome. Kershaw could tell that he'd had his nose broken and judging by the look of the man probably more than once.

Clive looked round.

"No problem, Billy boy. These two wanted some trouble, so we gave it to 'em."

Kershaw was a little startled when he heard Clive say 'we', but when he thought about it, he had helped, in his own little way, even if it was only pushing Ginger to the ground.

The landlord looked down at the pair on the floor.

Ponytail's upper lip had already swollen to almost twice its normal size and had turned a bright shade of purple. Ginger was looking okay, but he didn't seem to be in any hurry to get to his feet.

"Both of you, get out!" ordered the Landlord.

They helped each other up and as they passed Kershaw, they glared at him, venomously.

"Have you finished beating up on my customers, or is there anyone else in here you don't like the look of?" the landlord asked Clive.

The ex-soldier grinned at him.

"No, that'll do for now," and the landlord wandered off, muttering under his breath.

Clive bent down and picked up the Stanley knife from under the adjacent table.

"That bastard could have done a lot of damage with this," he said, holding the weapon in his hand.

"I guess I owe you one."

Kershaw felt so proud, he thought he would burst. So proud in fact, that it completely slipped his mind that Clive doing him a favour was what had kicked all of this off in the first place.

He tried his best to sound offhand about it.

"Well, buy me a beer and we'll call it quits."

"Sounds like a bargain to me," said Clive, slapping him on the shoulder.

"Did you say that you worked in a cash and carry warehouse?" asked Clive, as they stood at the bar with their drinks. Kershaw nodded.

"How many of those places are there around here?"

Kershaw thought for a moment.

"One, as far as I know. Why?"

"It's just that there's a guy I work with from time to time, he said he's got a job in one of those places. I thought, if you worked in the same warehouse, that you might have seen him. Be pretty hard not to, as it happens. He's about seven foot tall and built like a brick shit house. His name's..."

"Eddie," interjected Kershaw.

"So you do know him, do you?"

"Yeah, we work together, three of us, out on the loading bay."

Kershaw recalled the incident at the nightclub and Eddie working as a doorman.

"What sort of work do you do, then?"

"Security. Corporate functions, mostly."

Kershaw wasn't quite sure what a corporate function was and it must have showed on his face.

"Some big firm has its annual bash and hires a venue. You know, a hotel, a marquee in the grounds of a stately home, something like that. We get hired to make sure that things run smoothly."

Kershaw tried to picture Clive and Eddie as a pair. A truly awesome combination.

"It's window dressing, mostly. You hardly ever get any trouble at these things. We're hired to make sure that no one nicks the silver or draws moustaches on the Van Gogh's."

A light bulb came on over Clive's head and he wagged a finger at Kershaw.

"Come to think of it, we've got a gig on Saturday night, The Cafe Royale, in Regent Street, know it?"

Kershaw shook his head.

"It's a big place, five floors. Needs a lot of bodies to cover it. I'm sure if I spoke to the boss, he could use another man. You interested?"

"Me?" spluttered Kershaw.

"Sure, why not', said Clive. "You're tidy, you can look after yourself…"

"I thought you said there was never any trouble at these things?" interrupted Kershaw.

"No, I said there was hardly ever any trouble. Most of the time these hooray henrys are so shitfaced they can hardly stand up. There's nothing for you to worry about."

Kershaw knew that Clive was right. If there was any trouble, he'd hide behind him, or Eddie, or better still, behind both of them!

"Why not?" he thought to himself. It might be fun.

"Yeah, okay then" he said.

Clive smiled. "Good man. Hey, Billy! You got a pen and some paper back there?"

Billy slapped a biro and a scrap of paper on the bar and looked at Kershaw.

"You're not thinking of getting mixed up with this crazy man, are you?" he asked.

Clive pretended to be hurt.

"The only crazy thing about me, is that I'm still drinking in this dump."

"That's because you've been barred from everywhere else," retorted Billy.

Clive looked at Kershaw and grinned.

"Don't listen to him. I've never started a fight in my life."

"No, you just finish 'em," said Billy and walked off.

"Write your number down on there and I'll give you a call tomorrow, after I've spoken to the Guv'nor. There shouldn't be a problem, not if I recommend you."

Kershaw wrote his phone number down and Clive folded the piece of paper up and put it in his pocket.

"So is that all you do, work at these places?" asked Kershaw, wondering if there was a living to made out of it.

"No. They're pocket money. C.P. work is where you make the big bucks."

"C.P. work?"

"Close protection," Clive told him. "Some fat cat comes into town and wants a body with him full time. You know, drive him around, make sure no one tries to nick his Rolex, that sort of shit. The Arabs pay the best money. I get with one of them for a couple of days, I can make a fortune. They're paranoid about being assassinated. They've got their own bodyguards, but sometimes they prefer to have someone who knows their way around."

Kershaw thought about it for a moment.

"So, if someone does try to shoot the person you're with, you have to…"

"Make sure he doesn't," finished off Clive.

"So, it could be pretty dangerous, then?" asked Kershaw, realising what a stupid question that was, once he'd asked it.

The twinkle returned to Clive's eyes and he grinned.

"Yeah, great eh?"

The following morning, Andy and Kershaw were waiting in the yard for the lorry to arrive.

"So how did your paper hanging lesson go last night?"

Kershaw had toyed with the idea of redecorating his apartment, but he probably knew less about it than Andy. Now seemed like a good time to start picking his brains, getting a few tips for free.

"Did you learn anything useful?"

"Well," began Andy, with Kershaw listening intently.

"When you're pasting, it's best to put the paste on the hairy end of the brush."

Kershaw thought that he must have misheard what his friend said, until Andy burst out laughing."

"You want to see your face," he said, finding it hard to talk and laugh so hard at the same time.

"You silly fucker," swore Kershaw, realising that he'd been had.

Later, in the canteen, Kershaw was the first to take his seat, Eddie the second.

"I was with Clive last night," Kershaw told him, expecting the big man to be surprised that he knew the ex-soldier, but as usual, the Giant's face was expressionless.

"Good man, Clive," was all he said.

"He's going to see if they need any extra help for Saturday night."

This did get a reaction.

"You fancy some of that, do you?"

The tone of Eddie's voice made it sound as if Kershaw had signed on for some kind of punch up. It didn't help matters any that ever since he'd got out of bed that morning, he couldn't help feeling that he'd been a bit hasty in saying yes to Clive.

He knew full well that he wasn't cut out for this kind of work.

"Do you get much trouble at these kind of things?" he asked.

Eddie shrugged his massive shoulders.

"Depends."

Eddie's noncommittal didn't inspire Kershaw with confidence.

He'd said yes and he knew he couldn't give Clive some lame excuse as to why he'd changed his mind. He just hoped, that on the night, he wasn't called on to help out, if there was any trouble.

CHAPTER TEN

When Kershaw opened the door of his flat that evening, his phone was ringing.

"Hello Boy, it's Clive," said the voice on the other end of the line.

Kershaw often wondered why Clive called him Boy, even after he'd told him that his name was Bob. He guessed that was one of Clive's little idiosyncrasies.

"It's on for Saturday."

Kershaw wanted to tell him that he couldn't make it, but he didn't want Clive thinking less of him.

"Great," said Kershaw, hoping that he sounded enthusiastic.

"It's black tie. Have you got a dinner suit?"

"Uh, no."

"Have you got a black bow tie?"

"Er, no, 1 haven't got one of those either," said Kershaw, feeling a little inadequate.

"You've got a white shirt though, yeah?"

"Oh yeah, I've got one of those."

"Well that's a start. Looks like you're going to have to go shopping tomorrow, get yourself kitted out. It might set you back a few quid, but for most of these gigs, that's the standard dress code. You do two or three and it's paid for itself."

The mention of money made him feel slightly better about the whole thing.

"How much do we get paid?"

"It's nine 'til three and for that you get ninety quid. Not bad for just standing around looking pretty, huh?"

Kershaw hoped that that was all he'd be doing.

An hour later, he was drying himself after just having had a shower, when the phone rang again. To his surprise and pleasure, it was Penny.

"Do you remember that we talked about getting you a mobile phone?" she asked, after they had exchanged hellos.

"Yes."

"Do you have a lunch break where you work?" she asked.

"Yeah, from one 'til two."

"Can you make it into town, tomorrow?"

"I should be able to, yes."

"I'll meet you outside Boots, in the High street, about five past one. Can you make it then? You're not that far away, are you?"

It was true, he was quite near the town, but it would take him longer than five minutes to get there, even if he ran. He'd have to get Andy to drop him off.

He told her that he would be there and that he was looking forward to seeing her.

"Yes, I'm looking forward to seeing you, too."

"Can you drop me off in town, lunchtime?" Kershaw asked Andy in the canteen, the following morning.

"I suppose so," he replied, sullenly. "Are you ever going to get yourself a car?

I don't know how you manage without one."

"What do I need a car for? I've got you."

"I should charge you, really," said Andy, although his tone was a little breezier now.

"If it'll make you feel any better, I'll get in the back and throw up just as I'm about to get out."

"That'll be like a normal Saturday night, for you, then," retorted Andy.

"Are you shopping, or something?" asked Andy, as they drove into town.

"Yeah, and I'm meeting Penny as well."

Andy let out a short whistle. "You mean there's a chance that I might get to see the girl who's got you by the bollocks?"

Kershaw wasn't rising to the bait.

"I'm meeting her in the High street, so there's a possibility you might catch a glimpse, yeah."

"I can hardly wait," said Andy, wryly.

"You can drop me off here if you like," suggested Kershaw.

They were in the High street, a couple of shops down from where Penny said that she would meet him. He'd already spotted her, standing outside of Boots, but he didn't want to pull up next to her and have Andy staring at her through the car window, like he knew he would.

"Where is she then?" he asked, expectantly.

Kershaw pointed her out. She was wearing a grey skirt and matching jacket and he had to admit that she looked quite stunning.

Andy didn't say anything at first, he just looked.

"Is that her?" he asked, a note of disbelief in his voice.

"Uh huh. Still think I'm a fucking idiot?"

"No. I think you're a lucky, fucking idiot."

"Right, thanks for the lift, mate. I'll see you tomorrow."

Andy finally managed to drag himself away from staring at Penny.

"Tomorrow? You're not coming back today?"

"I've got the afternoon off. Boss man said I could come in tomorrow morning work it off then. After Penny and I have done our shopping, we'll probably go back to my place and well, you know."

"Don't have a nice time," said Andy, enviously.

"I'll try not to," Kershaw told him, winked and got out of the car. Penny spotted him before he got to her and smiled. He walked up to her and she kissed him on the cheek.

"Who was that?" she asked, nodding at Andy's car, pulling away.

"A mate from work. He gave me a lift down here. So, where are we going?"

"There's a phone shop further down," said Penny, starting to walk, Kershaw falling in beside her.

"We'll have to hurry though, if you have to be back by one."

"No problem. I'm on flexi time. I've got the afternoon off." When they entered the phone shop, Kershaw wasn't only amazed at the array of phones on show, but also the size of them.

"Look at that one," he said, pointing. "I've seen bigger matchboxes."

Penny laughed. "Pick one. I'll pay."

I can't let you do that."

He'd never felt comfortable with girls buying him gifts, it always made him feel as if he were some kind of pimp.

"I want to. It's a present."

She seemed rather insistent, and as she probably had a lot more money than him, just this once, he agreed.

"Okay, but I'm buying lunch."

He chose one that he liked the look of and that wasn't too expensive. Penny paid for it at the counter, along with a phone card.

Outside, Kershaw gave her a kiss and thanked her.

"You'll be amazed at all the things it can do," she told him. "They're not just phones anymore."

"They're not?" said Kershaw, coming to the conclusion that technology had left him lagging behind.

"When you get home, read the instructions and just keep playing with it. The more you use it, the better you'll become."

He grinned at her. "Bit like a dick, then?"

She stared back at him. "If that were the case, you must have played with yours an awful lot when you were young."

He took the backhanded compliment in the spirit in which he hoped it was intended.

They settled on pizza for lunch.

"So what are your plans for the rest of the afternoon?" he asked, hoping that they were going to be the same as his.

"Well, I have to call into the office a little further on down. They rang me this morning to let me know that they have some work for me."

"I thought you were looking rather business-like," he said, giving her outfit an appreciative glance.

"I prefer elegant," she told him.

"Anyway, there's a Burtons down there. While you're in your office, I can be in there. I have to get myself a dinner suit," he told her, hoping that she would be impressed.

"Dinner suit?"

"Yeah, I've got a job up in London tomorrow night. Security work."

"Security work?" repeated Penny, again, although this time, instead of sounding puzzled, there was a note of concern in her voice.

"It's my first job. I'm quite looking forward to it," he told her, which was partly true.

"What if there's any trouble? You could get hurt."

Kershaw was touched by her concern, but he needn't have been. She wasn't thinking of him, but of herself and the plans she'd made.

Not knowing this, he tried to put her mind at ease.

"Don't worry about that. There will be people there much better qualified than me to handle that sort of thing. I'm just there to make up the numbers."

Penny still wasn't looking too happy about the whole thing, but not for the reasons he imagined.

They carried on down the High street, until she stopped outside a temping agency.

"I'm going in here," she told him.

"And I'm going in there," said Kershaw, nodding to the other side of the street.

"Are you coming over, when you're finished?" he asked.

"I can't," replied Penny. "I have to be somewhere."

Kershaw was unable to hide his disappointment.

"I thought, seeing as I had the afternoon off, that we could go back to my place and er, entertain ourselves."

She touched him gently on the arm. "I only wish that I could, but I'm afraid it's just not possible.

She pointed to the box under his arm. "Don't forget to charge that up overnight"

It seemed that the discussion as to whether they were going back to his place or not was over, at least as far as she was concerned.

Penny opened her handbag and took out her pink notebook. Scribbling something in the back, she tore out a section of a page and handed it to him.

'That's my mobile number. I've got yours, the man in the shop wrote it down for me."

"He did? Shouldn't I know what it is?" he asked, still miffed that his plans for an afternoon of lust had been scuppered.

Penny smiled at him. "It's written down in the pamphlet that's in the box"

Are you upset because I'm working tomorrow night? Is that why you're going now?"

She reached up and kissed him on the lips.

"Of course not. Now, I really must be going. I'll ring you tomorrow okay?"

She was gone before he had a chance to tell her that it wasn't okay as she put it.

He was left standing alone on the pavement, feeling confused.

This wasn't how it was supposed to be, he thought to himself

Ah bollocks! Let's go and buy a suit.

He walked through the door of his flat, a large Burton's bag in one hand and a mobile phone in the other.

With the suit, he had decided to push the boat out and on the advice of the salesman had also bought himself a dress shirt with a wing collar and a suit bag.

He put the suit and all the extras on the bed and unpacked the phone.

He now wished that he hadn't made arrangements to have the afternoon off.

He wouldn't have had to go in tomorrow morning then, but he couldn't go back.

Andy would want to know why he wasn't spending the rest of the day doing the horizontal mambo with the beautiful Penny, a question that even he himself was unable to answer.

Following the instructions, he plugged in the charger and watched the battery symbol flash away on the phone's screen. Not exactly what he had imagined himself to be doing a couple of hours ago.

Reading through the instruction booklet, he began to understand what Penny had meant when she told him that it was more than just a phone.

It appeared that it could do almost everything, bar cook his dinner. After getting in from work the following morning, he decided that it would be a good idea to get his head down for a few hours, seeing as how he was going to be up 'til the early hours of Sunday morning.

The telephone woke him up around four thirty.

"Hello Boy. You alright for tonight? Get everything you needed?"

Kershaw told him that he was all ready to go.

"Give me your address," said Clive.

Kershaw told him where he lived.

"I'll pick you up at seven. We're getting changed up there, so carry your stuff, okay?"

Kershaw had nodded off again, when the phone rang for a second time.

Putting the receiver to his ear, all he heard was the dial tone, yet the phone was still ringing. Realising that the tone of the ring wasn't the usual noise his phone made, he guessed his alarm clock must be going off, yet when he leant across the bed, he found that silent as well.

It suddenly dawned on him that it was the mobile phone, on the table, that was making the sound he could hear.

By the time he'd rolled off of the bed and reached it, it had stopped ringing.

He had it in his hand and was studying the screen, when it began ringing again.

After reading the booklet, he at least knew how to take an incoming call.

Pressing the button, he spoke into it.

"Hello?" At once he realised how stupid that sounded. Penny was the only person who had his number, so it had to be her.

"How are you enjoying your new toy?" she asked.

'Uh, yeah, it's great."

"I'm ringing to see if you'd like to come over for lunch tomorrow."

What meet the family, sort of thing?"

He was stunned, one minute she didn't want to be with him and the next, she wanted to introduce him to her parents. He was having trouble working her out, but if he was looking for an easy exit this was it.

If he refused, the relationship, if it could be called that, would definitely be dead in the water.

"Yeah I'd love to" he replied, wondering why he couldn't get his mouth to say what he wanted it to.

"Can you get round here for one? Is that alright?"

He told her that one would be fine.

"Mummy's a fabulous cook; you're in for a treat."

Get tomorrow over with, Penny thought to herself, after she'd put the phone down and we can get the ball rolling.

CHAPTER ELEVEN

Kershaw showered, put his brand, spanking new suit in its bag, along with the shirt and bowtie and checked the time. It was ten minutes to seven.

Standing out on the steps of the house, he didn't know what vehicle he should be looking out for, but when an enormous, American style four by four, with tyres as wide as a swimming pool and enough spotlights to illuminate a football pitch turned into the road, he just knew that had to be Clive. Sure enough, when it thundered to a halt alongside him, Clive was at the wheel, with Eddie hunched up alongside him.

Kershaw put his suit bag in the back and climbed into the front.

Even though there was a bench seat spanning the width of the huge truck, with Clive and Eddie up front, there was still only just enough room for him.

Despite being above average height and build, Kershaw still couldn't help feeling petite next to these two.

"Squeeze in Boy," said Clive, as Kershaw jammed himself between the door and Eddie's massive shoulders.

He had never ridden in a tank, but he imagined that it was similar to being in this monster. He felt so high off the ground and when they stopped at traffic lights, he found himself looking down on all the other cars.

It was an uneventful journey up, which was just as well. If some poor soul had decided to have an attack of road rage, he would have received the shock of his life, when these two got out to face him!

They managed to find somewhere to park, which surprised Kershaw. He didn't think the streets of London would be wide enough to accommodate this beast.

They entered the Cafe Royale by the front entrance, and were directed by a member of staff to the kitchens below and then to a room where they could get changed.

Being the first time he had ever worn a shirt with a wing collar, Clive had to show Kershaw how to dress. Checking himself in the mirror, he liked what he saw, in fact he thought that he looked quite dashing.

Back upstairs, Clive left him and Eddie to one side as he went to talk to a large, thickset man, with a shaven head, wearing an earpiece and carrying a clipboard.

A couple of minutes later, he came back, holding what look to Kershaw like a pair of walkie talkies.

He handed one to Eddie.

"We're on channel one," he told the big man. "You're on the third floor. Your oppo's already up there."

Eddie nodded to Clive, then to Kershaw and walked off to the red, carpeted stairs.

"Who's that?" asked Kershaw, nodding at the man Clive had been talking to earlier.

"That's Ivor. He's running the whole show. It's a big firm of accountants here tonight. He's expecting seven hundred."

"That's a lot of accountants" said Kershaw.

"He's had dealings with this lot before. Apparently, last time, someone was found snorting coke in the bogs. That's where we come in."

Kershaw looked horrified. "What, we're in the bogs all night?"

Clive laughed. "No, in fact, we've got one of the best jobs, tonight."

Kershaw wondered why Clive should consider hanging around the gent's toilets all night, to be a good job.

"Normally at these gigs, you're static. You get put in one area and that's it for the rest of the night. It can be hard work and the time tends to drag, but we'll be on the move all night. Trust me, we've got the best of it."

"How's it going to work, then?" asked Kershaw, still not entirely convinced.

"Like I said, this place has five floors. We wait until everyone's in and seated in the restaurant, we give 'em fifteen minutes and then we get started.

We call in each toilet on the way up just pop our heads in to make sure everyone's doing what they should be doing, if you see what I mean" he said, smiling.

"When we get to the top, we make our way down, doing the same thing. We come back down here, hang around for a couple of minutes and then start again."

Put like that, Kershaw didn't think that it sounded quite so bad after all.

Clive checked his watch.

"It's seven thirty now. The coaches are expected at eight and they're sitting down at eight thirty. We'll get going around a quarter to nine."

Kershaw watched as Clive strapped the radio to his belt, under his jacket, ran the lead up the front, clipped the microphone to his lapel and inserted the earpiece.

"We've got to wait down here, we've got someone else with us. A coffee pot."

"Coffee pot?" asked Kershaw, sounding bemused.

Clive smiled. "Sorry, slipped into Army lingo for a moment, there."

"A female M.P., a Military policewoman. She's on leave, got bored and rang up the agency to see if they had any work on.

She'll be doing the ladies toilets, obviously."

With the conversation having come to a temporary halt, Kershaw took time to look around the foyer, at the paintings depicting Victorian London, old style slot machines and an enormous wood carving of a Red Indian chieftain. Just then, a woman walked through the front doors. She was dressed in a black skirt and jacket, with thick, clumpy shoes.

She had a similar hairstyle to Clare, Andy's girlfriend, but that was where the similarity ended.

She had a hard angular face and the makeup had been applied a little too thickly, obviously thought Kershaw, in an attempt to improve her looks.

It hadn't done the trick.

She looked like a man and walked like one as well.

She approached Ivor, who was checking something on his clipboard and spoke to him.

He looked over at Clive and nodded.

It made sense to Kershaw now. This was the Army policewoman he'd mentioned.

She walked over to them and introduced herself.

"Hi, I'm Janine. I'm with you tonight."

Well, at least she didn't sound like a man, Kershaw thought to himself.

"I'm Clive and this is Bob."

Kershaw was slightly taken aback, never having heard Clive use his given name before.

She held out her hand and Clive took it. Then she turned to Kershaw and shook hand.

He was surprised at how firm her handshake was, but then she was built like a small female gorilla.

When he looked in her eyes, he received a terrible shock.

He knew the signs. She fancied him. She held onto him for longer than was necessary and he had to gently pull his hand away from hers.

"You look very smart in that suit," she told him.

"Er, thanks," he replied, knowing that he was going to have to choose his words very carefully, if he didn't want her to get the wrong idea.

"I'm going to enjoy working with you tonight," she said and smiled at him.

Kershaw glanced at Clive, who was also smiling. He'd obviously read the signs as well.

Janine walked over to look at some of the pictures on the wall.

"You don't waste any time, do you, boy," said Clive grinning.

"It's not funny," said Kershaw seriously.

"Look at her she's a moose!"

"Hey, looks aren't everything," Clive told him. "For all you know, she could be a lovely girl deep down."

"If that's the case, why don't you have her?"

"You must be joking!" said Clive. "She's a moose!"

Kershaw was standing at the front door, watching the almost constant flow of traffic, stretched limos, black cabs, buses and rickshaws, when he realised that Janine was standing by his side, staring up at him.

"You're not wearing any rings," she said. "Does that mean you're single and available, like me?"

Shit! This called for some quick thinking.

"Uh, no, I'm married. I don't wear my ring at these things, in case I lose it, you know, in a scuffle."

Janine looked devastated and a little angry, almost as if she thought he'd been leading her on just by being there tonight. She walked off, without saying a word and Kershaw breathed a sigh of relief. Hopefully, that will have done the trick. The first guests began arriving around eight fifteen, in ones and twos at first and then the size of the groups began to swell, until it was an almost nonstop stream of girls in their posh frocks and men in their dinner suits. Clive, Kershaw and Janine stood to one side, watching as they all trooped in, laughing and shouting to one another. Some, it seemed, were already a little the worse for drink, either having had the coach stop off at a pub on the way, or had brought their own drink with them.

One pair of lads were louder than the rest. They were clearly drunk, their jackets and shirts unbuttoned and their bow ties hanging down.

Kershaw noticed that one of them had a ponytail. He was beginning to develop an unhealthy dislike for people with ponytails, unless they were female, of course.

They both gave the three of them a contemptuous look as they passed and then they spotted the Indian carving.

The one with the ponytail had some chewing gum in his mouth, which he took out and stuck on the end of the red Indian's nose, then stood back to admire his handiwork.

Janine walked over to him.

"Would you mind taking that off and putting it in the bin, where it belongs?" she asked.

He looked her up and down, arrogantly.

"Here, have you ever been mistaken for a man?" he asked, rudely.

Janine stared back at him. "No, have you?"

His companion roared with laughter, but the object of Janine's acerbic put down wasn't looking quite so amused. In fact, from where Kershaw was standing, it looked as though he was about to go for her.

Whether it was because he didn't want to hit a woman, even if she did look like Janine, or that he thought that if he did, she might well thump him back, it was hard to tell.

Either way, after staring hard at each other for a second or two, it was the man who finally broke eye contact.

With a derisory snort, he pulled the chewing gum off of the Indian's nose and dropped it in the waste bin on the floor.

"Satisfied?" he snapped and walked to the stairs, his pal following on behind.

"She's a cool one," said Clive, a note of admiration in his voice.

Kershaw nodded, but he couldn't help but feel sorry for any sylph-like debutante who was foolish enough to step out of line this evening. The awesome Janine would probably knock the stuffing out of her. The number of guests coming through the front door became less and less, until there was just the odd one, out of breath and checking his watch as he ran for the stairs.

Clive pressed his finger to his ear and listened to the message coming through.

"They're all seated. Time to get going."

"So where are you based?" Clive asked Janine, as they climbed the stairs.

"Aldershot."

"That must keep you busy. I hear those Para's can be naughty boys."

Kershaw caught Clive's knowing wink.

Clive explained the layout of the building to the other two as they walked.

"The first floor is the dining hall, the second the disco, then there's the casino, then the games floor. They've got the lot up there, even a mini go cart track. Everything a bunch of drunken yahoos need to keep themselves amused. The fifth floor is the guest suite. There shouldn't be anyone up there, but we'll have to check it, just in case."

Their patrol, from top to bottom, which was pretty uneventful, took them about half an hour, Clive stopping on each floor to chat with members of the security team that he knew.

On the third floor, Eddie nodded to both of them and Kershaw noticed that he gave Janine a longer look than normal, one which was returned.

Downstairs, Clive suggested that they go to the kitchens and get themselves a cold drink.

Twenty minutes later, they began their second patrol.

Things weren't so quiet now. With the meal over, there were people all over the place, walking and running from room to room and floor to floor.

When they reached the fourth floor, Kershaw thought that Clive wasn't going up any further, but he changed his mind and carried on.

Which was just as well.

When they got up there, there were two girls on the landing. Kershaw got the impression that they were nervous, especially when they caught sight of Clive.

"Are you with the party?" he asked.

They both nodded.

"You shouldn't be up here," he told them. "Better get yourselves back down."

As Clive walked towards the gents, the two girls hurried to the stairs, running down as fast as their outfits would allow.

The speed at which they left made Kershaw think that something wasn't right.

His suspicions were confirmed, when he and Clive walked into the toilet.

A short man was leaning over the sink and he appeared to be holding, what looked to Kershaw like some kind of straw.

Whatever it was he was doing, he failed to hear the door open.

"You shouldn't be doing this, son," Clive told him, obviously aware of what it was he was up to, which was more than could be said for Kershaw, who didn't have a clue.

The sound of Clive's voice made the man jump and cough at the same time and as his headshot up and he turned, Kershaw saw that the glasses he was wearing were covered in what looked to him, to be talcum powder.

The man was about five foot six, with short curly hair and even through the powder on his lenses, Kershaw could see that his eyes were wide open with fright.

"It's a party! I'm not doing anybody any harm," protested the man, wiping the cocaine dust from his glasses and from around his nose and mouth. Kershaw now knew what was happening and he suddenly thought of the two girls who had been nervously standing outside, as if on guard. Janine watched as the pair shot past her and she was thinking the same as Kershaw.

Something was wrong here.

The two girls flung open the doors of the games room, couldn't see what they were looking for and sped down the stairs, to the next floor.

Here, they found what they were after. A table with four large men at it, all drunk.

Their size was due to the fact that they were one quarter of the company's rugby team and the largest of the four was in the process of climbing onto the table, whilst balancing an empty bottle of champagne on his head.

One of the girls grabbed him before he could complete his ascent.

"Oscar's in trouble!" she shouted, above the noise.

"He was doing some coke and two of the bouncers have gone in. I think they're going to beat him up!"

Getting off of the table, his expression more serious now, he looked at the other three.

"Oscar needs our help, boys! What do you say?"

CHAPTER TWELVE

In the true spirit of rugby, the other three rose to the challenge of a prospective punch up and they all trooped out to the stairs.

"I think you'd better come with us," said Clive.

Oscar had tidied himself up, but was still looking a little hyper, after inhaling the equivalent of a week's wages for any respectable drugs dealer.

Oscar clearly didn't want to leave and began backing away, nervously looking from Clive to Kershaw and back to Clive again.

Out on the landing, Janine would have liked to have known what was happening in there but she guessed that whatever it was, the two boys could handle it between them and if not, Clive had a radio, as did she, so help would never be far away.

Just then, four rather large, rather drunk men, rushed past her towards the gents.

What was inside, plus these four, might a bit too much for the two boys, so she got on the radio and asked for someone to get up to the fifth floor, pronto. In the toilet, Clive was closing in on the retreating Oscar, when the door burst open and the four rugby playing musketeers burst in.

They split, two facing Kershaw and two in front of Clive. The first through the door was the largest, who squared up to

Clive, but looked over his shoulder at their coke sniffing friend.

"Get over here, Oscar."

"He's not going anywhere," said Clive, "Except out on the street."

The man glared at Clive. "You people. We come here to have a good time and all you want to do is fuck it up. Well, this time, it's you who's going to get fucked up."

Kershaw could feel his stomach beginning to churn, but it wasn't just because he thought he was going to be involved in a fight, but that Clive would see him for what he really was.

He couldn't let that happen.

He remembered the night in the disco and knew that he needed that same confidence now.

All four of the men who had burst in looked as though they could handle themselves and he knew that this situation wasn't going to go away.

This was exactly what he was hoping wouldn't happen, but now that it was here, he was going to have to deal with it.

The two facing him didn't seem to be in the least bit anxious and Kershaw knew that he had to appear as unruffled as them, make them believe that he was someone they shouldn't be tangling with.

"So what you're saying is, you've come in here to give us a good kicking?" he asked, doing his level best to keep his voice from sounding tremulous.

The man nearest him grinned.

"Too right, mate," he threatened.

Kershaw let out an audible sigh.

"Phew! That's lucky then. For a moment there, I thought that we were in trouble."

Rather than force his enemy to reconsider the consequences of his actions, Kershaw's sarcastic bravado was the spark that lit the blue touch paper.

Not taking kindly to having his fighting prowess slandered, the man stepped forward, aiming a punch at Kershaw's head.

The first lesson his athletics coach had taught him, was coordination, explaining that you wouldn't progress in any sport, no matter what it was, if you had arms and legs flailing about all over the place.

He'd spent months with Kershaw, getting his body to work as a single unit.

In the starting blocks, he taught him how to relax his body and his breathing, until he heard the starter's third and final word of command and then to tense his whole body and explode out onto the track.

With the javelin, it was the same. Relaxing as he took his approach run and then when he reached the board, to fire up all the muscles in his body in unison.

Although he hadn't been anywhere near a track, or picked up a javelin, for over two years, it was still there, like riding a bicycle.

Raising his left arm, he blocked the punch, the same time as he stepped forward with his right leg, bringing up his right fist and striking the man under the chin, all three movements performed at the same time.

The man appeared to grow an extra couple of inches, as Kershaw's uppercut lifted him onto his toes.

He was unconscious by the time he came back down and falling backwards, his pal behind had no choice but to grab him with both arms.

Kershaw couldn't believe how easy it had been to knock the man out and seeing that his friend had his hands full, he knew he had to finish it now.

Surging forward, he shoulder barged the unconscious man in the chest, the force of the impact, combined with the dead weight of the one in front, caused both men to stagger backwards, the one behind smashing his head on the hand drying machine on the wall.

Dropping his pal, he fell to his knees, groaning and holding the back of his head with both hands.

Seeing Kershaw kick it all off, Clive knew that the shit would be coming his way any moment as well.

Using his peripheral vision, he knew that Oscar was standing behind him and to the left.

Even though he was tiny, Clive knew that after sniffing coke, the little twat could be capable of anything. What he didn't need, at a time like this, was a loose cannon rolling around behind him.

Turning, he jabbed his elbow into the little man's temple.

Oscar fell to the floor, like a puppet with its strings cut.

Clive turned to face the big man, the leader.

They were about the same size and build, and they moved towards each other, cautiously.

All of a sudden, Clive threw both his hands up into the air. It looked weird, but it had the desired effect.

Just for an instant, Clive's opponent instinctively allowed his eyes to look upwards.

Clive swung his right leg around in a circle, about an inch off of the floor and swept both the man's feet from out under him.

He was very nearly horizontal when he crashed down to the floor.

Hitting the ground on a rugby field was one thing, but landing on a tiled floor was something else.

Even so, to his credit, he still rolled over and got to his knees.

Clive didn't want him getting back on his feet, so Queensbury rules went right out of the window. With the man on all fours, still recovering, Clive stepped in and kicked him in the ribs. He heard the air rush out of his mouth and the man sank back to the floor.

This left just one. The last man standing had looked quite confident, when he'd burst into the room with his mates, but now he wasn't looking quite so sure of himself.

With his heroic rugby captain down and not looking as though he was going to get back up again and his other two mates also out of the picture, he was looking decidedly nervous.

"Better get out now, while you can," Clive advised him.

He wasn't moving. It was clear by his stance that he was going to have a go, no matter what. That was, until the door opened and Eddie strode in.

He took one look at the giant and his courage, understandably, flew south for the winter.

"You still here?" asked Clive.

Leaving his mates behind, he turned, took one last look at Eddie, presumably, to make sure that he hadn't imagined it, and walked out the door, which Eddie was holding open for him.

No sooner had he left, than Ivor showed up. He eyed the carnage in front of him.

One unconscious, one flat out, one sitting, groaning and holding his head in his hands and one being sick.

"Christ! It's always you, isn't it?" he asked, looking at Clive.

The ex-soldier shrugged. "Just lucky, I guess," he replied, matter-of-factly.

"Are you alright?" Ivor asked Kershaw.

He nodded.

Ivor turned back to Clive.

"Unfortunately, one of those girls out there spilled the beans and the management got wind of it. They've called the law."

He looked back at Kershaw.

"Get yourself back downstairs. We'll deal with this."

Kershaw wasn't sure whether he should leave Clive to carry the can or not.

"It's okay," Clive told him, answering his question.

"We can sort this out."

Eddie and Janine were outside on the landing.

"Everything alright in there?" asked Janine.

"Yeah. Nothing serious just a few bruises and some dented egos! I shouldn't imagine," replied Kershaw.

On his way back down, Kershaw was having trouble believing that he had actually hit someone, something he'd never done before. Not only that, but how he'd felt afterwards, the excitement coursing through his body. It had felt good! He felt good!

He passed two uniformed policemen on the second floor and he imagined that Clive was used to dealing with situations like this.

He'd been standing by the front door for about ten minutes, when Clive appeared.

"Everything alright up there?" asked Kershaw.

Clive nodded. "Yeah. One of the company directors showed up. Those four are always getting into a mess of one kind or another. Plod's escorted them off the premises, as they say. As for the little coke sniffer, he wasn't so lucky. They did him for possession, so that's his weekend taken care of."

Clive was silent for a moment.

"That's one hell of a punch you've got there, boy."

Kershaw wasn't sure what to say. He could hardly tell Clive that was the first time he'd ever hit someone.

"I must have caught him just right, I guess."

The remainder of the night was uneventful, by comparison.

Ivor came down and told the pair of them that it would probably be best if they stayed where they were, for the rest of the night.

When the guests finally began to leave, Kershaw caught sight of the one that got away.

Their eyes met for an instant, then the man looked away and headed for the door.

That wasn't the only thing he caught sight of.

In the corner, Eddie and Janine were whispering things to each other, things that appeared to Kershaw, to be of a personal nature.

"Looks like Eddie's pinched your girl," said Clive, over his shoulder.

"Good luck to him," replied Kershaw.

"He's probably about the only bloke in here who could do anything with her and come away in one piece."

Nothing much was said on the drive back, all three of them caught up in their own thoughts.

After seeing Eddie bending almost double to give Janine a goodnight kiss, Kershaw had a fair idea what the big man had on his mind.

He himself was going over the evening's events and how they had made him feel and as for Clive, who knew what was going through his mind. After all that had happened that evening, Kershaw had completely forgotten about going to Penny's house for lunch. Laying his head on the pillow, he thought of her, but when he closed his eyes, all he could see were two men on the floor, where he'd put them.

Kershaw was sitting at the back of the bus, that morning, when his mobile phone began ringing. Taking it out of his jacket pocket, he knew it had to be Penny.

"Hello, Bobby? Where are you?" she asked.

"I'm on the bus, on the way to your place." He checked his watch.

"I should be about twenty minutes, it's still on isn't it?"

"Oh, yes. I'm ringing to ask you to please be on your best behaviour."

"Best behaviour?"

"Yes, no dirty jokes, or disgusting innuendo," she said, sternly.

"What, like how long it took me to scrub your lipstick off my…"

"Yes, thank you. That's exactly what I'm talking about. I've told you what my Father can be like."

Kershaw laughed. "Don't panic," he reassured her. "I promise I'll be good as gold."

When he rang Penny's doorbell, half an hour later, he felt almost as scared as he had been the night before. He mentally scolded himself for being so pathetic and was feeling slightly better when the door opened.

He instantly knew where Penny got her good looks from. The woman standing before him, was, not to put too fine a point on it, simply a vision.

At forty nine, Valerie Marshall was growing old gracefully. She still had a fine figure and the lines on her face seemed to add to her mature beauty.

She smiled and held out her hand.

"I'm Penny's Mother. You must be Bob. How are you?"

The old saying sprang into Kershaw's mind that if you wanted to know what a girl was going to look like in twenty years' time, take a look at her mother.

If it was true, then he guessed he'd better stick around!

"I'm fine, thank you," he replied, squeezing her hand gently.

A man was walking down the stairs the same time as Kershaw entered the house.

He was shorter than Kershaw, but as broad, if not broader. He had a handsome, squarish looking face, topped with a full head of hair that was beginning to turn grey.

Wearing a long sleeved shirt, with the top two buttons undone, Kershaw could see that he was incredibly hirsute, the hair from his chest creeping up around his neck like a fungus.

As he reached the bottom step, Penny came out from the kitchen and made the introductions.

"This is my Father," she said to Kershaw.

"You'd best call me George," said Marshall, holding out an apelike hand.

He had a crushingly confident handshake and Kershaw got the impression that he wasn't the sort of person you messed around with.

"Lunch shouldn't be too long, now," said Valerie, as all four of them stood in the hall.

"Why don't you two go and have a drink?" she suggested.

"What do you say Bob? Do you fancy a drink?" asked Marshall.

Kershaw got the impression that it was more than a simple invitation, as if Penny's Father were asking him if he liked to drink, as in getting drunk. The interrogation, it seemed, had already begun and Kershaw knew that he was going to have to choose his words very carefully.

"Yeah, a beer would be nice, thanks" he replied.

Marshall led him into the lounge, which, as Kershaw had expected, was every bit as impressive as every other room he'd seen, although, as far as Marshall knew, he hadn't seen any, least of all, the bedroom.

As Marshall walked over to a small bar, Kershaw noticed a plaque on the wall.

"Royal Hampshire Regiment," said Marshall, from behind him.

Kershaw turned, to find him standing with a glass of beer in each hand.

"I did my full colour service with them," said Marshall and nodded to a framed photograph hanging next to the plaque. Four rows of soldiers, all in their best dress uniforms.

Kershaw picked out a younger looking Marshall, sitting in the front row.

"I made W.O. 1," said Marshall, proudly.

Kershaw remembered Clive mentioning the Royal Hampshires one time, but he thought it best not to say anything about Marshall's beloved regiment, as when Clive had been speaking about them, the words sleeping bag and masturbation had been mentioned.

CHAPTER THIRTEEN

A pair of double doors opened on the other side of the room and Valerie appeared, announcing that lunch was ready.

The dining table was impressive, not just because of its size, but by the way it had been set. With glasses, napkins and what seemed to Kershaw to be every piece of cutlery imaginable, he felt as though he were walking into a high-class restaurant.

The table itself could easily have seated twelve, so they were well spread out.

The men were seated on one side, the women on the other, Kershaw facing

Valerie and Penny sitting across from her Father.

Valerie's cooking, as Penny had promised, was superb and Kershaw couldn't remember when he had tasted anything so delicious.

"So what do you do for a living, Bob?" asked Marshall, as they began on the main course.

Kershaw had to swallow a mouthful of food before he could answer.

"I work on the industrial estate, Whitman's cash and carry."

Marshall thought for a second. "Oh yeah, I know the place. Good job, is it? Good prospects?"

Valerie gave her husband a withering look, as if she knew what he was up to, which she did.

Kershaw shrugged. "It's okay. The money's good and at the end of the day, that's really what it's all about, I suppose."

"Not too stimulating, then?"

Kershaw guessed that being a military man, Marshall considered that the Army was the only worthwhile career to have, so he just smiled and carried on with his meal.

"So, how long have you two known each other?" asked Marshall.

"Must be about a month, now," replied Kershaw, glancing over at Penny for conformation.

She nodded. "Yes, it must be about that long now."

Marshall took a drink of his beer and nodded.

From then on, the conversation across the dining table consisted of small talk about nothing in particular. Kershaw was waiting for the questioning to begin again, but thankfully, it never did.

"Would anyone like a coffee in the lounge?" asked Valerie, when the meal was over.

"We're going to the cinema this afternoon, so we really should be going," said Penny.

Kershaw knew that that wasn't on the agenda, or at least, he didn't think it was, but he figured Penny must have her reasons for saying it, so he just nodded.

"That was a lovely meal, Mrs Marshall, thank you."

"Call me Valerie, please. I hope we'll be seeing you again."

"I'm sure you will," said Kershaw.

"Nice to meet you, George."

Kershaw held out his hand.

The handshake was still as firm, but now Marshall had a look in his eye, a look that said, mess with my little girl and I'll break both your kneecaps.

"We're not going to the pictures, are we?" asked Kershaw, as they drove out onto the road in Penny's Mini.

"No, I just wanted to get out of the house, although, I think Mummy must have had a word before you arrived. I've never known Daddy so subdued."

"So who wears the trousers in your house?" asked Kershaw, finding it hard to believe that a mere woman could keep a man like Marshall in his place.

"Oh, Mummy does, without a doubt," said Penny, correcting him.

They pulled up outside his flat and Penny applied the handbrake.

"I suppose we could go to the pictures…" she said and trailed off.

"Or we could go upstairs and interfere with each other," suggested Kershaw, hopefully.

"You really are a hopeless romantic, aren't you," she said, reproachfully.

"So, which would you prefer?" he asked.

Penny thought for a second. "Mmm, that's a hard one."

Kershaw winked at her. "Not yet it isn't, but I'm sure you've got a trick or two up your sleeve."

The following morning, Andy and Kershaw were in their customary position, perched on the edge of the loading bay.

"So how did it go Saturday?" asked Andy. "Bounce anyone?"

"Nah, it was pretty quiet, really," replied Kershaw, preferring to keep Saturday night's episode to himself.

"What, nothing happened at all?" Andy sounded disappointed.

123

"Well, I wouldn't say that. Eddie found himself a girlfriend."

"Blimey! What is she, a stilt walker?"

"No. She was working with us."

"What, a female bouncer? I didn't know there was such a thing."

"Well, you have to have at least one woman there, for obvious reasons," said Kershaw, sounding quite the expert.

"So what are they going to do, go down the gym and pump iron together?"

At that moment, Eddie walked out onto the bay.

"Well, here he is, why don't you ask him yourself" suggested Kershaw.

As they scrambled to their feet, Eddie approached, nodding to both of them.

"So what's this I hear about you hitting it off, you stud muffin you?" asked Andy.

"It wasn't me doing the hitting," rumbled the giant, looking at Kershaw.

Andy followed Eddie's gaze, looking at Kershaw suspiciously, waiting for some kind of explanation for Eddie's cryptic statement.

Kershaw shrugged.

"There was a scuffle. It was nothing."

Andy stared at Kershaw for a moment or two and turned back to Eddie.

"Anyway, don't change the subject. So did you... you know?" asked Andy, bending his elbow suggestively.

Eddie looked over his head at Kershaw.

"He can't help it," Kershaw told the big man. "He was upstairs reading his wank mags when the I.Q.'s were dished out."

Andy pretended to look hurt.

"Just trying to keep up with current events."

Eddie placed a massive hand under each of Andy's armpits and effortlessly lifted him up until they were face to face.

"Keep up with this current event," he growled.

"When the lorry comes in, I put you in one of the empty yorks and ship you off to Scotland."

Andy looked deep into his eyes.

"See you, Jimmy."

"Clare says that Angela's still waiting to hear from you," said Andy, when they were up in canteen, later that morning. "Are you still seeing that Poppy?"

"Penny," Kershaw corrected him, although he guessed that Andy knew her name.

"Whatever."

"Yeah, I went round her house for lunch yesterday."

"Oh, lunch," said Andy, putting on a la de da voice. "What was for afters, croquet on the lawn?"

"They're not like that," said Kershaw, in the Marshall's defence.

"Her Father's ex-army and not an officer either and the mother, wow! She really is a looker."

"Maybe you could have a mother and daughter three-way," suggested Andy, grinning.

"Don't be a dickhead!" said Kershaw.

Even as he was chiding his pal, the image of Valerie, Penny and himself, in the same bed was already piping itself into his mind and he knew he would have to erase it, or he'd end up with a stiffie.

"Anyway, how's your paperhanging course going?" he asked, the thought of something as tedious as decorating, helping to rid him of his perverted, yet delicious, sexual fantasy.

"I've got another two classes this week and I'm hoping to start on the first room this weekend. Clare said she'd come round and give me a hand."

It was Kershaw's turn to grin, salaciously.

"So you won't be getting much done, then?"

Andy shook his head. "Probably not. Might do a bit of stripping, though. She said she'd wear her uniform. Hubba hubba!" That evening, after finishing with the weights, Kershaw was about to make himself some toast, when there was a knock on the door.

He was surprised to find Penny standing there. His surprise quickly turned to concern when he saw the anxious look on her face.

"What's up?"

"Can I come in?" she asked, a slight tremble in her voice.

"Sure," he replied, standing to one side.

Once inside, she stood in the centre of the room, looking quite pathetic.

"I'm in trouble, Bobby."

Kershaw didn't know whether to feel worried or relieved. His first thought, when he saw the troubled look on her face, was that she had come to tell him that their little affair was over.

Now, he wasn't sure what to think.

"Sit down," he said, indicating the armchair.

He sat on the edge of the bed next to her.

"What sort of trouble are you talking about?"

"It's a long story. I used to take drugs."

Kershaw was shocked. He couldn't imagine her doing anything like that, anything that stupid.

His one and only contact with drugs had been last Saturday night. He'd heard the stories, seen the documentaries on television, but that was the extent of his knowledge.

He didn't know where to get them, or what to do with them, even if he could and the fact that Penny did, amazed him.

"I don't do them anymore," she told him, answering what was going to be his next question.

"But at one stage, I had to borrow money to pay for them. They rang me up today. They want their money by the end of the week and I haven't got it."

Kershaw thought for a moment. "I've got three thousand in the building society, you're welcome to that."

Penny took hold of his hand. "That's very kind of you, but I'm afraid it's not enough."

"Not enough? Why, how much do you owe, then?"

"Ten thousand."

Kershaw sat bolt upright.

"Ten thousand! You spent ten thousand on drugs?"

"No, I only spent two thousand on drugs," she told him as if that made things better.

"The other eight is interest."

If Kershaw could have sat any more upright, he would have done.

"Interest?" he repeated, incredulously.

"These are loan sharks, Bobby."

Kershaw was beginning to realise what a sheltered life he must have led.

Drugs, loan sharks, Penny moved in completely different circles to him, all the wrong ones, it seemed.

"Do you want me to try and have a word them?" he asked, gallantly.

Penny took a hold of his other hand.

"You're very sweet, but you're also very innocent, about some things, at least. These are not the kind of people you talk to. When they tell you that they want their money, you pay…or else."

"Or else what?" he asked, his heart beginning to beat slightly faster.

"I'm not sure, but it looks as though I'm going to find out," she replied, sounding quite philosophical about the whole thing.

Kershaw desperately wanted to help her.

"Have you told your Father?" he asked, thinking what George Marshall would do if he found out that someone was threatening his little girl.

Penny rolled her eyes. "Oh God! My Father. If he ever found out that I'd taken drugs, he'd throw me out of the house in an instant and Mummy wouldn't be able to help me either. I think one of his friends died from taking drugs. It's blinkered him, even towards me."

She shook her head, emphatically.

"I couldn't tell my Father, I just couldn't."

Kershaw thought that maybe Clive and Eddie could help, for a price.

"There is a way you can help, in fact, it'll help both of us," said Penny, interrupting his train of thought.

"There is?" he asked, although he couldn't for the life of him think what that might be.

He felt her squeeze his hands a little tighter.

"Daddy's a diamond merchant. He does little bits and pieces throughout the year, but once a year, he does one big deal that sets him up. He's doing it this weekend."

For one brief moment, Kershaw thought he knew where this was heading, but he was sure he'd got it wrong.

"He leaves for Amsterdam on Friday morning and gets back Saturday night. My Father is a creature of habit, if nothing else. He puts the diamonds in the safe when he gets in and transfers them to the bank on Monday morning."

Kershaw was getting that feeling again, only it was a lot stronger this time.

Penny squeezed his hands tighter still.

She confirmed his worst suspicions.

"Just think, Bobby. One hundred thousand pounds worth of diamonds! We could go to Spain buy ourselves a little beach bar. Wouldn't that be exciting?"

Kershaw pulled his hands away, as if hers were red hot and stood up.

"Are you sure you've stopped taking those drugs?"

"Steal your Father's diamonds! Are you mad?"

Penny seemed strangely unphased by his outburst.

"It'll be easy. I know how to turn off the alarm and the safe isn't a problem. All you'll have to do is walk in and walk back out again."

Kershaw shook his head and walked across the room.

"No, you're talking to the wrong person. I don't want anything to do with this hare-brained scheme of yours."

"Will you just think about it, please," she urged.

"There's nothing to think about. The answer's no now, it'll be no tomorrow and no every time after that. No!"

Penny stood up and casually smoothed down her skirt.

"Well, I had to ask. You do understand that, don't you?"

"No, l don't," he replied, angrily. "How could you ask me something like that?"

Penny shrugged. "Okay, then. Bye."

She turned and walked out, closing the door behind him.

Kershaw was speechless. Had she lost her marbles, or did she have some kind of split personality that he'd only now discovered?

Either way, he guessed he wasn't going to be seeing her anymore, which was just as well.

The last thing he wanted was some fatal attraction kind of crazy woman on his case.

Penny's Mini was parked a couple of yards down from the steps, but she walked straight past it and carried on until she came to a racing green Aston Martin, parked next to the kerb, it's engine purring.

She got in and closed the door.

"He said no."

CHAPTER FOURTEEN

Peter French was fast approaching his fiftieth birthday. At just under five foot nine, he wasn't the biggest man in London, but he was certainly one of the most dangerous.

Born in one of the rougher parts of the East end, he had grown up a street fighter.

Afraid of nothing and no one, at the age of twenty, someone suggested that he ought to try his hand at prize fighting, the illegal, bare knuckle kind.

After a few discreet inquiries, he turned up at the next venue, a barn, out in the wilds of Kent, somewhere.

Despite his opponent being taller and a great deal heavier, French won his bout comfortably. For this, he received the princely sum of fifty pounds, the promoter giving him the date of the next venue, telling him that he hoped to see him there.

He won his second bout just as emphatically, to the delight of over a thousand, bloodthirsty spectators.

When the word began to go round, that there was a new, exciting fighter on the scene, more and more people began travelling out into the deserted countryside to watch, which pleased the promoter, so much so, that he slipped French a few extra pounds, on the quiet, not wanting the other fighters getting wind of it.

By now, French was beginning to understand the mentality of the crowd.

They weren't interested in a quick knockdown, preferring instead, to see French demolish his opponent, piece by piece, round by round.

It was because he gave them what they wanted, that they kept coming back for more.

It was after his sixth consecutive win and when the promoter paid him his fifty pounds, plus a small bonus, producing both from a wad of money that French began to think that he might be on the wrong side of the fence.

Seeing that fat roll of paper money in the promoter's pudgy hand, French understood how the man could afford to smoke fat Havana cigars, wear a camel hair coat and travel around in a chauffeur driven Jaguar. At the end of the evening, when the promoter walked out into the cold night air, his bodyguard behind him, he found French waiting.

French explained the situation to the minder. He could either stay working for his fat, money grabbing boss, which meant that he was about to have his face rearranged, or he could come and work for him.

Having seen French in action, the minder, understandably, didn't take too long reaching a sensible decision.

French promptly beat the crap out of the promoter, telling him that he was taking over his business and his Jag.

At the next fight night, aware that there could be repercussions, the first thing French did was to increase the fighters' winnings and second, to offer the biggest and ugliest of them a job working for him.

With a small army of bruisers behind him, French decided to expand his empire, always at the expense of others.

Pretty soon, he was into anything and everything that could make him money, while at the same time, still taking part in the occasional prize fight, not just because he enjoyed it, but also to make sure that all his employees knew that he was still a force to be reckoned with and that if they messed with him, he'd mess with them.

His empire was a great deal smaller now, than it had been. Keeping the choice bits for himself, he farmed out the rest to his workforce, taking a small cut for himself.

His only legal concern was a used car business and that was just to keep the taxman happy, preferring to spend most of his time either in his villa in the Algarve, or down the gym.

The Police had had their eye on him for a good few years now, but as yet, he didn't have so much as a parking ticket against him, thanks to a very smart legal firm and loyal employees, who were prepared to give him an alibi for any time of the day or night.

He'd met Penny in one of the many night clubs that he owned, but didn't own, as far as the Inland Revenue were concerned.

He'd been attracted to her because of her beauty, she to him because he was dangerous.

Being with French meant living life on the edge. He didn't so much excite her, as scare her to death and she loved every minute of it. She sat in the passenger seat of the Aston, waiting for his reaction. He'd been staring through the windscreen and now he turned to her.

He had fair hair and a deep tan, thanks to his villa in the sun, which only seemed to make his piercing blue eyes even more penetrating.

"Did he now?" he replied, coldly.

"We'll just have to change his mind for him."

He flashed his main beam and the two front doors of a Vauxhall cavalier parked further up the road opened and two men got out.

"You're not going to hurt him, are you?" asked Penny.

He snapped his head round, the expression on his face making the hairs on the back of her neck stand upright.

"You're not going soft on this wanker, are you?"

"Of course not," she replied, although if she had taken the time to consider her response, the answer might have been different.

"He's no good to us if he can't walk," she said.

French gave her a wry smile.

He nodded at the two men walking down the road towards them. "They know what they're doing. He might be in a little pain, but he'll still be on his feet."

The two men walked past the Aston and on to the steps of the house.

"You might as well go home. He'll be calling you later, I guarantee it."

Penny got out of the car and walked back to her Mini. As she got in, the two men were climbing the steps, on the way to Kershaw's flat.

She had grown fond of him, she knew that, but at the end of the day, he was a means to an end and she had to put him out of her mind. Kershaw was still standing in the centre of the room, trying to get his head around what had just happened, when there was knock on the door.

He shook his head. It was probably that silly bitch come back to have another go at trying to get him to fall in with her.

Well, this time, she wouldn't even get through the door.

When Kershaw opened the door, he received his second surprise of the evening.

Instead of Penny, he was facing two men, two rather large men, one white, the other black.

The white man was wearing jeans and a leather jacket and sported a tightly trimmed beard.

The black man was wearing jeans and a jumper, without a shirt and had long, untidy dreadlocks.

"You Kershaw?" asked the white man, curtly.

He looked from one to the other. "Yeah."

"We need to have a word with you."

"Whatabou..."

Kershaw never got to finish his question. It was the man with the beard doing the talking, so while Kershaw was looking at him, he failed to spot the punch from his pal.

It caught him in the eye and for a moment, Kershaw couldn't see a thing.

He felt himself being lifted up by his arms and carried back into the room, where he was roughly manhandled on to one of his dining chairs and he felt a vice-like grip encircle his chest from behind.

His bad eye was beginning to close, not to mention hurt and his good one was watering like crazy. As his vision began to return, he saw the white man in front of him, which meant that the muscular black man was the one holding him in the chair.

"That posh tart you've been hanging around with owes money. She's asked you to help her and you said no. Well, now we're asking you. You're not going to say no to us, are you eh?" asked the man with the beard and kicked Kershaw's leg to get his full attention.

Kershaw couldn't believe that this was happening.

Who were these two and how did they know Penny? More importantly, how did they know about her madcap plan to rob her own Father?

It was all academic, anyway. They were here and it was obvious why.

As if to confirm Kershaw's thoughts, the man with the beard spoke again.

"You see, Leroy has a thing about beating up on white guys, don't you Sambo?"

The black man stared back at his working partner.

"Fuck you, man!"

The man laughed and looked down at Kershaw, smiling.

"You see? Leroy just don't like white folks."

The smile disappeared off of his face.

"So, either you do what you've been asked, or I turn him loose."

In all the confusion, one thing was perfectly clear to Kershaw. If he refused, they were going to beat the crap out of him. He had a choice. He could either sit there and allow it to happen, or he could put up some kind of resistance.

He'd probably still end up getting a beating, but at least he would have had a go.

Leroy's grip on his chest hadn't eased at all and Kershaw assumed it was there to prevent him from getting up, or more importantly, from moving forwards. He wondered what would happen if he went back.

Digging his heels into the carpet, he locked his knees and pushed with his legs.

The chair tipped backwards and he felt the grip on his chest slacken, enough for him to raise his right arm and punch Leroy in the side of the head.

He knew that there wasn't much power in it, not from that angle, but it allowed him to dig his heels in once more and push again.

He felt the chair begin to tip all the way back and pushed once more.

The top of the chair caught Leroy in the genitals, then carried on falling down his thighs, until it clattered over his knees.

As Leroy stepped back, Kershaw pushed once more and felt the chair tip pass the point of no return.

The top scraped down Leroy's shins and crashed down onto both his insteps.

Judging from the noises coming from behind him, Kershaw guessed that the man was in some considerable pain.

As the chair hit the floor, Kershaw rolled off to his right and kept on rolling, once, twice, three times.

His head was spinning and as things came back into focus, he found himself staring at the wall, standing up against which, was a broom handle that he used when he was exercising.

Figuring that it had to be better than nothing, he grabbed it, sprang up off of the floor and turned around.

Leroy was sitting on the carpet, rubbing his balls, his knees and his shins in rotation, in an effort to caress away the pain.

His accomplice was staring at him and then he turned to face Kershaw, fury in his eyes.

Kershaw held the broom handle out in front of him with both hands and stepped back.

The man didn't appear to be in least bit concerned that Kershaw had found himself a makeshift weapon.

"What do you think you're gonna do with that?" he asked.

Kershaw knew what he'd like to do. Throw it to the floor and run, but there was nowhere for him to go.

A smile played around the man's mouth.

"I'm gonna shove that so far up your ass, you're gonna be spitting out splinters."

He started to move towards Kershaw, who was trembling so much, he could hardly keep a hold of the stick, but he knew that having come this far, he had to see it through.

As the man came into range, Kershaw pulled the stick back behind his head and swung.

In fact, he drew it back so far, he might as well have sent the guy a postcard to tell him it was coming.

He ducked down and the stick whooshed, harmlessly over his head. Kershaw carried the movement on, bringing the stick back around behind his head again.

His bearded attacker, assuming that Kershaw was coming in for another harmless flypast, stepped in to grab him, while he had his arms up in the air.

At the last moment, instead of swinging the stick around for a second time, he stopped when it was behind his head and brought it straight down.

It wasn't much of a weapon, come to that, it wasn't much of a broom handle either, because it snapped in two when it connected with his opponent, but not before splitting his forehead.

The man stopped, groaned and put both his hands up to the inch long cut, the blood already beginning to seep through his fingers.

Kershaw stepped in and kicked him in the groin, bringing the man to his knees.

Left holding half a broom handle, Kershaw looked over at Leroy, who by this time had rubbed away most of the pain and was getting to his feet.

Three long strides and Kershaw was with him. With all of his considerable strength, he whacked Leroy around the ear, the blood almost instantly starting to run down the side of his face.

Just to even things up, Kershaw kicked him in the ribs, sending Leroy back to the floor.

Kershaw looked at both men, neither of whom looked as if they were about to get up.

His whole body was shaking and his breathing was coming in heavy gasps.

He thought he was about to collapse, due to a mixture of fear, excitement and relief.

Mixed in with this cocktail of emotions, was disbelief.

Had he really done all this damage, he thought, looking around him.

He certainly had and it made him feel quite proud.

These two had come to give him a pasting and he had shown them the error of their ways. Praise the Lord!

All that remained was for him to get them out.

Opening the door and still with the stick in his hand just in case he met with any resistance, he grabbed hold of Leroy's collar and dragged him out into the hall, the blood still flowing from his ear, leaving a trail of tiny dark red circles on the carpet.

Walking back into the room, the other man was on his feet, his face covered in blood, some of which was already becoming crusty.

The way in which he glared at Kershaw made him think that he was going to have another go, but then his eyes flickered down to the stick in Kershaw's hand and he thought better of it.

"Get out!" ordered Kershaw, never taking his eyes off of him.

The man sullenly walked past him and out into the hall. He turned around.

"You're gonna regr...," but Kershaw slammed the door in his face.

Walking back into the room, he was still feeling exhilarated by the whole episode.

Looking down at the brown stain on the carpet, he knew there was something that he had to do.

Ten minutes later, he was jogging down the road, on his way into town. He had to run. He knew that if he stopped and began walking, he might have time to change his mind about what he about to do, to see sense, maybe and he didn't want that.

CHAPTER FIFTEEN

Five minutes later, Kershaw arrived outside the café, the one with the pinball machine, the one he had told himself to keep away from.

Even though it was a chilly night, he was feeling warm, partly because he'd been running and partly because he was nervous.

The window of the cafe was slightly misted up, but as he peered in, he could make out what was happening inside.

There were a couple of people seated and someone was behind the counter, but it was the pinball machine that he was interested in.

Sure enough, the Skinhead was there, his longhaired, short assed little mate standing next to him.

As his hand hovered over the door handle, Kershaw could hear a voice inside his head telling him to forget this, go back home and to stop kidding himself that he was someone that he wasn't.

Thinking about what had happened ten minutes earlier, Kershaw knew why he was having doubts.

Those two back there had been strangers and it had all happened so quickly, it was over almost before it had begun. He'd had no time to think about it.

On the other hand, he knew the Skinhead and he knew that he feared him and standing outside of the cafe, he had the chance to consider what he was about to do.

This had to be done. Even if he came off worst, at the least the Skinhead would know that next time, if there was a next time, it wouldn't be such a pushover for him.

Taking a deep breath, Kershaw steeled himself and walked into the cafe. Johnny was concentrating on the pinball, but when the door opened, Mike turned around and recognised Kershaw instantly.

He nudged Johnny's elbow.

"Fuck off! I'm almost up to half a million."

As Kershaw approached, Mike thought that there was something different about him and it wasn't just the swollen eye. He seemed somehow more determined than he remembered him.

He took his life in his hands and nudged the Skinhead's elbow a second time.

Johnny took his eyes off of the machine and glared down at Mike.

"You do that one more time and I'm gonna..." He trailed off when he realised that Mike wasn't taking any notice of him, but was looking towards the door.

Following his gaze, a grin spread across his face when he spotted Kershaw.

The steel ball bearing rattled down the hole, but Johnny wasn't interested in his half a million score, not now Kershaw had appeared on the scene.

"Well, well, look who it is," said the Skinhead, smiling.

"If you're looking for a smack in the other eye, you've come to the right place."

After everything that had happened, Kershaw had completely forgotten about his eye.

Now that the Skinhead mentioned it, he could feel it throbbing, but it wasn't bothering him.

"No," said Kershaw, "I've come for my money. You owe me a fiver."

Johnny laughed in Kershaw's face. "Yeah, right," he scoffed and turned to face the pinball machine once more, paying Kershaw the ultimate insult. By turning his back he was saying that he didn't see Kershaw as any kind of a threat, quite the opposite.

"If there was a list by which you could measure people's worth, you'd come somewhere between a fork with no handle and a wasp," said Kershaw.

The Skinhead didn't seem to be too bothered, but Mike was starting to get a bad feeling about all of this. Something wasn't right.

The skinhead looked at Kershaw as if he were addressing him in an alien tongue.

Sarcasm's obviously lost on this thick bastard, Kershaw thought to himself. I'd better talk to him in his native language.

"You're a worthless piece of shit."

Johnny understood that alright!

"You fucking what?" he snarled, grabbing hold of Kershaw's jacket.

Kershaw knew what was coming next, in fact, he reckoned that if he took away the youth's head-butt, he was guessing that he didn't have much left in his arsenal.

He caught the slight movement, the same as the one outside of the chip shop, the one that he had been too slow to react to, but he was ready this time.

Remembering the episode in the pub with Clive, he thrust out his left hand, clutching the Skinhead under the jawline with his thumb and forefinger.

There are nerve centres all around the body, two of which could be found under jaw. When pressed, not only did they cause considerable pain, but they also cut off the air supply to the windpipe.

Johnny became motionless, his eyes and mouth wide open.

Kershaw kneed him in the groin and pushed him back, until he collided with the sharp metal edge of the pinball machine.

Kershaw thought it only fitting that he should be given a taste of his own medicine.

He'd never head-butted anyone before. How hard could it be?

As soon as he'd butted him, he realised that he must have done it wrong, because it hurt like hell and it hadn't affected the Skinhead at all.

He tried it once more and this time he got it right.

As a small cut appeared on the bridge of the Skinhead's nose, Kershaw released the grip on his jaw and punched him in the face with his right hand.

When he hit him a second time, he knocked him to the floor.

Looking down, Kershaw found it hard to believe that he had been running scared from this person for almost a month. He seemed pretty pathetic, lying down there on the floor.

He looked at Mike, who was also looking pathetic, as well as petrified.

"Where's my money?" asked Kershaw.

This time, it was someone else dipping into their pocket to save their own skin.

Mike brought out a ten pound note, which Kershaw took off of him.

"You want change?" asked Kershaw.

Mike stood there, not saying a word.

Kershaw turned and walked to the door. As he passed the cafe owner, he nodded.

The owner nodded back, as if in thanks for him giving the Skinhead what he deserved for tilting his pinball.

Outside, Kershaw took a lungful of the cold night air.

This was turning out to be quite an eventful evening, he thought to himself, and headed back to his flat, feeling immensely gratified. Penny had just reached the entrance to the Silvermere estate, when she did a u-turn and headed back the way she had just come.

She couldn't get Kershaw out of her mind. Over the past month, she had grown very fond of him, something that she hadn't planned on.

Despite the fact that she was using him, she still couldn't bear to think of him being beaten up. If she was quick, she might get back there before those two had the chance to do any real damage.

She'd tell them that French wanted them to leave him alone. If the two thugs thought that message had come from their employer, which she guessed, was what he was, they wouldn't dare question her.

Once Kershaw realised what sort of people he imagined that she was dealing with, he might just change his mind and agree to help her and if he didn't, then there would have to be a change of plan.

She simply didn't want him getting hurt, at least, not in the physical sense, anyway.

On reaching the house, she jumped out of her car and dashed up the steps to the main door. Inside, she ran up the stairs to the second floor and knocked on Kershaw's door.

She waited for a few moments and when there was no answer, she knocked again.

She put her ear to the door. There were no voices and she couldn't hear any movement.

Then she noticed the dark stain on the hall carpet. Bending down, she touched it with her finger. It was damp and her finger was red.

My god! What had they done to him? Had they taken him away somewhere, or had he dragged himself off to the nearest hospital?

She ran back down the stairs. Her mobile phone was in her car and she was praying that he had his with him.

Outside, she was just about to open the car door, when she spotted Kershaw walking down the street towards her.

She was relieved to see that he wasn't limping, he wasn't even hobbling and she couldn't see evidence of any bandages.

As he approached, she was able to see that he had a swollen eye, but it didn't really look that serious.

For his part, when Kershaw spotted Penny outside his flat, he felt like turning around and walking away. He didn't really want to see her.

On the other hand, it had been an extremely exhilarating evening. It seemed that the adrenalin had been pumping round his body at the speed of ten tall Indians since she'd first walked through his door.

He'd never experienced excitement like it, not even when he'd been competing at athletics.

Would he get the same kind of rush breaking into her house and stealing the diamonds?

He couldn't believe what he was thinking. He'd never done anything illegal in his life, hadn't even stolen sweets from the pick'n'mix, but when he thought about it, what was there here for him? Working in a cash and carry, unloading an articulated fucking lorry.

Did he really want to do that for the rest of his life, when he could be living in the sun, with Penny by his side?

If he did agree to it, and it wasn't definite yet, he wasn't going to hand it to her on a plate.

She was going to have to do a bit more grovelling first.

"I'm so sorry," she said, as she reached up and gently touched his cheek.

"I didn't want this to happen," she said, truthfully.

"So why send them round?"

He had to admit, he was angry that she could have done something like that.

"I didn't. When these people told me that they wanted their money, I stupidly told them about my idea to steal my father's diamonds and that you might be helping me. They must have followed me here and when they saw me leave, they quite rightly assumed that you had said no."

"Well, you don't have to worry about them now, I sent them packing," he told her, proudly.

Penny looked shocked. "What do you mean, you sent them packing?"

"I kicked them out," he replied, matter-of-factly and pointed to his eye.

"After they did this, that is."

"So what happens now?" she asked.

"What do you mean?"

"They're still going to want their money. Will you help me, please?"

"You mean that you're still thinking about stealing your Father's diamonds?"

She took hold of his hand.

"Think about it Bobby, somewhere in the sun, our own little business just you and I."

It was almost as if she could read his thoughts.

He nodded towards the steps. "Let's go upstairs and talk about it."

While he was fumbling for his keys, he noticed her looking at the bloodstain on the hall carpet.

"Don't worry," he reassured her. "It's not mine."

"My God, Bobby! What did you do to them?"

"I didn't murder them, if that's what you're thinking. I just knocked them about a bit, that's all."

Penny looked at him as if she were looking at a stranger, which was what he had become to her. He certainly wasn't the same person that she saw in the pub on that Friday evening.

There was something different about him, but it was something that she couldn't quite put her finger on.

"So how is this going to work?" he asked.

They were inside and in exactly the same position that they had been in just over an hour ago, she in the armchair and he sitting on the edge of the bed.

"My father will get back around midnight, Saturday. He'll put the diamonds in the safe and then transfer them Monday morning to the bank."

Kershaw interrupted her.

"One thing I don't understand. Why would you want to steal from your own Father?"

Penny let out a heavy sigh.

"My Father's a pig and I hate him," she said, resentfully.

Kershaw was surprised at her outburst. "I thought you two got on okay."

"You don't have to live with him, you don't know what he's like. Anyway, I don't want to talk about that now."

"Fair enough. Carry on," said Kershaw, sensing that if he pushed her any further on her relationship with her Father, she could well go into one.

"Do you remember, in the dining room, there are two sets of French doors?"

He nodded.

When you come round the back of the house, the first set of doors will be unlocked. My Father will have set the alarm before he went to bed, but I will have turned it off by time you get here.

Walk through the dining room and out into the hall. Do you remember Monty?"

Kershaw gave her a confused look. "Monty?"

"Field Marshall Montgomery, the bust in the hall."

"That's who it was!" he thought to himself. He knew he'd seen that face somewhere before.

"That's the safe," she told him.

"It is?" He couldn't remember it looking much like a safe.

"Yes. The head unscrews and it's hollow inside, but it's lead lined to make it feel as if it's solid.

Instead of unscrewing anti clockwise, as with most other things, you unscrew this in the opposite direction."

"Ingenious," he mumbled.

"The diamonds will be in there. You simply take them out, put Monty's head back on and go out the way you came in."

She sat back and smiled at him.

Kershaw had to admit, she did make it sound very easy, a little too easy.

"What's the catch?" he asked.

"There is no catch. It really is that simple."

"What about afterwards? I mean, we can't spend diamonds, can we?"

Penny smiled at him, knowingly.

"You don't have a Father who's a diamond merchant, without picking up a thing or two. I know someone who'll take them off our hands."

Kershaw looked mortified. "You're going to sell them to someone your father knows?"

"All diamond merchants are crooks, to a certain extent, at least, but the man I have in mind is a bigger crook than most. In fact, I wouldn't be surprised if he isn't around our house the following week, trying to sell my Father his own diamonds back."

Kershaw's nerve was beginning to weaken and his stomach felt as if it were going into meltdown. He wasn't entirely convinced that this was such a good idea.

"Say you'll do it, Bobby," begged Penny, reading his thoughts again.

He nodded, gingerly and she shot out of the chair and hugged him.

"We're going to have such fun together, you and I," she told him.

CHAPTER SIXTEEN

Penny had left soon after, telling him that she would call him during the week, but he knew that she meant would call him to make sure that he hadn't changed his mind. Was he doing the right thing?

She didn't seem to have any qualms about this and if it was as straightforward as she said it was, then it should be a piece of cake, but if anything should go wrong, he'd make damn sure that if he went down, she'd go down with him. In her car, Penny was having doubts of a different kind.

She was falling in love with Kershaw, of that she was certain. It hadn't been part of the plan but she was unable to help herself.

She couldn't see him go to prison, that would break her heart.

There was an embryo of a plan forming in her mind. It was daring, but it could work, although there were some people, who knowing the sort of person she was planning to double cross, would say that her plan wasn't so much daring as bordering on suicidal.

French had a luxurious apartment in a quiet mews in Richmond. It reflected the fact that he earnt between one and two hundred thousand pounds a year, on which he paid the lowest threshold of income tax, which in his case, was nil.

He had just poured himself a tumbler of scotch, when there was a knock on door.

Putting the glass down, he walked across the large living room to answer it.

When he opened the door, he found Leroy and his pal facing him, both looking the worse for wear, with dried blood on both their hands and faces.

"What the fuck happened to you two?" he asked, looking from one to the other.

"That Kershaw's not as soft as you said he was," said the one with the beard.

French looked both confused and angry at the same time.

"Kershaw did that to you?"

Both men nodded.

Just then, Penny appeared on the landing behind them.

Even though she knew that Kershaw had 'knocked them about a bit', as he'd put it, she still wasn't prepared for the sight of so much blood.

French glared at her.

"Seems like you've been shagging a regular superhero," he said, angrily.

Penny knew that he'd be upset and had decided that it would be best to bluff it out.

"Bobby did that to them?" she asked, pretending to be astonished.

"No, of course he didn't," said French, he voice heavy with sarcasm.

"After they beat the crap out of him, they fell down the stairs on the way out. What do you think?"

Penny looked at him calmly. "I think you sent the wrong people round."

"Get yourselves cleaned up and be round the club tomorrow morning," French told the two men and indicated that Penny should come in. French had two scars, a legacy from his prize fighting days, one down the side of his nose and the other under his right eye. When he was angry, really angry, they became more pronounced and right now, they were about as pronounced as they could get.

He took a large gulp of his whisky and swallowed.

"Sit down," he ordered.

"It's all right, he's going to do it," said Penny, sitting down on the sofa.

Penny had hoped that her news would calm him down, but it didn't have the effect that she thought it would.

"You still don't get it, do you? There are three gentlemen flying into Heathrow at the end of the week. These are not the kind of people you cancel on.

I don't want any cock-ups on this."

"There won't be," she assured him.

On the outside, she looked and sounded confident, but inside she was terrified.

She had experienced, second hand, French's fury in a pub one night, when someone had spoken to him out of turn and in a manner that displeased him.

She felt sure that he wouldn't hesitate to do the same to her, if she pushed him too far.

She had to keep him sweet, for the time being, at least.

"Everything will go according to plan," she told him, failing to mention, for obvious reasons that she was talking about her plan, rather than his. Kershaw had a fitful night's sleep, which was understandable, considering the circumstances.

He was torn between thinking with his head and thinking with his heart, although he was fairly certain that he would end up going through with this. The rewards were too tempting to ignore.

The following morning, Andy questioned him about his eye, which had developed into a classic shiner overnight.

"I walked into a door, didn't I?" he told him, making himself sound like a proper Charlie.

Not having any reason to suspect otherwise, Andy left it at that.

Kershaw wasn't sure what would be happening after Saturday, he hadn't thought that far ahead.

He guessed that as soon as Penny had turned the diamonds into hard cash that they would be off. It made him a little sad to think that he might not be seeing his chubby little pal anymore, but thankfully, as far as he was aware, that was the only real sacrifice he was going to have to make, but once he and Penny had got to where they were going, he was sure he could persuade Andy to fly out and see them.

It wasn't the end of the world, yet.

Penny phoned him on Wednesday evening.

"Hello Bobby, how are you?"

He thought that she sounded a little apprehensive.

"If you mean, have I changed my mind, no."

"No, well, yes and no, I suppose. I wanted to make sure that you were okay and to go through any last minute details."

"Like what?"

"Well, when you get through the gate, go to your left and keep as close to the trees as possible. That way, the security light won't come on.

When you come to the end of the trees, follow the hedge that runs down the side of the garden, again, keeping as close as you can. When you get level with the back of the house, cross over and keep your back to the wall, there are security lights at the back of the house as well.

You'll have to do the same on the way out. If the lights come on, they'll wake my Father. He's a light sleeper."

Kershaw didn't like the sound of that. "How light is light?" he asked, sounding concerned.

"Oh, he won't hear you in the house, but one of the lights is right outside his bedroom window and when it comes on, well it lights up the whole room. It's best that he doesn't discover that the diamonds are missing until he gets up, which will be sometime after midday. How are you going to get over here?"

Kershaw had been concentrating on what Penny was telling him and had been visualising himself crawling on all fours, under the hedge. Her question brought him back to the present.

He thought about it for a second and guessed that he could probably borrow Andy's car.

He'd lent it to him before and if he gave him some story about going away for the weekend and he bunged him a few pounds, it didn't think it would be a problem.

"I can get hold of a car," he told her.

"How will I know what time to come over?"

"I'll ring you. You won't have to answer, I'll let it ring three times and then hang up. That will tell you that my Father's been in bed for an hour, so he should be fast asleep."

"Should be?" asked Kershaw, sounding worried.

"He'll be asleep. Trust me."

There was a slight pause.

"So how much are these diamonds worth?" asked Kershaw.

"One hundred thousand."

Penny could tell by the silence on the other end of the line, that she had made the right decision in not telling him their real worth. That would really have freaked him out.

"What are you doing this weekend?" asked Kershaw, when they were up in the canteen the following morning."

"There's a nurse's party on Saturday night. Fancy coming? Angela's going to be there."

It was clear that Andy still hoped that the two of them might get together.

Kershaw shook his head. "No, I'm going away for the weekend, with Penny. That's the reason I asked. Can I borrow your car, if you're not using it, that is?"

"What, hasn't Lady Penelope got a motor, then?"

"Yeah, but hers is off the road. Will that be okay?"

"Yeah, I suppose so. Where are you going, anyway?"

"Up to the Lake district," he lied.

"It's not unlimited mileage, you know."

"Don't panic," Kershaw reassured him. "You'll have a full tank when you get it back.

Friday afternoon, Kershaw dropped Andy off at his house, thanked him again for the loan of his car and then headed for Twickenham, where he knew there was an Army surplus store.

There he bought himself a combat jacket and trousers. If he was going to be skulking around in the dead of night, he thought that he might as well look the part.

Wandering around the Aladdin's cave of military goodies, he picked himself up a cap comforter, the kind he'd seen soldiers wearing on the big screen.

On his way to the counter, he passed a box filled with green plastic pouches. Picking one up, he saw that it was camouflage cream.

In for a penny, he thought to himself.

He lay the items on the counter, while the assistant punched up the prices on the till.

"Going on exercise?" he asked, in a friendly tone.

Kershaw became flustered. He'd seen Crimewatch, seen a criminal caught, simply because someone remembered him acting strangely.

He gave a little laugh.

"No, paintballing."

"Good crack," said the assistant. "What company are you doing it with?

Why is he asking me all these bloody stupid questions? Kershaw thought to himself.

"Um, dunno," he replied, frantically trying to come up with an answer that sounded plausible.

"Someone else fixed it all up. A work's thing, you know?"

The assistant nodded.

"I'm looking forward to it, though."

"Yeah, I wear this stuff when I go," said the assistant, nodding to all the items on the counter.

"Looks better that a shirt and a pair of jeans."

Back in his flat, he tried it all on, all except the camouflage cream that is.

He checked himself in the mirror. A bit over the top, maybe, but what the hell?

He didn't have to go in to work the following morning, but he did anyway. It gave him something to think about, other than what he was going to be up to tonight.

Andy wasn't there, but Eddie was. They were out on the bay, when Eddie handed a slip of paper.

"Clive wanted me to give you this. It's his mobile number, he thinks that there might some more work coming up, if you're interested."

Kershaw thanked him and put the piece of paper into the pocket of his jeans.

He might just ring him, he thought to himself, but it wouldn't be about work and it probably wouldn't be from this country.

That evening he got himself ready. He didn't want to drive over there wearing combats.

There were two entrances to the estate, one off of the main road and one at the back.

The back entrance was a lot quieter, but it was also a good deal further away from Penny's house.

There was an unlit dirt track a little further down, on the other side of the road from the back entrance and he decided that he would park up there and get changed.

He stuffed the combats, the cap comforter and the camouflage cream into a holdall.

He had white horses in his stomach and he wanted to go to the toilet almost every two minutes, it seemed like.

When the phone rang, he could answer it and tell her that he had changed his mind. He could do, but would he?

George Marshall's silver Mercedes pulled into the drive just before eleven.

He was dog tired after what he considered to be a very successful shopping trip to Amsterdam.

All he wanted to do now was to have a hot drink and get to bed.

Once through the front door, he put his briefcase on the occasional table, opened it and took out a velvet pouch.

Unscrewing the head of the bust, he placed the bag inside and put Monty's head back on.

He walked into the kitchen, where his wife, having seen his car pull into the drive, was preparing him a coffee.

They sat at the table and chatted for a little while. It wasn't long, but it was plenty of time for Penny to creep downstairs and remove the pouch from the bust.

Up in her room, she lay on the bed, listening for her Father to finish in the bathroom.

Marshall thankfully slipped into bed, kissed his wife goodnight and rolled over.

He'd set the alarm downstairs, which Penny obviously knew about, but the last thing he did before he closed his eyes, was to reach down the side of the bed flick a small switch, which Penny didn't know about.

Kershaw had just come out of the toilet for the umpteenth time, when the phone rang.

Once, twice, three times. He checked his watch. It was a quarter past twelve.

Taking a deep breath and still wondering whether he was doing the right thing or not, he picked up the holdall and left the flat. Twenty minutes later, he was parked up the dirt track, in the pitch black, struggling to get his jeans off and his combats on.

When he finally got the jacket on, he buttoned it up to the top and put on the cap comforter.

Reaching into the bag, he took out the camouflage cream.

Never having served in the armed forces, he didn't know that camouflage cream, when applied correctly, was deigned to allow the wearer to blend in with the light and dark of the shadows. One small dab on each finger and the hand was down the face, creating a streaked effect.

Kershaw squeezed an enormous blob into the palm of his hand and covered his entire face in the stuff. Looking a little like a black and white minstrel, he started the car and drove out of the lane and into the estate.

He parked about two hundred yards from the top of Penny's road, feeling relieved that he hadn't seen any other vehicles.

He knew that on the way back, the distance between the house and the car, at a good sprint, would take him about twenty five seconds. He was happy with that.

He pulled on his gloves and got out of the car, leaving it unlocked. He didn't want to be fumbling for keys, when he had a hundred thousand pounds worth of stolen diamonds about his person!

He started walking down the road. If he saw the lights from another vehicle, he was ready to dive into the undergrowth, but it was quiet.

Reaching Penny's house, he looked up at the house. All the lights were off.

He placed his hand on the gate. He could still turn around, if he wanted to.

He opened the gate, steadied it as it swung open and walked it back to the trees.

Following Penny's instructions, he kept close to the whispering pines, as he began to make his way around to the back of the house.

CHAPTER SEVENTEEN

Kershaw moved slowly and silently from trunk to trunk. There was no moon, but a streetlamp out on the road helped to illuminate his path.

By the time he'd reached the end of the treeline, he was wishing that he'd never worn his combats. He was sweating heavily, partly due to the weight of his clothes, but mostly because he was as nervous as Hell.

The hedge was slightly taller than he was, but he still got down on all fours just as he'd imagined he would.

When he came level with the back of the house, he stood up and darted across the lawn. With his back to the wall and the heels of his trainers scraping the brickwork, he sidled along the patio, until he reached the first set of wooden French doors.

He could feel rivulets of perspiration trickling down the back of his neck and as he reached out for the door handle, part of him hoped that it would be locked, so he could pack in all this lunacy and go home.

The door opened silently and he stepped inside, closing it behind him.

None of the redeye's belonging to the motion sensors flickered. Penny had switched off the alarm after her Father had gone to bed and before she'd rung Kershaw on his mobile.

On tiptoe and barely breathing, Kershaw walked across the room, opened the door and stepped out into the hall.

His eyes had adjusted to the semi darkness inside the house and he could quite easily make out the shape of the bust in front of him. Looking up at the landing above, he stepped across the hall, still hardly breathing.

When he reached the bust, he had to think which way was anti clockwise, picturing a screw in his mind's eye. Placing his hand on Monty's beret, he began to turn the top of the bust in the direction that he had been told. After spending twenty two years as an infantry soldier, sleeping in fire trenches, under canvas, in the back of vehicles, semi consciously expecting to be roused at any moment, George Marshall could come awake at the drop of a hat.

Between the bed and his bedside table, a red light flashed and a buzzer, roughly equal in volume to that of a wrist watch alarm, woke him.

He was out of bed in an instant. Reaching underneath the valance, he pulled out a pick axe handle and headed for the door.

With Monty's head in his right hand, Kershaw plunged his left into the hollow bust. He swirled his hand around. Nothing. It was empty!

He groped around inside once more, but there was definitely nothing there. Penny knew that French hadn't got to where he was today by being a fool. She knew that he trusted no one and she wouldn't have put it past him to have someone hidden away outside somewhere, to make sure that Kershaw did actually enter the house.

Everything had to be as it was supposed to be which meant that Kershaw had to be seen coming in.

She would have preferred him not to, but she couldn't take the risk.

She guessed that once he discovered that the bust was empty, he'd simply leave and they could sort it all out in the morning. Kershaw wasn't quite sure what his next move ought to be. He had just screwed Monty's head back on, when the chandelier above him flooded the hall with light.

"Don't you fucking move!"

Whipping round, Kershaw saw George Marshall standing at the top of the stairs, a rather lethal looking axe handle hanging by his side.

Kershaw turned to run, when he caught sight of Penny, up on the landing, looking down. She had an astonished expression on her face, almost, it seemed to Kershaw, as if she was surprised to see him there.

With George Marshall and his big stick coming down the stairs, he wasn't about to hang around for an explanation. He ran back into the dining room, closing the door behind him. He didn't want Marshall chasing him around the garden. He had to slow him up, somehow.

Marshall had completed four tours of Northern Ireland with the Royal Hampshire's, three of which had been with the intelligence section. He knew who it was in his hall, he'd known who it was the moment he'd set eyes on him, despite the cam cream.

He'd spent almost twenty two years making snap judgments, some wrong, but most right and he'd known from the moment they'd met that Kershaw didn't have what it took to make him a threat. This meant that instead of coming down the stairs, wondering whether he should tackle the intruder or not, he could have his mind on other things.

Things such as, why was the alarm switched off, when he'd only set it an hour ago? He'd already spotted his daughter on the landing and guessed that the two of them must have set this up.

As he padded barefoot across the cold marble floor, in just his pyjama bottoms, he thought it best to let her think that he didn't know what was going on, which was why he hadn't called out Kershaw's name.

He guessed that Kershaw was leaving the way he'd come in, by the French doors. He would let him think that he was giving chase, then as soon as Kershaw got outside, he'd double back, go to the front door and catch the bastard when he got out onto the drive.

Kershaw stood on the other side of the door, his heart pounding. He couldn't allow himself to be caught. He waited until he saw the door handle begin to move down, waited until the door began to open, then slammed his shoulder into it, with all his might.

He felt the wood connect with something solid, heard a grunt and then the sound of a body falling to the floor.

Turning, he ran towards the French doors. Being in something of a hurry and not wanting to waste time with handles, he covered his face with his forearms and launched himself at the door.

Crashing through, he shot out onto the lawn amidst a shower of splinters and glass. He lost his footing on the grass, fell to the floor, got back up instantly and started running.

The security lights came on, bathing him in light for a second time that evening.

He sprinted around the house and onto the gravel drive. When he reached the gate, he risked a glance over his shoulder just as Marshall opened the front door and dashed out, still brandishing the pickaxe handle.

Kershaw ran out onto the road. Once on level ground, he really began to move. Under normal circumstances, the run from the house to the car wouldn't have been a problem, but with the adrenalin coursing through his body, trying to slow his heart down, Kershaw was finding it hard work.

At one stage, he didn't even think he was going to make it, but he knew that he couldn't stop.

By the time he reached the car, his breathing was ragged and as he fumbled for the car keys, his whole body was trembling so badly, he thought he was about to collapse. He got in and shut the door. It felt like he was going to be sick.

He started the engine and drove off.

He was in such a hurry that he missed the speed hump out on the main road that led to the exit of the estate. His head hit the roof of the car and when the vehicle came back down, Kershaw thought that the suspension was about to give out. He managed to keep control and as he reached the back entrance, he heard a siren in the distance.

Turning out onto the main road, he headed for the lane, where he parked up and switched off the lights.

His breathing was gradually returning to normal, although he was still shaking.

What the Hell had happened back there? Why was the bust empty and why had Penny been looking down at him like that?

He was just thankful that he had got away before Marshall had used the pickaxe handle on him.

He changed into the clothes that he had arrived in and was about to turn the car around, when he remembered that he still had camouflage cream on his face.

He risked using the interior light and when he looked at himself in the rear view mirror, his black face was now streaked with perspiration.

Searching through the glove compartment, he found some wet wipes and began cleaning himself up.

When he'd finished, he wound down the window and threw the black tissue out into the darkness. He pulled back out onto the main road and driving carefully, so as not to attract attention to himself, he made his way back to his flat, still unable to fathom out what had gone wrong.

Back at Whispering Pines, there were two vehicles in the drive, a marked Police car, its emergency lights still flashing and a brown Vauxhall Vectra.

Inside, two uniformed Police officers were checking over the shattered French doors, prior to the forensics team arriving.

In the lounge, George Marshall was sitting on the sofa, his wife by his side. He was holding a blood stained towel to his nose. He'd since put on his pyjama top, which was also stained red. Next to him, Valerie's eyes were red and puffy from crying. Penny sat in the corner, on her own.

Facing Marshall and his wife were two plain clothed Policemen, one old, the other a good deal younger.

Jack Dunn had been a Policeman for almost thirty years. Bald and sporting a tidy moustache, he was similar in build to Marshall, short and stocky.

At present, his rank was Detective Chief Inspector, although it probably would have been a great deal higher, had it not been for his problem.

He had trouble dealing with authority and didn't suffer fools gladly, most of those fools being his superiors. He was a good copper and had the respect of almost every junior rank in the Met, but the higher ranks saw him as a quarrelsome, insubordinate troublemaker.

It was due to his lack of respect, rather than his undoubted ability as a detective that had caused him to be overlooked for promotion on more than one occasion.

Not that Dunn was complaining. He just loved the job, except, apparently judging by the expression on his face, at one o'clock on a Sunday morning.

He had started out as a humble beat copper, but in the twenty eight years that he'd been a policeman, he'd spent time in nearly every arm of the force, including S.O. 14 and Special Branch, finally returning to C.I.D., because that was where he felt most at home.

The young man standing next to him was a good deal taller and had a lot more hair.

Allen Moreton had left university at twenty two, with a degree in economics.

He had planned to join the Army, but after a two week introduction course at Sandhurst, had decided that that the military life wasn't for him after all and had enrolled at Hendon.

The powers that be had thought that it would be a good idea to partner him up with Dunn. If the streetwise old copper had a young, inexperienced cadet with him, they thought, hoped, that it might make him toe the line, force him to set an example for the young officer to follow. To teach him.

Dunn had taught him alright. Unfortunately, what Moreton had learnt so far, he would never have been taught at Hendon, or any other school, come to that.

Dunn reminded the young detective of the rogue American cop in the television programmes that he had watched as a child, the one that would make and break the law as he went along.

On the odd occasion that Moreton had mentioned to the Inspector that he didn't think that what he was doing was strictly within Police guidelines, Dunn would simply laugh at him and tell him to stop acting like a big girl's blouse.

"So you say he was black?" Dunn was asking the questions, as befitted his status, whilst Moreton was taking notes, which befitted his.

"I don't say he was black, he *was* black," replied Marshall, his voice a little nasal.

He wasn't about to hand Kershaw over to the Police straight away. He wanted to have a word with him first, to explain to him that stealing was wrong and then teach him the error of his ways.

The Police could have him after that and he would probably give them his thieving daughter at the same time.

"Anything else you can tell me about him?"

"He was tall and judging by the way he went through my bloody French windows, strong as well."

Dunn looked at Valerie," Did you see him?" he asked.

She shook her head. "No, by the time I got downstairs, he'd gone and George was on the floor in the hall."

"Miss?" asked the inspector, turning his attention to Penny in the corner.

She was miles away. She'd heard her Father tell her Mother earlier that the intruder was a black man, which was a plus. At least Kershaw wouldn't be on the Police's list of immediate suspects, giving her time to try and sort this terrible mess out.

What was puzzling her was how her Father had known that Kershaw was in the house. She'd been awake and even she hadn't heard him.

She looked at the inspector, quizzically.

"Did you see the man who broke in?" asked Dunn.

"Yes, but I can't add anything to what my Father has already told you."

"And he could run like a bloody cheetah," said Marshall.

Dunn stood in the centre of the room, his hands in the pockets of his raincoat and looked up at the motion sensors that were in each corner of the room.

"You're absolutely sure that you set the alarm before you went to bed? No chance that you could have forgotten? You did say that you were very tired."

"You've asked me that already," replied Marshall, still dabbing the polka dotted towel to his nose, only less frequently now.

"I'm certain I set it, I always set it," he said, adamantly.

There was a knock on the lounge door and a uniformed officer poked his head around.

"We've had a good look at the French doors, Sir. There's nothing obvious that we can see. Do you want forensics around tonight, er, this morning I should say"?

Dunn looked at Marshall. The man was clearly tired and in need of some rest.

The Inspector knew that if he kept him up any longer, he would become irritable and uncooperative. He looked back at the officer.

"No, you get off, we'll take it from here."

"I suppose those French doors are going to cost a sodding fortune to get repaired," moaned Marshall.

"Speaking of fortunes, how much were the diamonds worth?" asked Dunn.

"A lot."

"Diamonds usually are. How much is a lot?"

For a moment, it looked to the Inspector as if Marshall wasn't going to answer his question, then he let out a heavy sigh and his shoulders visibly sagged.

"Three million," he replied, morosely.

CHAPTER EIGHTEEN

Back at his flat, Kershaw lay on the bed, still wearing his combats. He was trying to figure out what had gone wrong. The bust had been empty, there was no doubt about that.

So, either the diamonds hadn't been in there in the first place, in which case, why hadn't Penny told him to forget the whole thing when she'd called, or they had been taken out before he got there, in which case, why hadn't she told him when she'd called?

What about Marshall? Kershaw knew, when he'd looked in the rear view mirror of the car, that with the camouflage cream on his face, he'd looked a little different, but had it been enough to prevent him from being recognised?

He'd been sitting across the table from him only a week ago.

If Marshall had realised who he was, the Police could be here, well, anytime.

He didn't feel safe. He was going to have to leave his flat, for the time being, at least.

He'd take Andy up on his offer of a lodger. That would give him somewhere to hide until he decided what to do next.

He couldn't stay here tonight, though. He'd have to sleep in the car and go round to Andy's house first thing in the morning.

He took off his combats and along with the cap comforter and the camouflage cream, stuffed them all in the holdall.

He also put in his building society passbook, some clothes, a change of underwear and a few toiletries. Putting on a pair of jeans, a shirt and his black leather, he went back out to the car.

"One last question and then we'll let you get some rest," said Dunn.

Marshall's nose had finally stopped bleeding and his wife had gone out to the kitchen with the bloody towel.

Penny had excused herself and had gone back upstairs. It was just Marshall and the two detectives, alone in the lounge.

"We need the name of the person who sold you the diamonds."

Marshall looked surprised. "Gunter? What do you want to know about him for?"

Dunn gave a little shrug. "We need to check him out."

"He didn't have anything to do with this. I've known him for years, we're friends, good friends."

"I still need his name," insisted Dunn.

Valerie came back into the lounge.

Dunn looked at both of them. "You get some rest. We'll come back later today to finish off. If you could leave the French doors as they are, it'll make things easier for the forensics people when they turn up."

Sitting on the sofa, next to her husband, Valerie looked aghast.

"Do you mean we have to go upstairs without setting the alarm and with the French doors wide open?"

Marshall patted her on the knee. "It's alright, I'll get Billy over here. He can sleep down here tonight."

Dunn's ears pricked up. "Who's Billy?"

"He handles all my security," replied Marshall. He was reading the Inspector's mind.

"I know. If he had been here, none of this would have happened. I didn't think I needed him."

Dunn's eyebrows rose.

"You had three million pounds worth of diamonds in the house, and you didn't think that they needed looking after?"

Kershaw had moved the car further down the road, away from any streetlights.

If the Police did storm his flat in the middle of the night, he wanted to know about it.

Climbing into the back and using the holdall as a pillow, he put on his Walkman and slipped in Blink 182.

Dumpweed started playing and he curled up. The music helped him to relax and would hopefully, see him through what was going to be a sleepless night, or what was left of it.

Dunn and Moreton were in the Vectra, on the road outside of Whispering Pines.

"This stinks of an inside job," said Dunn.

"Not necessarily."

The Inspector looked across at Moreton. "How do you figure that?"

"A burglar breaks in, rifles through the house, looking for something to steal, thinks that the bust might be worth a bob or two, but when he picks it up, he realises that it's not all it seems." He looked at Dunn, expectantly, waiting for his reaction.

"Oh yes, the bust. Very clever idea, that. So you think that there could be some brick wielding, petty thief, sitting at home right now, playing tiddlywinks with three million quid's worth of diamonds?"

"It's possible."

Dunn stifled a yawn. "Take me home, then get some rest. Be back in at ten.

We'll give our Dutch cousins a bell, see what they can come up with on this…"

"Gunter," said Moreton.

Kershaw woke with the Walkman humming in his ears. He checked his watch.

Ten past nine. Getting out of the back of the car, he was as stiff as a board.

He stretched, then looked around him, hoping that no one was watching.

Looking down the road, he couldn't see any sign of the Police outside of the house.

He would have liked to have gone up to the flat, to see if they had paid him a visit, but he daren't.

Fifteen minutes later, he was outside Andy's door, ringing his bell.

It took a couple of minutes for Andy to open up and when he did, Kershaw could tell that he had come straight from his bed. He was wearing a pair of Winnie the Pooh boxer shorts, his hair was all tousled and he eyes looked as if they were still adjusting themselves to the daylight.

He blinked a couple of times. "Blimey mate! You're up early."

"Yeah well, I thought you might need your car."

Andy looked at his watch. "Not at this time of the morning."

Kershaw heard someone coming down the stairs and looking over Andy's shoulder, he saw that it was Clare.

She looked as half asleep as Andy, the only difference being that she was totally naked, obviously not realising that the front door was open.

When she saw Kershaw, she gave an embarrassed squeal and rushed back up the stairs.

Andy grinned, sheepishly. "She's been helping me decorate."

"Yeah? Get a lot done?"

Andy shook his head. "Not really."

"Anyway, look, are you still after a lodger?" asked Kershaw

"Yeah. Why, do you want to move in?"

"I thought I'd give it a try," said Kershaw and watched as Andy's chubby face lit up.

"Great! Well, move in anytime you want," Andy told him, clearly pleased at the prospect of having his pal staying with him, not to mention the help with the mortgage payments.

They stood staring at each other, until the penny dropped, for Andy.

"What, you want to move in now?"

"No time like the present. I'll just get my bag from the car, er, your car." When Kershaw returned, the front door was open and Andy was in the kitchen, making some coffee.

He looked at Kershaw's holdall, as he put in down on the floor.

"Is that it?"

"It'll do for the time being. I'll get the rest later. Two sugars in mine, thanks."

Penny put a jumper down by her door, so that if anyone wanted to come in, it would get caught up underneath, preventing them for opening the door all the way, which would give her time to conceal exactly what she was up to and it would appear less suspicious than locking herself in.

The velvet pouch wasn't that big, so she didn't think she'd have too much trouble concealing it about her person.

She checked herself in the mirror and when she was satisfied that the bag couldn't be seen, she picked the jumper up off the floor and left the bedroom.

"Are you going out, dear?" asked her Mother, who had come out of the kitchen at the same time as Penny reached the bottom of the stairs.

"Yes, I'm going to see Pauline," she lied.

"Are you alright now," she asked.

Valerie sighed. "I'll get over it, but I'm not so sure about your Father. I don't know how the insurance company's going to react over this."

Just then, Marshall walked out of his study, having just finished on the phone.

He stared hard at Penny, giving her the impression that he knew something, but he couldn't do, she thought to herself.

Saying good bye to her parents, she walked out of the front door and over to the garage.

Eventually, she would be going over to French's flat, but first she had to pay a visit to the crooked jeweller that she'd told Kershaw about.

He was a lascivious, weasel of a man, who, on the two occasions that he had called at the house, to do business with her father, had eyed her much like a dog would eye a juicy bone and it wasn't hard to tell what was going through his disgusting mind.

It wouldn't be too hard to get him to give her a fair price and if she had to give him a little sweetener, it would probably be worth it, however obnoxious it would undoubtedly be.

Moreton walked into the Inspector's office on the dot of ten o'clock.

"Morning, Sir," he said, sounding far too cheery for Dunn's liking.

As usual, the young detective was impeccably turned out. Clean-shaven, wearing a double breasted suit and a tie with a Windsor knot.

Dunn hadn't shaved, wasn't wearing a tie and felt like shit.

"Right, I want you to get back over to the Marshall's place. I want the details of every tradesman that's been at the house in the last month.

Builders, plumbers, the window cleaner, postman, the lot. Let's go on the assumption that someone saw Marshall using the bust and passed the information onto another interested party.

"I'm going to get onto the Dutch Police and see what they can give us."

"I think that we're going to have to clear this up as soon as possible," said Moreton, voicing his opinion.

"Why, because it's a private estate, filled with rich people?" asked the Inspector, scornfully.

"No, because the Chief Constable lives in the next road."

"Does he?"

Dunn looked at the young detective suspiciously.

"How do you know that?"

Moreton shrugged. "I guess I must have heard it somewhere. In fact, I'm surprised that he..."

Dunn's telephone began to ring.

"Morning Sir. Yes Sir, I know, it's terrible news. Yes, we're on it now. No, not yet, but it shouldn't be long. Yes Sir, I will Sir, Yes Sir.

Three bags fucking full Sir," said Dunn, after putting the phone down and making sure that it was properly back in its cradle.

He looked up at Moreton, who had the beginnings of a smirk on his face.

"You still here," snapped Dunn.

Penny's task hadn't been nearly as arduous and distasteful as she had imagined it would be.

The jeweller had rightly guessed that there was something not quite kosher about the diamonds that Penny was trying to sell and that was reflected in the price that he had offered her. As time wasn't on her side and his tender hadn't seemed that outrageous, she'd accepted it.

Now, on her way to French's apartment, she had two, identical velvet pouches.

One contained diamonds worth a King's ransom and the other didn't.

French was still in his dressing gown when he opened the door to her.

"Everything go alright?" he asked, closing the door behind her.

Penny took a pouch out of her handbag and held it out to him.

"Fine," she replied. Her hand was trembling, ever so slightly, but she managed to get it under control.

He walked over to the coffee table, undid the drawstring and tipped out the contents of the pouch. The diamonds twinkled and sparkled, as they spilled out over the table.

French picked one up in his finger and thumb and held it up to the light, a smile on his face.

"I should imagine Loverboy's down in the interview room, pissing his pants, about now."

When he didn't hear a reply, he turned to her.

Penny swallowed, hard. "He managed to get away, but it's alright, he had some stuff on his face and my Father thought that he was a black man, so the Police won't be looking for him."

French's scars began turning white. "No, but they'll be looking for someone, won't they?"

There was no mistaking the anger in his voice.

"That was the whole idea. The Police have someone in custody, so they're not out on the streets, going through the usual suspects, which will eventually be me."

His voice was growing louder, as Penny's heart was beating faster.

"It doesn't matter if he's black, yellow, or fucking rainbow coloured!

How the fuck am I supposed to do business with the Russian Mafia knowing that Plod could be knocking on my door any time of the day or night?"

Penny sat through his tirade, knowing that the best policy was to keep her mouth shut.

"But it's not just me, is it?"

When he looked at her, his ice blue eyes appeared to be more menacing than ever.

Penny wasn't sure what he was talking about. She gave him a quizzical look.

"Sooner or later, you're precious Bobby's going to catch the news or read a paper. What do you think he's going to do when he finds out that he's supposed to have had it away with three million quid's worth of diamonds?"

Penny began to see where this was going.

"I'll tell you what he's going to do," continued French, answering the question for her.

"He's going walk into the first cop shop that he comes across and tell them that it wasn't him. He's going to give them your name and sooner or later, you're going to give them mine."

Penny was about to tell him that she wouldn't do that, but he cut her off.

"It doesn't look as though I'm going to put this deal together, thanks to that little wanker, but I don't want the law on my ass for those," he said, pointing to the diamonds on the table.

"He's going to have to be dealt with."

A shiver ran down Penny's spine, when she heard French speak those words.

She was pretty sure what he meant by 'dealt with', but she asked, nonetheless.

"I can't have him running around, shouting his mouth off. Do I need to draw you a picture?"

Penny stood up.

"I'll speak to him, offer him some money to disappear," she suggested, trying not to sound too concerned over his welfare.

French had begun to put the diamonds back in the pouch. He turned to her, a trace of a smile on his lips.

"Oh, he's going to disappear alright. Don't you worry about that."

CHAPTER NINETEEN

The two boys were just finishing their coffee, when Clare walked into the kitchen, in her nurse's uniform.

She smiled at Andy, but ignored Kershaw. He guessed she was embarrassed after he'd seen her with no clothes on.

"Bobby's going to be moving in," Andy told her.

She glanced at Kershaw, but there was no warmth in her eyes. "That'll be nice for you."

She poured herself half a glass of orange juice from the fridge and drank it straight down.

Putting the glass in the sink, she walked over and kissed Andy on the cheek.

"I'll call you," she told him and gave Kershaw another cold look. "Goodbye."

After she'd closed the door, Andy gave Kershaw a weak smile.

"She's a bit pissed off with you, about Angela."

"Why? I haven't done anything."

"That's just it. Angela was under the impression that you were going to call her."

"I never told her that."

Andy shrugged. "That's women for you. You mess with her mate, you mess with her. What can you do?"

Despite the feelings that Penny now had for him, she knew that what French had said about Kershaw was true. When he discovered that he was considered to be the number one suspect in all of this, he was going to do his utmost to prove his innocence.

Unless she spoke to him first. He had been willing to go through with the plan, before it all went wrong. The only thing that had changed was the true value of the diamonds and that wasn't such a bad thing, was it?

She knew that she didn't have much time. French was going to get onto this as soon as possible.

"I've got to go home and pick up a few things," she told French, who was busy putting the jewels, one by one, back into the bag.

He stopped and looked at her.

"Stay away from Kershaw," he ordered.

"Of course I will," she lied. "I don't want to get caught up in the crossfire, do I?"

Detective Constable Moreton was in the kitchen at Whispering Pines, with Valerie Marshall.

He had just finished making a list of the people that she told him had been at the house within the past month, when he looked through the front window and saw George Marshall walking along the tree line, in conversation with a large, muscular man with a shaven head, earrings and what appeared to be more tattoos than skin.

"Who's that with your husband?" he asked Valerie.

She looked through the window.

"Oh, that's Billy."

Moreton was certain that he'd seen the man before, but couldn't remember where.

Throughout the journey from French's apartment to Kershaw's, although there was a huge difference between the two, Penny kept looking in her rear-view mirror.

She couldn't ignore the possibility that French had ordered someone to follow her, to ensure that she didn't disobey his command to stay away from Kershaw.

It was ten o'clock on a Sunday morning, so there wasn't that much traffic on the road.

It looked as though she was on her own.

She pulled in just before Kershaw's road and waited. There were no other cars behind her, so turning into the road, she parked up outside the house and ran up the stairs.

She knocked on the door with a certain amount of trepidation.

She was going to have to do some fast-talking, before he slammed the door in her face and she could hardly blame him if he did.

When there was no answer, she took out her mobile phone and dialled his number.

She could hear his phone ringing from inside the flat, but it wasn't answered.

Thinking hard for a moment, she went back down, got in her car and drove in search of a newsagents.

French pulled the drawstring tight and walked over to a bookcase. He wasn't an avid reader, the books were really only for show and to help detract attention from one book in particular.

Pulling out Dickens' A Tale of Two Cities, he opened it to reveal a cutaway inside.

The pouch fitted snugly inside and closing the book, he replaced it on the shelf.

He picked up the phone and pressed one of the memory buttons.

"Hello? Yeah, it's me. Where are you? Are you? What are you doing up there?

Oh, right. Anyway, I've got a job for you. It's urgent. How soon can you get down here? Good, I'll see you tomorrow."

He could put the deal together some other time, but to be able to do that, he had to have the diamonds. He wasn't about to lose them because of a prat like Kershaw.

He had to disappear and the man he trusted most to do the job properly, was on his way.

Moreton walked into Dunn's office, looking rather pleased with himself.

He noticed that since the last time that he'd seen him, the Inspector had found himself a tie, although in Moreton's opinion judging by the awful way it had been tied, he would have looked smarter without it.

The Inspector was looking over some papers.

"So what did you get?"

Moreton referred to his notebook. "I've got the names of a builder and a window cleaner, both of whom have been at the house in the last month. They don't have their milk delivered and the postman, well, that's going to take a bit of looking into, but it shouldn't take too long. Then there's this."

He placed a police evidence bag on the desk. Dunn screwed his face up as he looked at it.

It couldn't possibly be what it appeared to be, that would have been, well, too gross for words.

"What it is?" he asked, eyeing the bag with disgust.

"It's a wet wipe. Uniform was carrying out a search of the area and they found this in a lane, near the back entrance to the estate, along with a fresh set of tyre tracks."

"What the Hell have you brought it in here for?"

"The officer who found it, says that he's ninety nine per cent sure that it's camouflage cream."

Dunn felt a wave of relief sweeping over him. For a moment, he had thought that it was...he didn't want to dwell on it.

"That's the stuff that soldiers..."

"Yes, I know what cam cream is, thank you very much," said Dunn.

He took a closer look at the bag, with a little less revulsion this time and picked up one of the sheets of paper on his desk.

"Actually, that fits in quite nicely with this," he said, waving the paper at Moreton.

"What is that exactly, Sir?"

"This is the Marshall chronicles. The man's Military career. Twenty two years with the Royal Hampshire's."

Dunn put a finger on the evidence bag. "I find it hard to believe, that a man who's spent half his life as an infantry soldier, can't recognise cam cream when he sees it."

Moreton wasn't looking quite so pleased, now. He'd thought that he had come into the office with a significant piece of information, but it turned out that Dunn was way ahead of him.

"You think that he knew the man was wearing camouflage cream?" asked Moreton, in an effort to salvage something from the morning, before Dunn pulled the rug out from under him completely.

"More than that, I think he knows who it is, which brings us to this," said Dunn, picking up another sheet of paper.

"When you were at the house, either last night or this morning, did you notice a keypad for the alarm?"

Moreton thought for a moment and shook his head.

"No, you wouldn't have. It's hidden away," Dunn told him, waving the second piece of paper in the air, not unlike Neville Chamberlain.

"This is a record from the company who fitted the alarm. As an added security measure, Marshall got them to time exactly, to the last fraction of a second, how long it would take an able bodied person to walk from the front door to the panel, which, by the way, is hidden behind one of the paintings in the hall. Our black stroke white intruder came in through the French doors. There's no way he could have made it through the dining room and out into the hall in time. The alarm would have gone off."

"So you think Marshall forgot to set it?"

Dunn shook his head.

"Twenty two years in the Army and then a diamond merchant? No, security's in the man's blood. A small fortune, or rather a large fortune, in diamonds, he doesn't think that they need watching over and then he forgets to set the alarm? I don't think so. He set it alright, then somebody else turned it off, before our burglar arrived."

"The daughter?"

"She's the obvious candidate, but who did she turn it off for? Who was she expecting to enter the house? Was she there this morning?"

"No," replied Moreton, guessing what was coming next and knowing that he was going to look like a fool.

"Did you ask the Mother if she's got a boyfriend?"

Moreton shook his head, feeling like a fool.

"So why would Marshall have lied? Do you think he's going to go after the man himself?"

"I hope not," replied Dunn. "People start fucking about with the law and all Hell breaks loose."

Moreton saw an opportunity to make some small contribution to the morning.

"If Marshall's considering exacting his own revenge, then he's got the right man for the job. Billy was there, the same time as I was. You know, the man who Marshall told us handles all his security?

I knew I'd seen him somewhere before and I was right. We've had him in here on a couple of occasions, both times for assault. He's not a very nice man, by all accounts."

Dunn pushed his chair back, stood up and put on his crumpled jacket.

"Looks like we're off to Whispering Pines again. I have to inform Marshall that this is a vigilante free zone and you have to find out from the Mother about the men in her daughter's life."

After finding what she had been looking for, Penny drove back to Kershaw's flat and parked outside.

Sitting in her car, using the writing pad that she had just bought, she composed a letter.

She started off by apologising and asking him for forgiveness.

Then she went on to explain about French and the whole plan. She told him what French was planning to do and for him to get away, as far away as possible, then for him to phone her on her mobile, if he still wanted anything to do with her.

Apologising once again, she signed the note and slipped it into an envelope.

Upstairs, she knocked on the door, in the vain hope that he might have returned whilst she had been gone.

When there was no answer, she bent down and slipped the envelope under the door.

She hoped and prayed that he read it in time.

When Valerie Marshall opened the door, it was clear that she wasn't pleased to see the Police, so soon after their last visit, but she was still pleasant.

"Inspector, back again?"

"I'm sorry about this, but I need to have a word with your husband. Is he in?"

"Yes, he's in his study."

She was about to walk across the hall, when Moreton gently took her by the arm.

"Which door is it?" asked Dunn.

Valerie pointed to the third one along and looked at the Inspector and then at Moreton, clearly anxious.

"I'm absolutely parched," said the young detective, pleasantly.

"Is there any chance of a cuppa?"

Valerie watched Dunn walk across the hall towards her husband's study, then turned to Moreton, smiling weakly.

"Of course, come into the kitchen."

Dunn knocked at the door and walked in, not waiting for an invitation.

Marshall was sitting at his desk, Billy standing by the window.

The Inspector recognised him just as Moreton had.

"Ah, Inspector, do come in," greeted Marshall, smiling.

"Any news?"

Dunn took the evidence bag out of his jacket pocket and threw it down on Marshall's desk.

"Well, there's that, for a start."

Marshall looked at the bag, much as Dunn had, when he'd first seen it.

"I'm not with you. What is that?"

"It's cam cream. Your intruder was wearing it last night, but then, you already know that, don't you?"

Billy took a step towards Dunn, who turned and glared at him.

Dunn had been around too long to worry about a bruiser like Billy. The Inspector was a lot tougher than he looked.

Marshall held up his hand and Billy stopped where he was.

Dunn turned back to the desk.

"I'm sure I don't need to remind you that obstructing the Police is a criminal offence," warned the Inspector.

Marshall looked as if he couldn't care less. "I don't know what you're talking about."

"Don't give me that load of old bollocks! You know who it was in here last night and you're planning to send laughing boy there over to give him a beating," said Dunn, managing to control his temper, in spite of Marshall's supercilious attitude.

"Where's your daughter?"

For the first time since Dunn had walked into his study, Marshall looked concerned.

"What do you want her for?"

It was Dunn's turn to act nonchalant. "Just routine."

"She's out," said Marshall, curtly.

The Inspector leant forward, both palms on Marshall's desk.

"If I find that you're giving me the run-around. I'll see you in court."

He turned and walked towards the door.

"Inspector?"

Dunn looked round, to find Marshall smiling. "Love the tie."

Out in the hall, Dunn could see Moreton and Valerie talking in the kitchen.

Catching the young detective's eye, he nodded towards the front door, indicating that it was time for them to leave.

Valerie walked out of the kitchen with Moreton.

"Is everything alright, inspector?" she asked, sounding no less anxious than when they had when they'd first arrived.

"Everything's fine," he reassured her. "We'll have this wrapped up in no time, don't worry."

Smiling nervously, she watched them leave.

"Any luck with Marshall, Sir?" asked Moreton when they were in the car.

"I don't know. I don't think he was taking me seriously, but he will if he starts fucking me about. What about you?"

Moreton nodded. "The daughter's got a boyfriend, alright. All the Mother could tell me was that his name's Robert and he works at Whitman's cash and carry. He's tall and well built, although those weren't the exact words that she used.

Oh, and he's white."

CHAPTER TWENTY

Fifteen minutes after the two Policemen had left, Penny pulled into the drive.

She opened the front door as quietly as possible. She was hoping to get in and out without seeing either of her parents, her Father in particular.

Upstairs, she grabbed a few clothes and stuffed them in an overnight bag.

As she reached the bottom of the stairs, her Mother came out of the kitchen.

"Hello dear. How's Pauline?"

For a brief moment, Penny was baffled by her Mother's question, then she remembered what she had told her when she'd left, earlier that morning.

"Oh, she's fine. I'm on my way back there. We're going out for the evening."

Just at that moment, her Father came out of the study, followed by Billy.

"Ah, Penny. That guy you brought over for lunch, last Sunday. What was his name?"

"Bob."

"That's right, Bob. Are you going to be seeing him this week?"

Penny didn't like the direction that this conversation was taking, especially with Billy, standing behind her Father, leering at her.

"Probably, why?" she asked and she was actually telling the truth, at least, she hoped so.

"I might be able to put some work his way, security work. Billy can show him the ropes."

Yes, and then he'll most likely hang him with them, she thought to herself, looking over her Father's shoulder at the violent bodyguard.

She had a pretty good idea why her Father wanted Kershaw at the house and it had nothing to do with work. He knew, she was sure of it.

"I'll ask him if he's interested."

Saying her goodbyes, she walked out the door.

Getting in her car, she couldn't help feeling a little sad, as that was the last time that she would be in that house, the last time that she would see her parents.

She was going to miss her Mother, but as for her Father, he could rot in Hell, for all she cared.

Andy and Kershaw were in the lounge, watching the early evening news.

As usual, it was all doom and gloom and Kershaw wasn't paying much attention to it.

Then the local news came on and his heart skipped a beat, when he heard the newsreader mention the Silvermere estate.

If his heart had missed one beat, then it missed half a dozen, when a picture of Penny's house appeared on the screen.

His jaw dropped when he heard that a thief had broken in during the night, stealing diamonds estimated at three million pounds. The newsreader continued by saying that the Police were looking for a black male.

Kershaw couldn't believe what he was hearing!

He hadn't taken anything and if he had, the diamonds were only worth one hundred thousand and he wasn't black!

Andy gave a short whistle. "Wow! That's a Hell of a lot of diamonds to have hanging around, eh?"

He might as well have been talking to the wall, because Kershaw couldn't hear him.

His head was buzzing and he was having problems thinking coherently.

He could hear a voice in the background, which turned out to be Andy.

"Huh?" Kershaw mumbled, his mouth hanging open.

"What's up? You look as though you've just seen a ghost."

Andy looked nervously around the room just to make sure that they were on their own.

For a moment, Kershaw thought that he's been struck dumb, he seemed unable to speak.

"Uh, no...uh, no, I'm alright."

"Do you fancy a pint?" asked Andy.

"There's a nice place just round the corner, with a proper pool table, you know, tips on the end of the cues, chalk, everything. I'll give you a thrashing, if you like."

Kershaw knew that he had to try and act normal, for the time being at least and that meant not staring at Andy with his mouth wide open.

"Yeah, okay," he replied, trying to calm himself down after the shock he'd just received.

By the time they'd got out of the front door, Kershaw had come to terms with what he'd heard on the television. That bitch Penny had obviously been stringing him along, although why and to what end, he had no idea, but he sure as Hell was going to find out.

The pub was literally two minutes away and when they walked in, being early Sunday evening, it wasn't that busy.

Drinkers were dotted around, either at the bar, or sitting down and two lads were having game of pool.

Andy walked over and put his pound on the edge of the table, then joined Kershaw at the bar.

"We're up next," he informed him, "And mine's a pint of lager."

Inside, Kershaw was fuming, but he had to keep it under control, at least until he had decided what to do next, which he guessed was to get his hands around Penny's throat and throttle the conniving cow.

"So how are you and Clare getting along?" he asked, while they were waiting to be served.

"Great!" replied Andy, enthusiastically. "We're having a really good time."

"I'm glad for you," said Kershaw, putting on a brave face.

It seemed as though Andy's life was getting better and better with each passing day, while it looked as if his was about to turn to dog shit.

They got their drinks and Kershaw paid.

"I'm going for a wizz, find us a seat, yeah?"

Kershaw stood at the urinal. He still couldn't believe it. Being stood up and messed around by a girl was fair enough, he'd done it to them on countless occasions, but what Penny had done was out of order. She'd overstepped the mark and he wanted to know why.

No one knew where he was and the newsreader had said that the Police were looking for a black suspect, that had to be something to do with the camouflage cream, he guessed.

So he was safe for the time being. He might as well enjoy his pint, it could be his last for some time, he thought, rather melodramatically.

When he walked out of the toilets, he noticed that there were two different men at the pool table.

"I thought you said that we were on next?" he asked, sitting next to Andy.

He shrugged. "Ah, they got there before me."

"But you put your pound on the table. That means that we're before them."

Andy seemed embarrassed.

"They said that they were going on next."

Kershaw looked over. One of them was standing at the far end of the table and the other, who was racking up the balls, turned to Kershaw and smirked.

Kershaw couldn't help noticing that the man had a ponytail.

All this shit was kicked off by a guy with a ponytail. He could feel the anger welling up inside him.

He could have controlled it, been like Andy and just let the guy go first, but why the Hell should he?

"We'll see about that," he said, taking a mouthful of his pint and placing it back on the table.

"No, leave it..." Andy tried to grab hold of his arm, but he was too late, Kershaw was already walking.

The guy saw Kershaw approaching the table and turned away. Having racked up the balls, he placed the white on its spot and began cueing up.

Pulling back his arm, he was about to make his break, when Kershaw placed his hand on the table, between the end of the cue and the white.

Still leaning over the table, the guy looked up at Kershaw.

"I think we're on next," Kershaw told him.

The man gave a heavy sigh and was about to straighten up, when Kershaw whipped his hand off of the baize and smacked him in the face with the back of his fist.

There wasn't much power in it, but it stung enough to give him time to get in another one.

Hitting him again with the back of his fist, this one was stronger, splitting the man's top lip.

As the man staggered backwards, Kershaw whipped the cue out of his hands, to prevent it from being used as a weapon against him, rather than wanting it for himself, but now that he had it, why not?

He drove the thickest end of the cue into the man's face just below the eye, cracking his cheekbone. As he yelled in pain, Kershaw hit him across the side of the head, the cue breaking in half.

The man fell to his knees at the same time as Kershaw heard Andy calling out his name.

"The Landlord's called the Police! Let's go!"

At the mention of the word, Kershaw flung the half of the cue he had in his hand onto the pool table, scattering the unbroken balls to all four corners.

He looked down at the man on the floor, curled up, cradling his head in his hands and then at his pal, down the other end of the table, who clearly didn't want to get involved.

"You're stripes," said Kershaw, as one of the balls dropped into the corner pocket.

Andy was holding the door open for him, clearly eager to get moving.

Kershaw ran out the door and headed back to Andy's house, his slightly overweight pal trying desperately to keep up, but falling further and further behind.

By the time Andy finally reached his front door, breathless and perspiring, Kershaw was there, waiting for him.

"What...the Hell was...all that back...there?" asked Andy, between gulps of air.

"That's not like...you."

Andy was right. Under normal circumstances, Kershaw would have reacted just like him.

He would have let the guy with the ponytail go first, without a word of protest.

"What's going on? You turn up here at the crack of dawn wanting to move in and all you've got is a holdall. Then you beat the crap out of that bloke back there, like you've been doing it all your life."

Andy held his palms upward. "What gives?"

Kershaw was living in his house, so he figured that it was only fair that he knew what had happened. At least that way, he'd know why the Police were breaking down his door in the middle of the night.

Kershaw nodded his head at the front door.

"Let's go inside. There's something you need to know."

While Kershaw told him everything, Andy listened intently, his eyes wide open in disbelief.

When Kershaw finally finished, ending with why he'd beaten the guy in the pub around the head with a pool cue, Andy blinked a couple of times and swallowed.

"Blimey, mate! You have got yourself into a bit of a pickle, haven't you?"

Kershaw smiled. From where he was standing, a pickle didn't begin to describe the mess that he was in, but he felt as if a great weight had been lifted from his shoulders just by telling Andy the whole story.

"Yeah, and all over a pretty face," said Kershaw, sorrowfully.

Andy let out a short laugh, stood up and clapped him on the back.

"Delilah did it to Samson and it's been happening ever since. You won't be the last guy to be taken in by a woman. Look at me. That she bitch almost hung me out to dry."

"Yeah, but at least you didn't have the Police chasing after you."

"No, and neither have you. You said that they were looking for someone black, remember? As long as no one tells them otherwise, why should they come after you?"

Kershaw put his elbows on the table. He didn't want to feel sorry for himself, but he couldn't help it.

"Are you going into work tomorrow?" asked Andy.

"How can I?"

Andy shrugged. "What's the worst that can happen? If they do come and pick you up, at least it'll be over and if they don't, well, you live to fight another day, so to speak, but if you stay here all day, thinking about it, it'll drive you bonkers."

Kershaw nodded in agreement of his pal's advice.

It felt good, knowing that he had at least one person on his side, one person who believed him.

Kershaw lay in bed, staring up at the ceiling. Was everything that Penny had said to him a lie? He gave a little nod. Probably. He couldn't very well call at her house and he wasn't sure where she was working. He would have to risk a visit to his flat tomorrow evening, where he had her mobile phone number written down somewhere.

He'd ring her, although he doubted very much, after all that had happened, after all that she had done, that he would get much out of her. Certainly not the truth.

He tried to imagine where she right at this moment, what she was doing. Then he fell asleep.

Strangely enough, Penny was thinking about him. She too was lying on her back, but instead of a duvet on top of her, she had French.

He was grunting and thrusting, then he climaxed, rolled off of her and went straight to sleep.

Sex with French had been exciting, at first, simply because of the man himself and who he was, but as a lover, compared to Kershaw, he really stank.

Kershaw was gentle and considerate, while French was brutal and selfish.

Kershaw went out of his way to pleasure her, putting her needs before his, whereas French only thought of himself. Like most bad lovers, he thought he was the best.

Penny missed Kershaw, something that she hadn't planned for. She missed his smile, his touch, his humour.

A lump came to her throat at the thought of never seeing him again, alive.

When she woke, French was gone. She looked at the clock by the bed and guessed he had gone to the gym, as he did most mornings.

Getting out of bed, she put on her dressing gown and padded into the lounge, where she received a shock.

Sitting on the sofa, eating a bowl of cereal, was a man that she had never seen before.

"Hi, I'm Ali. I guess you must be Penny." When he spoke, he had a thick, Mancunian accent.

He had short, dark, curly hair and an unkempt curly beard. Even though he was sitting down, Penny got the impression that he was quite tall and a little on the lean side.

He was dressed in jeans and a black tee shirt, with Motorhead emblazoned across it.

It made him look a little like a hippy student, but Penny noticed that even though he was smiling benignly at her, the warmth never reached his eyes.

They were cold and heartless.

Penny knew, immediately, that she didn't like this man and she involuntarily pulled her dressing gown tighter around her body.

"Pete's gone down the gym," he told her, swallowing a mouthful of cereal.

"But being old, he shouldn't be too long. It's okay. I'm quite safe."

Penny imagined that safe was the last thing that this man was.

Just then, the door opened and French walked in, wearing a tracksuit and carrying a sports bag.

He looked at the two of them. "Getting to know each other, huh?"

"Yeah, but your girl seems a little nervous," said Ali, still sitting on the sofa.

French glanced at him and smiled.

"Yeah, most people tend to get nervous when you're around."

He looked over at Penny.

"Why don't you go take a shower? Me and Ali have some business to discuss."

Penny knew that it wasn't a request, but she didn't mind.

She was just happy to get away from Ali. He gave her the creeps.

As she shut the bathroom door behind her, she knew that if this was the man French had hired to deal with Kershaw, then her secret lover was in real danger.

CHAPTER TWENTY-ONE

French went into the kitchen, poured himself a glass of orange juice, walked back into the lounge and waited until he heard the shower running.

"Right, there's an industrial estate, on the outskirts of Brentford. Do you know it?"

"No, but I'll find it."

"Kershaw works in a cash and carry, down there, alright?"

"What does he look like?" asked Ali.

French thought about that for a moment. "I dunno. I asked Penny what he was like and she just said that he was okay. Anyway, someone will point him out to you?"

Ali's eyes grew wide. "Yeah, and then someone will point me out. She must know what he looks like, she was fucking him, after all."

French seemed a little dubious.

"Ah, she gets funny whenever his name's mentioned. I don't know what's got into her. Best to leave her out of it.

Anyway, you're getting paid well over the odds for this one, a damn sight more than you'd normally get for just pulling the trigger. Use your initiative, do whatever you like, just make sure that by this time tomorrow, Kershaw's resting in peace."

Ali stood up. Penny's first impression was right, he was tall, around six foot.

He handed French the empty cereal bowl.

"Righto, I'll see you later," he said and walked out the door.

If it had been anyone else, French would have broken the bowl over their head, handing it to him like that!

As much as he hated to admit it, if he tried that with Ali, he could end up taking a hammering.

Ali was an expert in most of the martial art disciplines and French had seen him at work.

He had all the grace and poise of a ballet dancer and despite his lean frame, the strength of a mountain gorilla, but his laid back, almost lackadaisical attitude, sometimes brought his efficiency into question, although French was prepared to overlook that.

What really impressed him about Ali, was his total lack of compassion.

It was said, that if you going to kill a man, you should never look him in the eye.

Ali would never look anywhere else. It was almost as if he were trying to figure out what was going through his victim's mind, when he, or she, knew that they were about to die.

He could kill someone as easily as he could eat a hamburger.

French was confident that if he wanted Kershaw out of the picture, he had the perfect man for the job.

Kershaw, on the other hand, was far from being the perfect man for the job, at least, not this morning. He couldn't keep his mind on anything and he constantly had his eye on the door, expecting half the local Police force to come barging in, shouting his name.

Andy had to keep reassuring him that no one was coming to take him away and that tonight they'd work out together, what it was he should do.

The fitter had just replaced four new tyres on an old Fiesta, when a black Mercedes with tinted windows, pulled up to the kerb.

The passenger window slid down and Ali leant across.

"Excuse me," he called out politely.

The fitter sauntered across to the car.

"Is there a cash and carry warehouse around here?"

The fitter took a drag on his cigarette and thought for a moment.

"Oh yeah. Second turning on your left, about halfway down."

Ali thanked him and the big car glided off, leaving the fitter wondering how much a motor like that would cost him, on his salary.

Ali had bought the Mercedes outright, with the payment from his last job.

He liked his work and the hours suited him, one day on, six months off, but this little outing was better than most.

For some reason, French was paying him a lot of money for this one and Ali figured that it would get him a couple of months in the Bahamas. Just what the doctor ordered, he thought to himself, as drizzle began to fall on the windscreen.

He pulled up outside the warehouse gates and studied the notice that gave the opening times. The warehouse closed at six. Checking his watch, he saw that he had a few hours to wait. He'd go and do a spot of shopping, have some lunch, then find himself a quiet spot and grab forty winks, before returning.

Andy and Kershaw were on their way up to the canteen, when Andy's mobile phone started to ring.

"I'll catch you up," he said to Kershaw, taking the phone out of his pocket.

"Get us a cuppa."

Ten minutes later, Andy sat next to Kershaw and began stirring his tea.

"That was Clare on the phone. She's going to come round tonight for a meal."

Kershaw nodded, but he got the impression that Andy had something else to say.

He was right. "I told her to bring Angela along. That's okay isn't it?"

Kershaw didn't think that he'd be very good company right now, but he knew that all Andy was trying to do was to make him feel better.

He guessed that a night with Angela, who, if he recalled, was quite pretty, might help to take his mind of off the shit that was rolling downhill towards him.

"Yeah, we'll make a night of it."

Andy grinned. "It'll be a laugh."

At a quarter to six, the black Mercedes rolled up on the other side of the road to the warehouse, about fifty yards away.

Ali had just applied the handbrake, when he thought that he might have spotted the answer to his dilemma.

Swanning down the road towards him, was a young boy, who Ali figured must have been twelve, maybe thirteen.

As with most kids his age nowadays, he was kitted out from head to toe in designer labels and he walked with a cocky swagger.

As he approached the car, Ali lowered the window.

"Hey kid, want to earn yourself some money?"

Clearly having had the dangers of talking to strangers drummed into him, the lad's cockiness seemed to vanish. With a distrustful look in his eye, he took a sideways step away from the car and carried on walking, ignoring Ali's question.

"Hey, it's okay. You don't have to get in the car. I just want you to do me a favour, over there," said Ali, pointing towards the warehouse gates.

The kid stopped and looked at Ali warily.

"How much?"

"A tenner."

The light was beginning to fade and the drizzle was coming down again.

The boy flipped up the hood on his Nike top and waited, expectantly.

Ali looked across the road and noticed that some people had already come out onto the bay and were walking along to the steps at the end.

He knew that he was going to have to be quick, or he's miss his mark.

He saw a big, fat woman, who must have come out before the others, standing by the gates, as if she were waiting for a lift.

"See that woman over by the gates," said Ali, looking back to the boy.

"What, the one with the great big tits?"

Ali smiled. "Yeah, the one with the great big tits."

"What, you fancy her?" asked the boy, cheekily.

"No, I want you to go over and get her to point out Robert Kershaw to you, okay?"

With his curiosity whetted, combined with his lust for pocket money, the boy came a couple of steps closer to the car.

"You going to thump him?"

The kid was starting to get on All's nerves.

"No, I just want to have a word with him, but I don't know which one he is, alright?"

The lad seemed disappointed that he wasn't going to witness a punch up in the middle of the road. He nodded and trotted away.

Ali watched as the boy went up to the woman. She smiled sweetly down at him as she listened to what he was saying.

Looking up, she pointed to a couple of men who had just walked out of the gates, heading towards a red Mazda, parked on the road.

So, it's one of those two, is it? Ali thought to himself.

Now, what had French said? He wanted Penny to pick someone who wasn't likely to give them any trouble.

The big guy looked like he could be a bit of a handful and if Ali wanted an easy time, he certainly wouldn't have picked him, which meant that it had to be the Billy Bunter wannabe.

The kid ran round the front of Ali's car and came up to the window.

Ali started the engine.

The two men, having had a quick conversation across the roof of the car were getting in.

"The woman said that…"

"Thanks, kid," laughed Ali and putting his foot on the accelerator, he pulled away after the Mazda.

Ali pulled up about fifty yards away and watched as Andy and Kershaw got out of the car, outside of Andy's house.

They were oblivious to the Mercedes, with the tinted windows, as they had been on the trip home, when it was behind them.

If the big one was just visiting, then he could have a long wait, Ali thought to himself, but if he actually lived there, then that could be a little tricky.

He couldn't do both of them, he'd only been paid for one and he wasn't in the habit of handing out freebies, not even for French.

Kershaw came down the stairs, after having had a quick wash.

"I'm going to need to get some cash from the hole in the wall, okay if I take the car?"

"Yeah, help yourself", said Andy, from in the kitchen.

Picking up the car keys from off of the hall table, he walked out the door.

"Oh, sweet," muttered Ali, as he saw Kershaw walk out of the house, get into the Mazda and drive away.

Time to book myself a holiday, he thought to himself.

The Mercedes crept silently along the road, until it was level with Andy's front door. It was almost dark now and as well as the drizzle still hanging in the air, it had grown colder. Ali preferred it when the weather was like this, it meant that he could use his favourite coat.

Getting out of the car and leaving the engine running, he walked to the boot and took out a full-length, black leather coat. Underneath, was a heavy roll of plastic, which at first glance, looked as though it should contain the car's jack.

Putting on the coat, he unrolled the plastic. Instead of a carjack, it contained a sawn off shotgun and half a dozen cartridges.

He wouldn't need those, as the weapon was already loaded. He slipped the gun into the right hand pocket of his coat, which had no lining. This enabled him to walk with his hand in his pocket, holding the gun at his side, undetected under the coat.

Buttoning up the three top buttons, leaving the bottom two undone, he closed the boot and walked casually across the road.

He rang the doorbell and waited.

He could hear movement inside and then the porch light was switched on.

Andy opened the door.

"I bet you've forgotten your..." He trailed off when he saw the tall man standing in the porch. He was about to ask him what he wanted, when the shotgun appeared out of the bottom of the coat.

Ali emptied both barrels full in Andy's face.

The report of the gunshot echoed down the hall, followed by a spray of blood and fragments of bone, mixed in with various other bits and pieces.

As the blood splattered all over Andy's newly decorated hallway, his lifeless, almost headless body, fell backwards onto the carpet.

Leaving the hall filled with smoke and reeking of cordite, Ali walked just as casually back to his car. Turning around in the road, he drove off, whistling to himself and thinking of the Bahamas.

"I still don't think that this is a good idea," said Clare, as she was waiting for a gap in the traffic, so that she could turn into Andy's road.

"Why not?" asked Angela.

Neither of them paid any attention to the black Mercedes that pulled out of the road and sped away.

"He's nice."

"Yes, I know," said Clare, "But he's also a charmer. You know that he's seeing some rich girl, don't you? When Andy asked me to bring you, I should have said no."

"I can make up my own mind," said Angela, sounding a little miffed.

There was a gap in the traffic and Clare turned.

"That's funny," she said. "Andy's car isn't here, but the front door's wide open."

They had only taken a couple of steps from the car, when they spotted the body in the hall.

"Oh my God!" exclaimed Clare and they ran into the house.

Working in accident and emergency, both girls were used to seeing victims of traffic accidents, industrial injuries and the like, so it wasn't the fact that they were looking at a body with only half a head, the other half spread up the walls that shocked them, but that it could be someone that they knew.

"It is Andy, isn't it?" asked Angela.

"I recognise his clothes, so I suppose it must be," replied Clare.

She reached into her handbag and took out her mobile phone. As nurses, they both realised that there was nothing they could do for the body on the floor, which they knew to be lifeless.

Clare was trembling slightly as she dialled the emergency operator and Angela could see that her eyes were becoming watery.

On getting through, she told the operator which services she required and what they could expect to find on arrival.

Angela put an arm around her friend, to comfort her.

"We'd best wait in the car," she said, gently.

Although gruesome, Clare didn't want to leave and Angela had to tenderly ease her away.

Driving back from the cash dispenser, Kershaw was feeling slightly better about things.

He hadn't had his collar felt and was beginning to believe that maybe he wouldn't after all.

He had a pocket full of money and was about to spend the evening with a pretty girl.

Andy wasn't the only person whose life could improve, he thought to himself.

When he turned in to the road, his world came crashing back down round his ears.

"Shit!" he swore, when he saw the police car, its emergency lights flashing, bumped up on the pavement, outside the house.

How the Hell had they managed to find him?

He did a U-turn and drove back to the main road.

Because of the way they were facing, the two girls failed to see Andy's Mazda careen and swerve its way back out into the traffic.

CHAPTER TWENTY-TWO

Chief Inspector Dunn was on his way to the canteen. Despite bringing the chef's culinary skills into question at every opportunity, he had most of his meals there, having neither the time nor the inclination to cook at home, a maisonette, where he lived alone.

He had been married for ten years, almost the length of time that he'd spent in uniform.

The marriage had been fine, until he began experimenting with other branches of the force. It was then that it began to flounder.

The even more unsociable hours, the late night drinking sessions and the unexpected, yet strangely, expected phone calls, to inform his wife that he had been injured and was in hospital, of which she had received two, began to take its toll.

His wife had begged him to return to being a regular copper again, but he hadn't listened.

He came home one morning, to find the house empty and a note, telling him that it was over. He felt sure that things could be patched up, if he acceded to her requests, but looking back, he realised that he had been too wrapped up in his career to consider anyone else but himself.

It had been fifteen years since the divorce. There had been the odd fling, but for the most part, he was alone.

He heard his name being called and when he turned, he saw Moreton jogging down the corridor towards him.

"We might have something, Sir," said the young detective, sounding excited and a little out of breath.

"There was a shooting about half an hour ago, in Firwood road."

Dunn nodded. "Yeah, I heard that in the cad room."

"Anyway, the unit who answered the call were carrying out a search of the house and they found a holdall, containing a set of combats, a cap comforter and a passport, in the name of Robert Kershaw, who happens to be five foot eleven and a half."

Moreton shrugged. "It might be nothing, but I thought that you ought to know."

Dunn was looking thoughtful, not just about what Moreton had told him, but that if they left now, he could get something to eat while he was out. He fancied fish and chips.

"Might be worth looking into," he graciously conceded.

When French answered the door, Ali sauntered in and sat down on the sofa, opposite Penny, who was in the armchair, reading a magazine.

"Well?" asked French, expectantly.

Ali shrugged. "It's done."

Penny looked up from her magazine. She had hoped that Ali wouldn't have been able to find Kershaw before she did, but it seemed as if French had been right to put his faith in him.

Ali smiled at her. "I must say, I didn't think that you'd go for a porker."

When Penny appeared puzzled. Ali assumed it was because she was unfamiliar with the term.

"You know, a fat bloke?"

Penny knew what a porker was, but that would have been the last word she would have used to describe Kershaw.

"Bobby wasn't fat."

French was looking at the two of them and he didn't like the direction that this conversation was taking.

Ali shrugged. "No, I suppose I shouldn't talk ill of the dead. Maybe not fat, then.

Let's say cuddly."

Penny put her magazine down. "Bobby didn't have an ounce of fat on him, in fact, he had the body of a gymnast," she told him, while at the same time, thinking the unthinkable.

French was looking even more anxious now and Ali wasn't looking too comfortable, either.

"This Bobby, tall is he?" asked Ali.

"Yes, he's about six foot."

Ali looked at French and made a sucking noise. "Oops!"

French stared at him, incredulously.

"Oops? What the fuck is that supposed to mean?"

Ali looked at him, sheepishly. "I think I've done the wrong one."

"For fuck's sake!" exclaimed French, staring up at the ceiling.

"We all make mistakes," said Ali, as if he'd done nothing more sinister than to buy the wrong newspaper.

It was difficult, but Penny managed to hide her relief. If Kershaw was still out there, then all might not be lost.

"So where's Kershaw now?" asked French, still fuming, but managing to keep it under control.

"The last I saw of him, he was alive and well and driving around in a red Mazda," replied Ali.

Kershaw was alive and he was driving a red Mazda, but he was far from well, in fact, he was feeling a little queasy.

Before he'd disappeared onto the main road, he'd toyed with the idea of turning back and handing himself in, if only for Andy's sake. He felt sure that his pal wasn't too pleased at having Policemen traipsing through the house, searching every room, but he knew the mess he was in and that none of it was none of his fault. Andy would understand.

What was he going to do though? He couldn't go to his flat and he didn't fancy another backbreaking, muscle knotting night in the car. He needed to find an out of the way, nondescript bed and breakfast, where he could hole up for the night, like the fugitive that he had undoubtedly become.

He would find Penny tomorrow, he didn't know how, but he had to and if he didn't, then he would have to turn himself in and hope that he could convince the Police that he was innocent.

Dunn and Moreton parked next to the patrol car and made their way to the house.

As Dunn lifted the black and yellow tape that had been strung across the path, he gave the two girls in Clare's car a cursory glance.

Outside the porch stood a well worn uniformed Sergeant, his lined face resembling a relief map of the London underground.

The Sergeant nodded to Dunn. "Hello Jack," he greeted the inspector, informally.

"Alright Dave," replied Dunn.

"It's a bit of a messy one in there," the Sergeant told him and glanced at Moreton.

"I thought I'd better mention it, in case you're thinking of sending the boy in. I wouldn't want him throwing up all over your…," he cast an eye over Dunn's crumpled jacket and lurid tie, that looked as though it had been knotted by a chimpanzee.

"Your best outfit."

"Kiss my ass!" said Dunn scowling at him. He looked at Moreton.

'You're not going to puke, are you?"

"No, Sir," replied the young detective, staunchly.

Dunn turned back to the Sergeant. "See?"

Dunn opened the door and they walked into the house.

When the Inspector pulled back the sheet, that one of the officers had placed over the body and Moreton caught a glimpse of the near faceless corpse, the first thing he did was vomit.

Dunn took a step back. "Jesus! Will you watch where you're throwing that stuff."

He turned around to find the Sergeant, standing by the door, grinning.

Dunn had seen too many corpses in his career, from finding them still warm, through stiff, to decomposing, to react in the way Moreton had just done.

He was still affected, but in a different way. Whenever he came across a murder victim, it filled him with a sense of pity, knowing that someone had been robbed of the most precious commodity in the universe, life itself.

Although, in a strange turnabout, he was a staunch advocate of capital punishment, firmly believing that if someone took a life, then they should forfeit their own.

Knowing that his feelings fell and would always fall, on deaf ears, he kept them to himself.

Hearing footsteps, Dunn looked round to see two uniformed officers making their way down the stairs.

"One of you found a holdall?" asked Dunn.

"Yes, Sir," replied one of the officers, a giant bear of a man.

"It's in here," he said, opening the door to the lounge.

Leaving Moreton being supported by the wall, his skin ashen and slightly waxy, Dunn followed the big officer in to the room.

"Got any gloves?" asked Dunn.

The officer nodded and pulled a pair of white latex gloves out of his jacket pocket.

Dunn snapped them on and unzipped the holdall.

He rummaged through the bag. Combats were combats were combats and he doubted very much that he would get any information from them here and now.

It was the passport that he was interested in. Finding it, he opened it up and stared at the photograph inside.

The Inspector had been a policeman long enough, to know that a copper's hunch was not a myth, something that was discussed in whispers, up in the canteen.

Looking at the picture of Kershaw, looking at the eyes, Dunn knew that this man was not responsible for the body in the hall. That was someone else's handiwork.

"There's two girls in a car outside, Sir," said the officer from behind, disturbing Dunn's train of thought.

"They're the ones who found the body. One's the girlfriend."

Dunn nodded and checking the address in the passport, he placed it back in the holdall.

"Take that with you, when you go and log it in."

The officer nodded and took out another pair of gloves. Outside in the hall, Moreton wasn't looking much better than when Dunn had left him.

The young detective was determinedly keeping his eyes averted from the body and the wall that had Andy's brains pebble dashed all over it.

"Come on," said Dunn, unsympathetically, "You can wait in the car, while I have a word with these two girls."

214

As they walked out of the door, the aged Sergeant clapped Moreton on the shoulder.

"Don't worry about it, son. I puked when I saw my first gruesome body."

The Sergeant's admission seemed to offer Moreton some comfort.

"Did you?"

"Oh, yeah. I'll never forget it. It was on my honeymoon night, when the missus took her teeth out. Gawd, it was horrible!"

Dunn laughed, but the pasty faced Moreton didn't find the Sergeant's attempt at humour, at his expense, quite so amusing.

"Hey, Jack," called out the Sergeant.

Dunn stopped and turned around.

"Love the tie."

"That's Chief Inspector Jack, to you, asshole."

"Do you know Bourne road?" asked Dunn, when the two of them reached the car.

Moreton shook his head.

"Get in the passenger side. I'll drive, after I've had a word with these two girls."

Two pairs of eyes watched him as he walked towards Clare's car, opened the rear door and got in.

"I'm Chief Inspector Dunn," he said, holding up his warrant card.

"Do you know who that is in there?"

It was clear that Clare had been crying and Angela was looking a little upset as well.

"His name's Andy Parkin," said Clare, between short sniffs.

"Do either of you know a Robert Kershaw?"

The silence and the quick glance, exchanged between the two girls, told him what he needed to know.

"Can you describe him to me?" he asked.

"He's tall, has dark hair and he's well built," said Angela.

"You don't think he had anything to do with this, do you?"

"We don't know anything at the moment, that's why we need to speak to him.

Were they friends?"

Angela nodded. "They worked together at Whitman's cash and carry and Bob was Andy's lodger. He moved in yesterday morning."

Dunn's eyebrows rose a fraction. "Yesterday morning?"

He considered this for a moment. "Would you know where he is now?"

"He was supposed to have been here, but Andy's car is missing, so I guess he must have it."

Angela was doing all the talking, she knew that Clare wasn't up to it.

"What car is that?"

"It's a red Mazda."

"You wouldn't happen to know the registration number?" asked Dunn, hopefully.

"No, I'm sorry, I don't."

"Miss?" asked Dunn, this directed at Clare.

She turned around to look at him, clearly not having heard a word of what had been said.

"Do you know the registration number of Mr. Parkin's car?"

Clare just shook her head.

"I'm going to need both of you to make a statement, at some time. Just pop into the nearest Police station, within the next couple of days. Someone there will take them down and forward them on to me. In the meantime, I'm afraid that I'm going to need someone to make a formal identification."

Clare turned around. "He has an ex-wife up in Nottingham. Her address is in the house, somewhere."

It was obvious that neither of the girls wanted the onerous task of identifying Andy's body and were angling for a way out.

Dunn could understand that.

He nodded. "That's okay, we'll find it."

"You two might as well get off home."

Dunn had lost count of the number of times he'd had to deliver bad news to someone, concerning a relative or loved one and it never seemed to get any easier.

He put a hand on Clare's shoulder.

"I'm sorry about your boyfriend," he said.

Clare looked at him, smiled and her chin began to tremble.

"You feeling better, now?" asked Dunn as they drove off.

"Yes, thanks." replied Moreton, his voice a little husky.

Having spent some time in the Army, all be it a fortnight and having only just passed out from Hendon, Moreton found it strange that a junior officer should address a superior by his Christian name. He said as much to Dunn.

"Dave Ryder's been a copper even longer than I have. He was happy to stay as a Sergeant, I wasn't. There's nothing that man doesn't know about Police work, and I feel privileged that he calls me by my first name. When there's no one about, of course."

"Where are we going, Sir?" asked Moreton.

"Kershaw's flat, see what we can come up with."

"Do you think that's wise, without back up, I mean?"

The Inspector smiled. "Don't worry, Kershaw's not our shooter."

217

"How can you be so sure?" Moreton was happy for the Inspector to go rushing in, all gung ho, if that's what he wanted, but he preferred to keep his head where it was.

"Trust me," Dunn reassured him, "Kershaw's harmless, but I've got the feeling that there's more to this than meets the eye."

CHAPTER TWENTY-THREE

By the time they reached Kershaw's flat, the colour had returned to Moreton's face.

Dunn knocked on the door and waited.

When there was no reply, he glanced at Moreton and nodded towards the door.

"Kick it in."

The young detective looked horrified. "Isn't that illegal entry, Sir?"

"I don't have time for all that bollocks! Just open it."

Moreton had only been a Policeman for two months, so he hadn't had many copper's hunches, in fact, this was his first.

He had a hunch that the Inspector was in no mood to be argued with.

Taking a step back, he kicked the door with the sole of his shoe and bounced off, stumbled and managed to regain his balance, before he fell flat on his back.

Dunn stared at him blankly.

"Well, go on then. Kick it harder this time."

Taking two steps back, Moreton launched himself at the door. This time, when his shoe made contact with the area around the lock, he heard the wood splinter and the door burst open, Moreton flying into the room, out of control.

The door swung all the way back, hit the wall and began to return, Moreton catching it before it knocked him back out into the hall.

Dunn instantly noticed the envelope on the floor that Penny had pushed under the door yesterday morning.

The Inspector picked it up.

"To Bobby. I wonder what we've got in here?" he said, tearing it open.

Moreton felt like saying something about other people's mail, but decided against it, instead walking into the room and looking around for anything that might be useful to them.

As Dunn began reading the letter, his eyes grew wider and wider.

"Oh, I don't fucking believe this!"

Moreton walked over to see what had made the Inspector so animated.

Dunn handed him the letter and walked over to the bed.

"Peter French? I've heard that name somewhere before."

"I'd be surprised if you hadn't," said Dunn.

"French makes the Krays look like Morecambe and Wise. I've been trying to pin something on that bastard for the last ten years, but he's as cunning as a barrel full of monkeys, but according to that...," he pointed to the letter, "That could be just what I'm looking for."

"So, according to this, Kershaw didn't steal the diamonds," said Moreton, holding out the letter.

"No, and as he obviously hasn't read that yet, he probably imagines that we still have him down as the number one suspect and I should imagine that he also assumes we think he had something to do with the shooting this evening as well."

"So he's on the run, when he needn't be?" asked Moreton, feeling a twinge of pity for the innocent Kershaw.

Dunn shook his head. "Oh, he needs to be on the run, alright. He's got French up his ass. The man wants to close him down. He's tried once, he won't let it rest there. If Kershaw's anywhere within a fifty mile radius of here, French'll find him. We just have to make sure that we find him first.

And as for Penny Marshall, if French ever finds out that she wrote that, he'll cut her up and post her back to her father.

We need to find them both, before French goes on a killing spree.

In fact, I think it's time we paid Mr. French a visit, rattle his cage a bit."

The colour seemed to be draining from Moreton's face again.

Dunn smiled. "Don't worry. French has never done time and he's not about to start now and certainly not for anything as petty as assaulting a Police officer.

He's got his reputation to think of."

Kershaw finally found what he was looking for, a bed and breakfast, in Hawthorne road.

It backed onto the recreation ground, which he liked.

If it came to it, he could get around the back and sprint across the field and away.

He rang the bell and a couple of seconds later, the porch light was switched on.

A woman answered the door.

Kershaw placed her somewhere between her late forties and early fifties.

Blonde, curly hair framed a face that had once been attractive, but sadly, she hadn't aged gracefully.

She had the beginnings of bags under her eyes and her face was heavily lined, but the clothes she wore, made it all too evident, that her face was the only thing that Father Time had done the dirty on.

Her body was full and voluptuous and the expression not looking at the mantelpiece while stoking the fire, came into Kershaw's mind.

It was clear by the look in her eye that she didn't find him half bad, either.

"Can I help you?" she asked.

"I was wondering if you had a room for a couple of nights?" although, he'd be surprised if a place like this was ever full.

"Oh, I'm sure I can fit you in," she said, smiling and with a slight emphasis on the word you.

"Come in," she said, standing to one side.

Kershaw had trouble getting through the door, without brushing against her, which seemed to disappoint her slightly.

She looked behind him before closing the door.

"No bags?"

The only thing Kershaw had managed to salvage during his flight to freedom, was his Walkman, which he held up to show her.

"Only this," he replied. "I like to travel light."

She didn't seem to be overly concerned at his lack of belongings. He guessed that as long as he paid, that was good enough for her.

"It's fifteen pounds a night. The kitchen's down there," she told him, pointing to the end of the hall.

"Breakfast is between seven and nine. If you follow me, I'll show you your room."

Her skirt was far too short for a woman of her age, but she had the legs to carry it off, along with everything else, Kershaw didn't wonder.

As he followed her up the stairs, he caught more than a glimpse of stocking.

There was a voice in his head telling him that he didn't need this right now, but it was being shouted down by another, louder voice, asking why the hell not?

The room was small, but it was clean, if maybe a little sparse.

A single bed, a table and one chair, a small black and white television, that must have been fifty years old, at least and an electric kettle with a cup and saucer.

"I'll have to have the money in advance," she told him.

"I don't want you running off with my state of the art, home entertainment centre," she said, pointing to the old television.

Kershaw laughed.

"You've got a nice smile," she told him. "My name's Sylvia."

"Bob," Kershaw introduced himself.

They shook hands, Kershaw getting the impression that she didn't want to let go.

Eventually, she released his hand. "I'll see you in the morning, then," she told him.

Kershaw lay back on the lumpy bed and surveyed his surroundings. How the Hell had it come to this? He had no idea how long he was going to be staying here, in fact, he wanted to leave already, but at least he was safe here, for now.

He picked up the Walkman and checked the disc inside.

AC/DC's Powerage. That should help him take his mind off of things.

He'd go to the agency where Penny picked up her assignments. They might be able to give him a lead on her whereabouts. It had to be worth a try.

He put in the earphones, pressed play and then random.

Up to my neck in you, was the first track to play. Very appropriate, Kershaw thought to himself.

He was certainly up to his neck alright and sinking fast.

Dunn was driving, as he knew the way. He'd been to French's luxury apartment at least a dozen times and had come away with nothing every time.

He'd be coming away with nothing again this evening, but this time, it was from choice.

He wasn't planning to arrest French, or even take him in for questioning, he just wanted him to know that he was on his case.

The Inspector knew that he wouldn't have any trouble getting the Chief Constable to authorise some over time, to put a man on French. The Fat Controller wanted French behind bars even more that the Inspector did.

Dunn knew how smart French was, but he was hoping that his visit might stir him up.

People who think that they're untouchable always slip up in the end.

He took a right off of Richmond Hill, into a quiet side road and parked outside of a small apartment block.

He didn't want to alert French, by using the entry phone thus allowing him time to compose himself and prepare answers to any of Dunn's questions.

A light was on in one of the ground floor flats, so he walked over and tapped on the window. The curtains were pulled back and a middle aged woman peered out.

Dunn put his warrant card up against the glass and pointed to the front door.

The woman scrutinized Dunn's identification, checking the photo against the face at the window, then nodded.

A couple of seconds later, the buzzer sounded and both officers walked into the building.

"This is a nice place," said Moreton, as they climbed the stairs.

There was plush carpeting throughout, healthy, well-tended house plants on the landings and tasteful prints, dotted about the walls.

"Yeah well, the thieving scumbag makes more money than we do," said Dunn, bitterly.

He stopped outside of a burgundy door.

"When we get in, if we get in, don't look at anything, don't touch anything and let me do all the talking. Is that clear?"

Moreton nodded.

Ali had popped out to find a pub and to get away from French, ten minutes earlier.

Penny was watching a documentary on television and French was about to run himself a bath, when the doorbell rang.

"Are you expecting anyone?" asked French, knowing that Ali hadn't been gone long enough to be coming back already.

"You'd better get out of sight. I don't want anyone knowing that you're here."

He waited until Penny had disappeared and then answered the door.

The Inspector thought that he saw a fleeting look of shock on French's face, then it was gone.

"Inspector Dunn," said French, grinning.

"It's Chief Inspector Dunn."

French feigned surprise. "What, they promoted you, even though I've been giving your sorry ass the run-around for the last ten years?"

"That's academic now. There's rumours going around that you're past it, over the hill."

"You wish," said French scornfully.

225

French looked at Moreton. "Bob a job week come round already, has it? No, don't tell me this is a copper? What are they doing, recruiting at primary schools now?"

Moreton could feel his face warming and his stomach turning.

He'd done all the usual public relations exercises at Hendon, with off duty recruits acting as drunks or rioters, throwing empty beer cans and toilet rolls.

Since he'd been on the streets, Moreton had dealt with two late night revellers, fighting outside of a nightclub and one cowardly wife beater, but French was the real Macoy.

Moreton felt intimidated and French knew it.

So did Dunn.

"Never mind him," he snapped.

French's expression turned to stone instantly. "What do you want?"

"Just need to ask you a couple of questions. Mind if we come in?"

"Be my guest. I have to apologise for the state of the place, though," said French, standing to one side.

The two officers walked into the flat, which was immaculate.

"Doesn't look that bad to me," said Dunn.

"That's what I mean. I apologise for the state of it, 'cos it's probably ten times better than the shithole you live in. You want to think about taking a few backhanders. Bent coppers always have a better lifestyle that the straight ones."

"I'm here to talk about Penny Marshall."

French made an exaggerated pretence of trying to recall the name.

He shook his head. "Don't know the name, should I?"

"Do you know Robert Kershaw?" asked Dunn, knowing full well what French's response would be.

French shook his head again. "Nah."

"What about Andrew Parkin?"

A flicker of recognition came into French's ice blue eyes. "Wasn't he the one who won gold in the hop, skip and jump?"

The two men stared at each other and the animosity between them, was almost tangible.

"Is that it? Is that what you came here for? To see if I knew a couple of people you pulled out of the fucking phone book?"

A smile played around Dunn's mouth.

"When you try to sell those diamonds, I'll be waiting."

"Have you been on the pop?" asked French, angrily.

"I'll be seeing you," Dunn told him and turning, he nodded to Moreton to indicate that they were leaving.

Penny was standing on the other side of the door, listening to the conversation.

Her heart skipped a beat at every name that the Policeman mentioned.

How could he know all of that, about her and Kershaw?

When she heard the word diamonds, the horrific realisation came to her.

They must have broken into Bobby's flat and found her letter!

French would never believe that the information hadn't come from her, no matter what she told him.

She was on the first floor. She looked at the window behind her. There was no way she could climb down and get away. She was stuck in a flat, with a violent man, who knew she had betrayed him.

She could walk out now and turn herself over to the Police, or she could try and bluff her way through this, after they'd gone.

She heard the front door close, but no one had said that they were leaving.

"You can come out now," she heard French say.

"That wasn't very successful," said Moreton, as they walked down the stairs.

"On the contrary, now he knows that we know. I'll get someone round here within the next half hour, to watch him. With any luck, he'll make a mistake and then we'll have him."

Penny walked out of the room and she could feel her knees trembling.

She was expecting French to be raving, but he appeared to be calm, which somehow made it seem all the more terrifying.

"Where did they get all that information from?"

"I don't know," replied Penny, trying to stop her voice from quaking.

She was mesmerised by his piercing blue eyes, so much so, that she didn't see the slap coming. It knocked her to the floor.

"You fucking lying whore!" he shouted, his face now hideously distorted with rage.

Penny wanted to cry, but she was determined not to give French that satisfaction.

She didn't want to cry because he'd hurt her, but because she felt sure that she wasn't going to get out of there alive.

CHAPTER TWENTY-FOUR

Penny realised that she had made a grave error of judgement. She should have come out while the two Policemen were still in the flat. At least she would have been safe.

If she could just get out onto the landing, she'd scream the building down.

Someone would come out and then she could get away.

To where, she neither knew nor cared.

"You think you're so tough, don't you?" she said, from down on the floor.

"Bobby's more of a man than you'll ever be."

French stared down at her for a second, then threw his head back and roared with laughter.

She scrambled to her feet, her right cheek red and stinging and when he brought his head back down, she slapped him across the face.

French froze, not because it hurt, but that she had dared to strike him.

Penny made a dash for the door, but he was too quick for her. He grabbed her by the wrist, almost pulling her shoulder out of its socket as he yanked her back towards him.

She felt his hands around her throat. The pain was unbearable as she gulped and gulped again, in an effort to get air into her lungs.

She tried to break his grip, but he was far too strong for her. She couldn't reach his face, but rained blows down on his forearms, but to no effect.

She was barefoot and almost on tiptoe, as he pulled her up. She kicked out, frantically at his shins, but even if she had been wearing boots with steel toe caps, French still wouldn't have felt anything.

He was in the grip of an all-consuming fury, the only thing occupying his thoughts, to choke the life out of the person who had tried to give him up to the Police.

Tiny droplets squeezed themselves out of the corners of her eyes and everything started to become misty. Her movements became weaker and weaker, until they stopped altogether and her tongue lolled out of the side of her mouth.

French let go and Penny's lifeless body dropped to the floor like a puppet with its strings cut.

Ali let himself in and closing the door he came around the sofa.

"The pubs round here aren't up to mu..." He stopped when he saw Penny lying on the floor, her arms and legs splayed out in different directions.

"Wow, she must have really pissed you off'.

French stood there, staring down at the body, his chest heaving.

After a couple of seconds, he acknowledged Ali's presence.

He snapped his head around. "We're leaving," he told him.

"We are? Where to?"

French walked over to the bookcase, took down his special book and pulled out the diamonds.

"To a safe house. This has all gone to shit and back. In the morning, I'm getting a flight out to Portugal and you can go back to wherever it was you came from."

"What about that?" asked Ali, pointing to the floor, as if Penny's body were no more than a stain on the carpet.

"I'll get someone to deal with that in the morning."

"Tell me, if I find Kershaw, do you still want me to get rid of him?" asked Ali.

French laughed. "You, find Kershaw? You couldn't find your ass with both hands."

He thought for a moment. If Kershaw had laid down, like he was supposed to, he, French, could be on his way to becoming a multi-millionaire by now.

Every time he heard the name Kershaw, his stomach knotted up. He hated the man, even though he'd never met him. The bastard deserved to die.

French looked at Ali. "Okay, if you can prove to me that you've done him, you'll get your money."

"Sweet," said Ali, smiling.

Five minutes later, French had stuffed everything that he needed into a sports bag.

Taking one last look around and taking little or no notice of the body on the floor, he headed for the door, Ali following behind.

"Are we going back to the station, Sir?" asked Moreton, after they had been on the road for a few minutes.

"No, we're off to see Marshall. It's only fair that he knows who he's dealing with and then, hopefully, he'll back off and let us handle it." George Marshall answered the door. "Ah, the dynamic duo. Got any news for me?"

"We have, as it happens," replied Dunn.

"Where's your wife?"

Marshall looked puzzled. "My wife? She's out doing her aerobics, or Pilates, or whatever the hell it is she does. Why?"

"It's best that she doesn't hear what I've got to say."

Marshall's brow furrowed, slightly. "You'd best come in, then."

In the study, he sat behind his desk, arms folded across his chest.

To Dunn, he was a nobody, who thought he was a somebody. The inspector couldn't help feeling that he was going to derive a certain satisfaction from taking the wind out of his sails.

"So what is this news, that's so devastating that my wife wouldn't want to hear it?" asked Marshall.

"Let's stop messing each other around, shall we? You think Kershaw stole your diamonds, but he didn't, your daughter did."

Marshall didn't bat an eyelid, he just stared at Dunn, impassively.

"So tell me something I don't know."

Oh yes, too cocky by half, thought Dunn.

"Kershaw was being used. Your daughter took those diamonds for someone else."

Dunn could see that he had Marshall's attention.

"Who?" he asked, sitting up and unfolding his arms.

"Do you know a man by the name of Peter French?"

The look of concern on Marshall's face, told Dunn that he did.

"What's he got to do with all of this?"

"Your daughter's been seeing him. That's who she took the diamonds for."

Marshall tried to laugh off the Inspector's statement.

"Don't be ridiculous! Penny wouldn't have anything to do with a man like him.

She doesn't even know people like that exist."

When the Inspector didn't speak, Marshall looked distraught and Dunn couldn't help feeling sorry for him, despite himself.

"Why don't we ask her?" suggested Dunn.

Marshall looked lost. "She's not here. I haven't seen her since Sunday."

"And that doesn't bother you?" asked Dunn.

"Not until now. She's always off visiting her friends, staying the weekend. Do you think she's with him now?"

Dunn shook his head. "No, we've just come from him, we think she's with Kershaw, but I'm afraid it gets worse."

Marshall's eyes opened wide. "How much worse can it get?"

"There was an incident tonight, a shooting. We think Kershaw was the target, but there was a mix up. French wants Kershaw out of the way and if your daughter's with him, she could be in serious danger. We need to find them both. Where does your daughter work?"

Marshall seemed on the verge of becoming suicidal. He shook his head.

"She temps. I don't know where she is from one week to the next, she never tells us anything."

His face brightened up slightly. "I think I've got their address here, somewhere," he said, rummaging through one of his desk draws.

"Yeah, here it is." He handed Dunn a business card with the name and number of a temping agency on it.

"Good. We'll pop in and see them first thing tomorrow morning," said Dunn, taking the card and slipping it into his breast pocket.

"In the meantime, I suggest that you back off and allow us to do our job."

The Inspector stared down at Marshall with serious intent. "You don't know French, I do. You mess with him and he won't just bury you, he'll bury your whole family."

Marshall looked a shadow of the man he had when Dunn had first arrived and the Inspector wasn't surprised.

"We'll see ourselves out, thanks."

Moreton opened the door and both men walked out of the study, leaving Marshall sitting at his desk, wondering how the Hell he was going to break the news to his wife that their daughter was on a gangster's hit list. Dunn pulled into a lay by, outside a fish and chip shop, on the way back to the station.

"You fancy anything?" he asked Moreton.

The young detective still had visions of brain splattered wallpaper and vomit covered carpet flashing through his mind.

"Uh, no thanks," he replied.

When the two of them walked into the station, they noticed that Sergeant Ryder had brought himself in from the cold and was now on desk duty.

The Inspector placed his fish and chips on the counter.

"Mmm, that's smells good," said Ryder.

"Yeah, and it's going to taste even better," Dunn told him.

The Sergeant looked at Moreton. "Not eating?"

"Just having a bit of fun with you, lad. Don't take what happened out there to heart. You have to roll with it. Comes with the job."

Dunn placed both his hands on the counter. "So Dave, got any budding detectives in your crew?"

Ryder thought for a moment. "Well, there's Benson he's eager to get out of uniform. He wants to become a living legend like you."

"Is he in?"

Ryder looked at the duty chart and then behind him at the clock on the wall.

"He should be back in about ten minutes."

"When he gets in, can you send him up to my office?"

Dunn and Moreton walked to the door leading to the inside of the station.

"Anything exciting, Jack?" called out Ryder.

Dunn turned. "You want exciting?" He held out his thumb and forefinger, with a quarter of an inch gap in between.

"French is this far from going down. Is that exciting enough for you?"

The Sergeant let out a long whistle.

"You'll be a hero, Jack."

Dunn smiled. "I'm already a hero, I'm your hero."

When Kershaw opened his eyes, the room was pitch black and for a second he wasn't sure where he was. The events of the day slowly began to return and he slowly got his bearings.

Checking his watch, he saw that it was nearly ten o'clock. He'd been asleep for almost two hours. He guessed that the events of the last few days were beginning to catch up with him.

Switching on the light, he took his shirt off and hung it over the back of the chair.

He was going to have to get himself something to wear tomorrow, but in the meantime, he didn't want what he had getting too messed up.

He heard a noise, a strange kind of tapping and he realised that it was coming from his door.

He knew that it wasn't the Police. If they came knocking on his door, it would be with a size eleven boot.

When he opened the door, he found Sylvia standing there.

Her eyes nearly popped out of her head, when she caught sight of his naked, muscled torso and he couldn't help looking surprised, either.

A roll of cellophane would have been less opaque than the nightdress that she was wearing. It left nothing to the imagination, which was exactly what she was wearing underneath.

"I was wondering if you fancied a nightcap?" she asked.

The twinkle in her eye told Kershaw that drink was the last thing she had on her mind.

If he was looking for a distraction, to take his mind off of the world that seemed to be crashing down around him, he could do a lot worse than fool around with the sultry Sylvia.

It made her sound like a blow up doll and he imagined that she would be every bit as accommodating.

"Yeah, okay"

She turned and headed for her room. Closing his door, he padded down the hall after her.

"Do you think we'll have any trouble with Marshall, Sir?" asked Moreton, when they were in the Inspector's office.

Dunn shook his head. "No. As long as we keep him updated, he'll stay out of it and the missing link, Benny, Billy, whatever the Hell his name is, he's not going to want to mess with French, either."

There was a knock at the door and a uniformed constable walked in.

"Benson, Sir. Sarge' said that you wanted to see me."

He was around five foot eight, with a crew cut and an intelligent, fresh looking face.

"What time did you come on duty?" asked Dunn.

"Eight this evening, Sir."

"Fancy some overtime, a spot of C.I.D. work?"

The young constable's face lit up. "Yes Sir," he replied, eagerly.

"Do you know Peter French, know what he looks like?"

The young constable wasn't fazed when he heard the name French. He nodded, still as keen as mustard.

He's definitely up for it, this boy, Dunn thought to himself.

"Richmond Mews, off of Richmond Hill. He's got himself an apartment there. Get over and sit on it, but don't make it too obvious. French can smell a copper a mile off. I want to know when he leaves and where he goes. Got that?"

Benson nodded, chomping at the bit almost.

"Do not, under any circumstances approach him. I just want to know his movements. Moreton here will relieve you at six tomorrow morning. Any questions?"

Benson shook his head.

"Right, get changed and get over there. You're going to have to use your own car, so don't forget to put in a claim."

"Yes, Sir," replied Benson and left.

"You don't mind getting up at six tomorrow, do you?" Dunn asked Moreton.

"I didn't think I had a choice."

"You don't."

French told Ali to pull up outside of a terraced house in Merely Road, Twickenham.

When the door opened, Ali understood why French had called it a safe house.

Filling the whole doorway, was the biggest black man Ali had ever seen and he'd seen a few in his time.

"Hello Mr. French," boomed the giant. Despite being seven foot tall, if he was an inch, the huge black man still afforded French the respect that befitted his position as a gangland boss.

"Alright Errol? I need a place to stay for a couple of nights. Okay if I bed down here?"

Errol looked over French at Ali, eyeing him with suspicion.

"It's okay, he's with me."

Errol nodded and stood well back to allow the two men room to enter the house.

"You got a problem, Mr. French?" asked Errol.

"Nothing that a good undertaker can't fix."

CHAPTER TWENTY-FIVE

Moreton drove past Benson's car and parked further down the road. He was dressed a lot more casually, this morning.

Dunn had told him to sit tight, until he heard from him and Moreton didn't want to crease up one of his suits, sitting in a car, for God knew how long.

He walked up to Benson's car and the young constable wound the window down.

"Anything?" asked Moreton.

Benson shook his head. "Not a peep."

"Okay, you get off and get some kip. Be back here at twelve."

Benson looked a little concerned. "This is alright, isn't it? You know, me being here. It's just that I've got a shift to do this morning."

"Dunn's cleared it with the Chief Constable. You're with us until you hear otherwise."

Benson nodded, looking more relieved.

Now it was Moreton's turn to sit outside of a flat that contained a dead body and nothing else.

Kershaw woke around eight, aching and famished. Sultry Sylvia had lived up to his expectations. Her lovemaking had been voraciously adventurous, but thankfully, Kershaw had had youth on his side and eventually, Sylvia had cried uncle and reluctantly sent him back to his own bed at two o'clock in the morning.

He had a quick wash and went downstairs, following the wonderful aroma of coffee and bacon.

In the breakfast room, sitting in one of the corners, were two burly men, dressed in overalls and wearing fluorescent vests. They both looked at him as he walked in.

"Tis a grand breakfast that she does here, sir," one of the guests informed him.

"Worth every penny, so it is," he said, tucking into a huge fried breakfast.

Just at that moment, Sylvia walked in from the kitchen, carrying two large mugs of tea.

She winked at him, gave the workmen their tea and came over to his table.

"Hungry?" she asked.

Kershaw smiled and nodded.

"I'll bring you a nice big breakfast. You need to keep your strength up."

Kershaw wondered what she used to keep her strength up. He couldn't help thinking that an older, less fit man than himself, could well have died in that room last night.

Perhaps one already had!

As he was eating the huge breakfast that Sylvia had put before him, he thought about work and suddenly remembered that he still had Andy's car.

His pal had probably cadged a lift, or caught the bus, but Kershaw bet he was cursing him all the way there.

He remembered seeing a pay phone in the hall, by the front door. He'd leave Andy a message on his answerphone, explaining and apologising and telling him that he'd return his beloved Mazda back to him just as soon as he could.

Having managed to wade through the mountain of bacon, sausage, eggs, baked beans, mushrooms and toast and after washing it all down with a cup of coffee, he thanked Sylvia, told her that he'd see her later and went in search of the phone.

He dialled Andy's number and waited for the recorded message to start, but the phone just kept on ringing. He thought that was rather strange as Andy always flicked the switch when he left the house, turning it off when he got back in.

Kershaw let it ring for a little while longer, then hung up. He'd try again this evening. He drove into Brentford town centre, found a parking space and went into the first clothes shop that he came to.

All he needed for the moment, were a couple of shirts and some underwear.

He bought two casual shirts that he liked the look of, put one on in the changing room and carried his old one out with him. He put it in the carrier bag that the assistant gave him along with the other new shirt and the underwear.

He went back to the car, put the bag on the back seat and headed off for the temping agency that Penny used.

Walking down the High street, he spotted two uniformed Police officers on the other side of the road, walking towards him.

He turned and looked into the window of a travel agent, watching the reflection of the Policemen in the glass.

He didn't know whether they had a description of him or not, but he wasn't taking any chances, at least, not yet.

When he came to the agency, he stopped outside. If he came out of here empty handed, he might as well catch those two Bobbies up and turn himself in. Moreton had just checked his watch for the umpteenth time, thinking that maybe this C.I.D. work wasn't all it was cracked up to be, when Benson drove past him and parked further up the road. It was only half past ten and Moreton wondered what the Hell he was doing here, so early.

"I've had some sleep and seeing as I didn't have anything else to do, I thought I'd come and relieve you. That's alright, isn't it?"

Moreton was only too pleased to get away. If the mug wanted to sit here for another six hours, then good luck to him.

"Anything happening?" asked Benson.

Moreton shook his head. "No. In fact, I'm beginning to think that French isn't even in there."

He thought for a moment. "I might not be able to reach the Inspector over the radio, so you stay here and I'll go back to the station and see what he wants to do, okay?"

Kershaw opened the door and walked in. There was a girl on reception, busy on a keypad.

He knew that he was going to have to be at his most charming, if he was to get the information that he was after.

"Hi," he greeted, smiling down at her. She was a bit on the dumpy side, with straight, black hair and large glasses.

She seemed slightly flustered, when she looked up at the handsome man standing in front of her.

"Yes, can I help you?"

"I'm looking for Penny Marshall."

"She doesn't actually work here. She's one of our temps."

"Yes, I know, but I need to get in touch with her and I was hoping that you might have her mobile number."

"I'm sorry, but I can't give out that kind of information," she told him.

Kershaw took a deep breath. "Okay, I'll come clean. She worked for the company I was with a few months ago. She had a certain rapport with the clients, you know, they all seemed to like her. Anyway, I've since left that company and set up on my own and I wanted to ask her if she'd like to come and work for me and hopefully lure some of my old company's customers my way. Totally unethical, I know, but all's fair in love and business."

Kershaw sat on the corner of her desk and smiled.

"If you were to give me her mobile number, I'd be...ever so grateful, er, I'm sorry, I don't know your name."

"Paula," she told him. She seemed to have a more authoritative air about her, all of a sudden. She gazed up at him, through her spectacles.

"How grateful?" she asked.

Kershaw gave a little shrug. "You name it."

"Dinner and a fuck?"

Kershaw almost fell off the desk. If Paula had been Diana Prince, twirling round and becoming Wonder Woman, she couldn't have made more of a transformation than she had since he'd walked through the door.

Paula had changed from shy, flustered receptionist, into a lust hungry vamp.

"Okay," he agreed, regaining his composure.

He picked up one of the office business cards from out of a box on her desk and wrote down the first six numbers that came into his head.

"That's my home number," he lied. "Ring me this evening."

"I will," Paula assured him.

Looking around to make sure that no one was paying any particular attention to them, she swivelled her chair around, opened a filing cabinet and pulled out a manila file.

"You'd better be worth it," she told him, taking another cautious peek behind her.

"I don't have her mobile number, but I do have her home address."

Kershaw's heart sank. "No, I can't contact her there."

Paula turned the page over. "I do have another address, where she can be contacted."

Kershaw couldn't hide his surprise.

"Another address?"

"Yes, Richmond Mews, off Richmond Hill, apartment number four."

"Okay, I'll try there. He gave her hand a gentle squeeze. "You've been very helpful. Ring me," he reminded her and headed for the door.

When Moreton walked into the Inspector's office, Dunn checked his watch.

"What are you doing here?" he asked.

"Benson came and relieved me. Said he had nothing better to do, so I let him get on with it. I needed to get back here. There's been someone outside since ten last night and we haven't had a peep out of French. I'm beginning to wonder whether he's actually in there."

Dunn considered this for a moment.

"Well, you can come with me to the agency and I'll get our supercop to hang on for a while longer. If there's no sign of him by midday, we'll have to go in." Fifteen minutes had passed and Paula was still tapping away on the keypad, when Dunn and Moreton walked through the door.

She got the impression that they hadn't come in search of a typist.

"Can I help you?" she asked, for the second time that morning.

Dunn held out his warrant card. "I'm Detective Chief Superintendent Dunn and this is Constable Moreton. We're trying to locate Penny Marshall."

"My, she's a popular girl this morning," said Paula, cryptically.

"What makes you say that?" asked Dunn.

"You're the second person this morning who's been looking for Penny."

"Who else was in here?" asked the Inspector, looking concerned.

She suddenly realised that her date for this evening hadn't even told her his name.

"He didn't say."

"Can you describe him?" asked Dunn.

"Well, he was tall, very good-looking..." she said, wistfully, trailing off, a sinking feeling in her stomach telling her that she wasn't going to see him this evening, after all.

"What was he wearing?"

"Uh, jeans, a blue checked shirt and a black leather jacket."

"And what did you tell him?"

"That Penny had another contact address, in Richmond." When the policemen had left, Paula dialled the number that Kershaw had given her.

As she expected, the operator told her that the number she had dialled had not been recognised.

With Moreton driving, Dunn got on the radio to Benson.

"In about fifteen minutes, a man is going to be entering that apartment block. He's tall, with dark hair and he's wearing jeans and a black leather jacket. If he comes out before we get there, follow him. Got that? Don't do anything else just follow. Right?"

"Yes Sir," crackled Benson's voice through the handset.

"Going on the letter that Penny Marshall wrote, Kershaw doesn't know about French," said Moreton.

"Well, let's hope for his sake that you're right and French isn't there."

Ten minutes after Benson had received the message from Dunn, Kershaw turned up.

Seeing that there was an entry phone system on the front door, he pressed the button for number four. He waited, but there was no answer. He had to get in there somehow.

He pressed one of the other buttons.

"Hello?" said a woman's voice.

"Parcel," said Kershaw, into the microphone.

He knew that everyone had a parcel at some time or other and most people had forgotten that they'd even ordered anything. People always opened up for a surprise.

The buzzer sounded and he pushed the door.

On the drive over he'd been trying to figure out why Penny had given this place as a contact address, but couldn't come up with an answer. Hopefully, he'd get one upstairs.

The whole place looked very upmarket, which didn't surprise him, knowing Penny.

When he got to apartment number four, he took a deep breath and knocked on the door.

Benson was going over the Inspector's orders in his head, wondering if he shouldn't try acting on his own initiative, when a white van pulled up outside the block.

Two men got out, dressed in green overalls and opened the back doors.

They took out a large roll of something, it looked like it could be carpet, inside of a long, black, plastic cover.

Heaving the roll on to their shoulders, they made their way to the front door.

The lead man didn't press a call button, he just punched a number into the keypad and pushed the door.

What with this Kershaw chappie and now these two, Benson got the feeling that something was going on in there. He rubbed his chin.

Should he go in, or should he wait out here, like the Inspector had said?

He decided that he had better wait in the car.

When Kershaw didn't get an answer, he was about to walk away. No, he had to get in there, had to find out something, anything.

Deciding that adding criminal damage to the list of charges that the Police probably already had against him was the least of his problems, he backed up to the wall and flew at the door. When his foot connected, he felt it give slightly, but it didn't open.

Taking a couple of steps back, he tried again. This time it gave out and he stumbled into the flat.

When no one appeared to investigate the noise, he guessed that the place was empty.

It was a very impressive apartment and he wondered where he should start looking, to find some kind of clue.

He walked around the sofa and froze. He couldn't believe what he was seeing.

His stomach knotted up as he stared down at Penny's body on the carpet.

He'd seen a dead person before, when he was younger, so he knew that Penny was beyond help.

The eyes, open and lifeless, the lips, nose and ears, tinged with blue, the face grey.

Then he spotted the bruising around her neck. Somebody had strangled her.

He felt the anger rising up inside of him, like a tidal wave.

When he found out who did this to her, he was going to do the same to them.

He knew that he couldn't remain here, nor did he want to. The last thing he needed right now, was to be found in an empty flat with a dead body, the body of a person that the Police, by now, must know that he had been seeing.

Jesus! What if they thought that he had killed her? That they'd had an argument over the theft of the diamonds?

That decided it for him. As much as he hated to leave Penny there, like that, he had to get out.

He walked out into the hall and came face to face with Leroy and his mate, carrying what appeared to be a roll of carpet on their shoulders.

CHAPTER TWENTY-SIX

The man with the beard, whose head Kershaw had split with a broom handle, recognised him instantly.

"You, you bastard," he swore.

He was about to throw the carpet off of his shoulder, to free his hands, when Kershaw struck him on the side of the jaw.

As the man's knees buckled, Kershaw grabbed hold of the carpet with both hands and shoved it hard. Leroy still had it on his shoulder and he stumbled backwards, crashing into the wall behind him, next to a large arched window.

Even though Leroy had come to a standstill, the slippery, plastic covered carpet kept on sliding over his shoulder and crashed through the window.

Down in the car, Benson was considering what to have for his dinner, when the carpet came through the first floor window in a shower of glass, like some kind of airborne torpedo.

"Bloody Hell!" he swore. He guessed that he was left with no choice. He had to get up there and see what was going on.

Leroy and Kershaw squared up to each other and Leroy was about to push himself away from the wall and leap at Kershaw, when Benson appeared on the landing, brandishing his warrant card.

"I'm a Police Officer! Both of you, stay where you are," he commanded.

Kershaw knew that he couldn't be arrested here, not with Penny's body only a few yards away.

"Watch out!" he shouted, pointing at Leroy. "He's got a gun!"

Leroy looked around him, to see who the white-fool was talking about, when he realised that Kershaw must be referring to him.

Kershaw's shocking revelation caught Benson completely off guard.

His Kung Fu for beginner's classes hadn't reached the catching bullets in the teeth stage yet, so he figured he could be in a spot of bother.

As he turned to Leroy, wishing now that he had stayed in the car, Kershaw leapt at him, punching him in the side of the head.

Benson staggered back, but was still on his feet. Kershaw moved forward and kicked him in the stomach.

Benson went back another step and doubled over, gasping for breath, after being winded.

Kershaw would have loved to have hung around and beaten some answers out of Leroy as to what he was doing here and why Penny's dead body was in the flat, but he had just assaulted a Police Officer.

Not only that, but if there was one Policeman here, Kershaw figured that there would be more on the way.

He jumped over Benson, lying on the floor, who made a half-hearted attempt to grab his ankles, but missed.

Kershaw ran out of the apartment block and as he dashed to Andy's car, he heard a siren in the distance.

He'd just put the key in the ignition, when a patrol car came hurtling around the corner, its lights flashing.

His heart thumping, he started the car and drove off. He turned right onto the main road and thirty seconds later, Dunn and Moreton turned in from the left.

Dunn was less than impressed with the sight that greeted him, when he reached the first floor landing.

The two uniformed officers who arrived on the scene moments earlier, had Leroy and his pal, who was still slightly groggy, up against the wall and Benson was just getting to his feet, still holding his stomach, but there was no sign of Kershaw.

Dunn was fuming. He glowered at Benson. "You, wait downstairs," he ordered.

"I'll speak to them in a minute," the Inspector told the two officers, pointing at French's employees.

He glanced at the door, almost hanging off its hinges and walked into the apartment, Moreton following.

When he spotted Penny's body, his reaction was the same as Kershaw's had been and like Kershaw, he too noticed the bruises around Penny's throat.

He'd imagined that he'd paid his last visit to Whispering Pines, but it looked as if he was wrong.

"Damn! Why did the stupid girl get mixed up with French in the first place?" Dunn asked, of no one in particular.

"Well at least we know why he's not here," said Moreton.

The Inspector walked back out into the hall.

"Do you work for French?" he asked the man with the beard and then looked at Leroy, to indicate that he was asking them both.

Neither of them replied.

Losing Kershaw and finding another dead body, clearly murdered by French, his bête noire, was bringing Dunn to the boil. "What, you think this is a fucking game?" he bellowed at the two men, the officers holding them jumping slightly at the sound of the Inspector raising his voice.

Still they didn't respond.

"I wouldn't waste your time being loyal," Dunn told them.

"Loyalty's not going to do that bastard any good, not where he's going."

Their continued silence drew a heavy sigh from Dunn.

"Take them away," he told the two officers, "And get another car over here, pronto."

Dunn looked at Moreton. "You wait here," he said and walked to the stairs.

Moreton had a pretty good idea where the Inspector was going and he was glad that he wasn't in Benson's shoes right now.

"I thought I told you to wait in the car?" said Dunn, angrily.

"There was some kind of trouble up there and I thought…"

"I don't give a rusty fuck what you thought! If you had followed orders, you'd be tailing Kershaw now, but instead, we don't have a clue where he is."

Benson's face was flushed and he was looking everywhere, but in the Inspector's eye.

"Get back to the station and get back into your uniform and be grateful you've still got that. If I had my way, you wouldn't even get a job as a fucking lollypop man!"

Back upstairs, Dunn cast an eye over the damaged door, one more time and shook his head.

"For an innocent man, this Kershaw fellow is becoming a real pain in the ass.

It seems that everywhere he goes, a dead body turns up."

"Jesus! He's worse than the grim reaper."

Driving back to his bed and breakfast hideaway, Kershaw was having trouble getting the image of Penny's dead body out of his mind.

There hadn't been many women who had captured his heart, but Penny certainly had and to such an extent that he'd imagined them together for a long, long time.

He felt a lump in his throat, when he realised that she was gone forever.

His grip on the steering wheel became tighter and tighter, until his knuckles became white.

He would find the person responsible and when he did, God help them! He crept into his digs, managing to avoid seeing Sylvia. He couldn't face seeing anyone right now.

Lying on his bed, he made a momentous decision.

Tonight would be his last night of freedom, so to speak. He'd go out, have a few beers, chat to a few women and when closing time came around, he'd turn himself in.

He hadn't stolen anything and he hadn't murdered anyone, so things weren't all that bad.

All he was guilty of was breaking into the Marshall house, assaulting George Marshall, criminal damage at the apartment and assaulting a Police Officer.

Christ! They'd throw the book at him.

He slipped on his Walkman and allowed Bon Scott's dulcet tones to wash his troubles away, as he screamed out Gimme a Bullet. As he was leaving for the evening, he bumped into Sylvia in the hallway.

"Just popping out for a while," he told her.

She smiled, salaciously. "I'll see you later though, won't I?"

"Probably," he lied.

What he wanted was a busy pub, where he could lose himself.

He plumped for the White Swan, on the Twickenham road. It proved to be a good choice.

The place was packed.

He smiled to himself as he walked in. A month ago, if he had come in here, on his own, he would have been terrified that someone would try and pick a fight with him, but now, if somebody wanted to have a go, well, that was their lookout.

He confidently muscled his way up to the bar and got himself a drink.

Finding a space against one of the walls, he stood there and just watched.

Suddenly, he thought that he'd spotted someone he recognised. Peering through the sea of heads, he caught sight of Angela's curly, auburn hair and slightly freckled face.

She appeared to be having an animated conversation with three men seated at a table on the other side of the room.

Unbeknown to him, the man in the middle was Alex, Angela's ex-boyfriend and the argument they were having was over some money that he had stolen from her, the day she'd kicked him out of her house.

She wanted it back, but he'd spent it.

His two pals, sitting either side of him, seemed to be taking a certain pleasure from his obvious discomfort.

Finally, Angela picked up Alex's half empty pint, threw it in his face, put the glass back on the table and headed for the door.

Wiping the beer from his face, Alex looked at his two mates and they all put their heads together, spoke and then turned to watch Angela walk out the door.

As the door was closing, all three of them got up and followed her.

It looked to Kershaw as if they were out to get some of their own back.

It was nothing to do with him. He had enough on his plate, without involving himself in somebody else's problems.

How would he feel, if tomorrow, he found out that she had been assaulted, or worse and he could have done something to prevent it?

Ah, bollocks! He thought to himself. I'd better go and have a look.

Putting his pint down on the table nearest to him, he too headed for the door.

Outside, he couldn't see Angela, or the three that had followed her out.

He walked round to the right and looked in the car park, but there wasn't a soul around.

Turning back, he walked past the pub in the other direction. Where the building ended, there was an alleyway.

Peering down, he realised that he had been right to come out.

Angela was being pinned up against the wall by the two pals, while Alex stood in front of her.

He had his legs against her legs, to prevent her from kicking out at him. Her blouse had been ripped open and he had his hand up her skirt.

Keeping to the shadows, Kershaw crept a few yards into the alley, then coughed, loudly.

All four figures froze, then as one, they turned their heads in the direction of the noise.

"Is this what they call unsociable behaviour?" asked Kershaw, stepping out of the shadows and into the centre of the alley.

"Who the fuck are you?" asked Alex, clearly upset at having his fun disrupted.

"I've come to make a citizen's arrest, if that's alright by you."

Alex blinked. "A citizen's arr…"

He looked at his two friends. "I think this wanker's asking for a kicking," he suggested.

The two pals hurled Angela to one side, hoping to come back to her, after they'd dealt with the gate crasher.

As the three men approached him, Kershaw's first thought was that he might have bitten off more than he could chew.

Looking to his left, he saw a large, industrial waste bin. It was about his height, with four wheels and a handle on each side.

Getting behind, stretching his arms around and grabbing hold of both handles, he began pushing it towards the three of them.

Luckily, it hadn't been designed on the supermarket trolley, all four wheels moving in different directions. Instead, it moved smoothly and quickly began to gather momentum.

Alex moved to the left and one of his pals to the right, but the one in the middle, was like a rabbit caught in the headlights of a car.

He couldn't make his mind up which way to go and by the time he did, it was too late, Kershaw was already on him, with his homemade battering ram.

The alley wasn't that wide and before he knew it, the guy was being pinned up against the wall.

Kershaw gave one more heave and let go. The bin was up against the man's chest, his arms and legs splayed out on either side, so that the only way he was going to move the bin, which was full and therefore quite heavy, was with his head.

He called out for his mates to help him, but they were preoccupied.

Now that the odds had been reduced slightly, Kershaw felt a little happier.

As he prepared to take them on, Angela came flying out of the darkness, screaming like a demented banshee.

Whether she was after Alex or not, was hard to say, but as it was, she jumped onto the back of her ex-boyfriend's pal, wrapped her legs around his waist and dug her nails into his cheeks.

The two of them went round and round, Angela still screaming and the man screaming as well now, but for someone to get her off of him.

As Alex turned to look at them both, Kershaw leapt in and punched him on the side of the jaw. He staggered back and Kershaw hit him again, square on the jaw this time, knocking him to the floor.

Angela and her piggyback ride were still going round. He was desperately trying to shake her off, but she was hanging on like a limpet and there were trickles of blood running down his face, where her nails had punctured the skin.

As if he were standing in front of a revolving door, Kershaw waited until the man turned to face him and then kicked him in the groin.

As if having a mad woman on his back wasn't enough, he groaned and fell to his knees.

Getting off, Angela looked over at Alex, who was on his hands and knees and in the process of getting to his feet.

Walking over, she kicked him in the ribs. "Bastard! She swore down at him and he sank back down to the floor again.

Kershaw had rescued Angela from what could have been quite an ordeal. He wasn't expecting her to drop to her knees and worship him, but he didn't think a small show of gratitude would have been out of place.

Instead, she was staring at him as if he were Frankenstein's monster.

"You shot Andy!" she accused.

At first, Kershaw imagined that she must be delirious.

"What?"

"Why did you kill Andy?" she asked, the terrified look still in her eyes.

Kershaw let out a little laugh. "Andy's not dead, he hasn't been shot."

"Yes he has. Claire and I saw his body, last night."

Kershaw thought back to the previous evening, feeling anxious.

He remembered the Police car, bumped up on the kerb, its lights flashing.

He took a step towards her, but she retreated, like a frightened child.

He thought about the answerphone being switched off.

Jesus! This was turning into a nightmare!

"I didn't shoot him," he pleaded, as everything began to dreadfully fit into place and he made sense of what Angela was telling him.

"I wasn't there, I went out to get some cash. When I came back and saw the Police car I thought that they'd come for me and got out of there."

The panic stricken look in her eyes began to fade and he was about to take a step towards her, when it returned.

"Why would the Police be looking for you?"

CHAPTER TWENTY-SEVEN

Pinning her blouse together with her fingers, where the buttons had been ripped off, Angela was still looking far from comfortable.

Kershaw let out a heavy sigh. "It's a long story. You want to hear it?"

His defeated expression appeared to calm her slightly and she looked around her.

"I don't think we should hang around here anymore," she suggested.

"I don't live very far away. I need to change, anyway," she told him, indicating the torn blouse and walked past him in the direction of the main road.

As he turned to follow her, the guy behind the bin was still trying to get free.

Kershaw gave the bin a kick and the movement stopped.

Dunn and Moreton were in the Inspector's office. The room was silent, both men occupied with their own thoughts, Dunn wishing that he didn't have to inform George Marshall and his wife of the death of their daughter and Moreton hoping that the Inspector wasn't going to get him to do it.

Suddenly, Dunn slammed both his hands down on the desk, causing Moreton to almost fall off of his chair.

"I've had enough of this running around bollocks!" he declared and picked up the phone.

He looked at Moreton and then at his watch.

"I'm going to ring the local news station, get them to put Kershaw's photograph on the nine o'clock news. If he knows that we think he's innocent, maybe he'll come to us."

"It's worth a try, Sir," said Moreton.

Angela had arrived at the pub by taxi, so they drove back to her house in Andy's Mazda.

On the way, Kershaw told the whole sorry story, for a second time, all the while thinking of Andy. This had to be connected, but why shoot him? What the Hell had he done to anyone?

"You have to go to the Police," said Angela when Kershaw had finished.

"I'm sure they'll believe you."

"I was planning to do that after closing time, but now…"

"What are you going to do?" she asked.

"I could do with a cup of coffee," he said, looking across at her, expectantly.

"What, like a last request, you mean?" asked Angela, a slight smile on her face.

Kershaw laughed. "Yeah, something like that."

The expression, 'it's a small world', was never more true than when Ali walked into the White Swan, ten minutes after Kershaw had walked out.

There were ways and means of tracking Kershaw down and he had some favours to call in. There was no real hurry, he'd find him eventually and then he'd pick up his money.

The world shrunk even more, when he sat at a table next to three guys.

One looked a bit of a mess, with fresh cuts on his face and another had a swollen jaw.

Ali had just taken a mouthful of his drink, when one of the men swore and pointed up at the television screen in the corner.

Ali couldn't believe his eyes. It was a picture of Kershaw, the big guy he'd seen coming out of the warehouse with the late Billy Bunter.

The three guys seemed to recognise him, so he decided to chance his arm.

He leant over. "Do you know him?" he asked Alex.

All three of them turned to look at him.

"What's it to you?" snapped Alex.

All could sense that there was some hostility here. It couldn't be towards him, he'd only just walked in.

"He's a friend of mine. I've been looking for him all day."

"She said they were going back to her place, didn't she?" asked the man sitting to the right of Alex. Angela's ex-boyfriend glared at him. It was bad enough that they'd taken a beating from him, without being reminded that he'd walked off with the stupid tart.

Ali sensed that he could be on to something here.

"He didn't do that to you, did he?"

Their silence told him what he wanted to know.

"He's always getting into scrapes like this. He's a footballer, plays for Luton Town."

Ali didn't know whether these three were ardent football fans or not. If he told them that Kershaw played for a Premiership club, they might wonder as to why they hadn't recognised him.

"You know what these footballers are like," he said jokingly.

The man on Alex's left, whispered something in his ear and he nodded.

When he turned back to Ali, he seemed to have mellowed out.

"Well, we'd had a bit to drink, he'd had some as well. You know how it is."

Ali smiled and nodded.

"The thing is, your mate dropped his wallet in the car park. I put it in my car for safe keeping. If you want to come out with us, I'll give it to you and you can get it back to him.

Ali had a fair idea what these three were up to and it suited him just fine.

"That's great," he said, beaming. "He'll probably be in here tomorrow night to buy you boys a drink."

All four of them headed for the door.

With his stupid Metallica tee shirt and his soft benign attitude, the three boys figured that Ali was an easy target. If he was a friend of the bastard who'd ruined their evening, they intended to take him outside and give him a good kicking.

It might not achieve anything, but it would make them feel a whole lot better.

Out in the car park, Alex pointed to the far right hand corner, which, by a strange coincidence, happened to be the darkest, worst lit area.

"My car's over there," he told Ali.

The three of them were walking in front, Alex said something to his pals and they all laughed.

Then, the one on the left stopped, making a pretence of tying his shoelace.

As soon as Ali had passed by, he got up and began to close in behind him.

Ali allowed himself a little smile. These three fools were amateurs, but they were about to find out what it meant to deal with a professional.

Kershaw pulled up outside a small terraced house in a quiet, out of the way cul-de-sac.

"Is this your house?" he asked. This would probably have been the sort of place he would have bought for himself, but he didn't think that he would be needing any sort of accommodation for a while, not where he was going.

"Yes, an aunt of mine left it to me in her will."

"That was very nice of her."

"Yes, I thought so," said Angela, taking a bunch of keys out of her handbag.

She was about to open the door, when she stopped and looked at Kershaw.

"You don't have anything against dogs, do you?"

"Only the ones that bite me," he replied.

"You don't have to worry about that. Russell's a big softy."

"Russell? Why Russell?"

Angela looked a little embarrassed. "I named him after Russell Crowe. I think he's a bit of a hunk."

She opened the door and blocking the hallway, was a muscle quivering, mountain of Doberman Pinscher. Its ears pricked up the moment it caught sight of Angela and when it spotted Kershaw standing behind, it cocked its head onto one side, its eyebrows twitching.

She walked up to the dog, wrapped her arms around it and kissed it on the top of the head.

"Hello darling. Have you missed me?"

What there was of its tail brushed across the carpet. She turned and smiled at Kershaw.

"You see, he's a big pussy cat, metaphorically speaking."

Kershaw came in through the doorway.

"Just don't touch his nose," she warned.

Kershaw stopped where he was. "Why not?" he asked, imagining what sort of damage a dog like that could wreak, if someone were stupid enough to upset it.

Angela opened the lounge door and ushered the dog in, where it headed straight for its basket in the corner.

"When I first had him, I was doing some ironing and you know what puppies are like, into everything. Anyway, I turned my back for a second and he started playing with flex. He pulled the iron off of the board and it hit him on the nose."

"Ouch!" said Kershaw, wincing.

"Yes, exactly. It didn't do any real damage, but now, not only does he not like irons, but he hates anyone touching his nose. If you touch it once, he'll bare his teeth. Touch again and he'll start to growl."

"What happens if you touch it a third time?"

"I don't know, I've never tried it."

The man came up behind Ali and grabbed him in a bear hug.

"I've got him!" he shouted to the other two, who stopped, turned and started walking back.

Ali knew what was about to happen, when he saw the man fall behind.

Using his peripheral vision, when he saw the man's arms begin to encircle him, took a deep breath, expanding his chest.

The man's grip was tight, but when Ali breathed out, constricting his chest, the bear hug became loose. Spreading his legs and dropping into a low stance, Ali slipped down out of the man's grip. He drove his elbow straight back, striking him in the groin.

As he grunted and bent forward, Ali stood back up, grabbed hold of his left arm, twisted his hips and effortlessly, flipped the man over his shoulder. When the guy hit the concrete, he shattered his hip, causing him to scream out in agony.

As Alex's other pal moved towards him, Ali used the man on the ground as a springboard, launching himself off of him, performing a bicycle kick and striking the second man full in the face, breaking his jaw.

After watching his two pals hit the floor, Alex knew that he'd be next, unless he got in there quick.

As Ali came back down to earth, landing on the balls of his feet, his balance perfect, Alex rushed towards him, aiming a punch at his face.

Ali spun around and caught Alex square in the chest with a reverse kick.

Spinning again and rolling off of Alex's body, Ali ended up behind him.

He stamped down on the back of Alex's leg, bringing him to his knees.

Thrusting his own knee into the small of his back and cupping his hands under Alex's jaw, Ali bent him backwards, so much so, that he was able to lean over and look into Alex's eyes, staring back up at him.

"Where does this girl live?" asked Ali, his voice no more than a whisper.

Alex was in agony. The pain from his neck and his back was shooting through his body and he was still having trouble breathing, from where he had been kicked in the chest.

He had trouble speaking, but he knew that the sooner he told this man what he wanted to know, the sooner the pain would stop.

In between grunting in pain and gasping for breath, Alex gave Ali Angela's address.

Staring down into Alex's eyes, which now not only registered pain, but fear as well, Ali smiled.

"Thank you. You've been very helpful."

Alex had wanted the pain to stop and he got his wish.

Jerking his knee forward and yanking up on his jaw, Ali watched as the pain and fear left the man's eyes. He let go and Alex crumpled to the floor, his neck broken.

Russell was curled up in his basket, his head resting over the edge, watching his mistress and the stranger. He was looking at her the way that she looked at him.

Angela wasn't sure that she was doing the right thing, allowing a man that she had only known for an hour, into her bed just because he'd helped her out and she was feeling sorry for him and Kershaw wasn't sure he was doing the right thing, involving Angela in all this mess, but neither of them cared. It somehow felt right.

They kissed passionately and Russell snorted.

Angela broke away. "You said you wanted a cup of coffee."

Kershaw smiled. "Yes please."

"I'll get changed and then I'll put the kettle on. You and Russell can get acquainted."

She left Kershaw sitting on the sofa, staring at Russell who had begun to snore. He'd been sitting on the sofa for about ten minutes. He'd heard Angela go upstairs, heard her move about and come back down. She'd gone into the kitchen and Kershaw was about get off the sofa and see if he could get friendly with Russell, taking great care to avoid his nose, when he heard Angela call out his name.

"Can you come in the kitchen a moment?" she shouted.

The lounge door was closed, and he closed it behind him, leaving the dog asleep in its basket.

"What's the problem? Having trouble with…"

He froze, his mouth hanging open.

The back door was ajar and Ali was up against the kitchen top, a petrified Angela in front of him. He had one arm around her chest and was holding a carving knife to her throat with the other.

"My, Bobby, you're a hard man to find," said Ali, smiling.

Kershaw stared at him, a puzzled expression on his face.

"Who the Hell are you?" he asked.

"That's not really important, is it? What is important is that I've found you. Now I can collect my money."

Having been a nurse for over ten years, Angela knew how the human body worked.

When she felt Ali move his arm from her chest up to the side of her neck and begin to apply pressure, she knew that he intended to put a sleeper on her.

She waited until her vision began to get blurred and as everything started to become white, she let her whole body go limp.

Her ruse worked. Thinking that she had passed out, Ali threw her to one side.

Angela was well aware that unconscious people, when they fell to the ground, didn't break their fall, so she knew that if she did, the mysterious intruder would smell a rat.

When she hit the cold, hard floor, it hurt her elbows and her hip, but luckily, she managed to get away without banging her head.

She lay on the floor, not moving a muscle, her head spinning.

Ali moved towards Kershaw, the smile still on his face.

The first thing Kershaw noticed, was the way in which his attacker was holding the knife.

Whereas, most people would hold a knife with the blade pointing forwards, Ali had the blade pointing backwards, running parallel with his forearm.

Kershaw guessed, with a certain dread, that this was the way someone accustomed to using a knife would hold one.

He glanced across at the kitchen door and then down at Angela. He could probably make a dash for it and maybe get away, but he couldn't leave her here with this maniac.

He knew now, that he should never have allowed her to get involved.

Ali began to move towards him, like a panther, stalking its prey.

Kershaw's eyes kept flickering from Ali's face, to the knife and back to his face again.

Suddenly, Ali make a quick movement in his direction and Kershaw mirrored it, by stepping backwards.

Ali brought his left leg from behind, making a roundhouse kick, aiming for Kershaw's ribs.

As Kershaw brought his right arm down to block it, Ali switched, bringing his foot up and clouted him around the side of the head.

It knocked him sideways and he had to grab hold of the worktop, to stop himself from falling. His legs gave way beneath him and he slumped to the floor.

In front of him he could see two attackers, both armed with a knife.

Ali flipped the knife into the air, let it spin, then caught it. Holding the weapon in the conventional manner, he closed in on Kershaw.

Sitting on the floor, he felt dizzy and nauseous. He tried to kick out, to keep Ali at bay, but he felt so feeble from the crack on the head, that the movement was little more than a twitch.

He wished now that he'd given himself up to the Police when he'd had the chance.

CHAPTER TWENTY-EIGHT

The Inspector was in the canteen, eating what had been described on the board as cottage pie. He was thinking that the chef, if he had a right to be called that, had got the cottage bit right, when Moreton sat down at his table.

He was looking as if he'd just won the lottery.

"I think that we might have a lead," he told Dunn, unable to conceal the excitement in his voice.

"Whatever you've got has to be more interesting than this crap," said Dunn sourly, tapping the plate with his knife.

"The White Swan, on the Twickenham road."

The Inspector nodded. "Yeah, I know it."

"There was a fight in the car park, earlier this evening. Apparently, it was three on one, but it turns out that they picked on the wrong man. One ended up with a shattered hip, one with a broken jaw and the third's dead. Had his neck broken."

Moreton was waiting for some kind of reaction from Dunn, but the inspector just stared at him blankly.

"Well, anyway," continued Moreton, "When a patrol arrived, obviously the dead man wasn't saying anything." Dunn's eyebrows rose a fraction.

"The guy with the broken jaw wasn't saying much either."

Dunn was seriously considering going up for seconds just to get away from Moreton's rambling.

"But the one with the broken hip, told the officer that the fight was over the man whose photograph had been on the nine o'clock news. Kershaw."

Moreton could see that he'd finally got the Inspector's attention.

"What else did he say?"

"That Kershaw went off with a girl, to her house."

"Which is where?"

Moreton shook his head. "The guy passed out before he said anything else."

Dunn closed his eyes, clearly frustrated at having lost Kershaw once again.

"The only other thing we've got is from a guy who was in the car park, on his mobile. He's the one who reported the incident. He told one of the officers that it looked like something out of a Jackie Chan film."

Dunn was about to put a forkful of food into his mouth, when he froze.

"Is there a description of the guy doing all the damage?"

Moreton checked his notebook.

"Yes. He said that he was tall, leanish and had a beard," he said, putting his hand up to his chin.

"This just gets better by the minute," said Dunn, even more sourly.

"Do you know who it is, Sir?"

"Going by the description, I'm fairly certain that it's a man by the name of Alistair Simmonds. He's for hire, if you can afford him. He's a wily Northerner who we're convinced is responsible for at least two hits down here, but he covers his tracks too well to be caught. He's worked for French before, so

I'm betting the big man's brought him in to save himself from getting his hands dirty."

Moreton considered this for a moment.

"Do you think he's got something to do with the Parkin shooting?"

Dunn nodded. "Now that we know he's down here, I'd say it was all connected, somehow."

"So what's all this about Jackie Chan, Sir?"

"Simmonds is a martial arts whizz kid. I saw him in action, once. It was a couple of years ago. I was driving back to the station, when a report came over the radio of a disturbance outside the Night Owl. That was a club in the town centre.

It was closed down a while back.

I was close by, so I thought I'd pop round. On the way, 1 picked up two uniformed beat officers, who were responding. When we got there, Simmonds was outside, although at the time, I didn't know who he was. He was ringed by five men.

In the time it took me to get out of the car and cross the road, it was all over.

Those poor bastards never knew what hit them. I have to say, it was spectacularly impressive, but like I said, he's smart.

I guess he must have been down here on...business," said Dunn, making inverted commas with his fingers. "He must have seen us arrive and didn't want to end up behind bars, while he was on the job, so to speak.

In order to save himself from a beating, he used the minimum amount of force required to defend himself, but I got the impression, that if we hadn't have turned up, those five would have ended up like the three at the White Swan this evening.

Anyway, we got a statement from someone working in the club. The five guys had tried it on with Simmonds, but he walked away. When he left, they followed him outside.

We had nothing to charge him with.

We took him in anyway and it turned out that he has black belts up the ying yang.

He's got a black belt in this and a black belt in that and so on.

He uses weapons, but he doesn't have to, his hands and feet are weapons in themselves.

You could call him an all-rounder, but anyway you phrase it, Simmonds is one seriously dangerous individual."

"And you think that he's after Kershaw, Sir."

"It certainly looks that way. Where's the man with the broken hip, now?"

"He's at the hospital, undergoing surgery."

"Right. You get down there. I want to know the minute he's able to talk. Got it?"

Moreton nodded.

"It's even more important now, that we find Kershaw, before Simmonds does."

Moreton was about to get up out of his seat, when Dunn slapped himself on the forehead.

"Christ! He's done it again!"

Moreton looked puzzled at the Inspector's outburst.

"He's gone to the White Swan, disappeared and we're left with another dead body. We'd best be careful, if we ever catch up with this Kershaw fellow, one of us could wind up on the slab."

Moreton looked horrified. The Inspector smiled and gently placed a hand on the young detective's arm.

"I know what you're thinking and I'm touched, but there's no need to worry, it won't be me."

Angela opened her eyes, slowly, just in time to see Ali kick Kershaw in the head.

Watching him go down on the floor and seeing Ali walk towards him, she knew that she had to do something, or they would both end up dead.

Ali would have preferred a quick kill, but with Kershaw waggling his legs about, it might prove awkward trying to get in there. The easiest thing would be to slice the femoral artery and let him bleed to death. That would mean he would have to kill girl too. It was a shame, but he couldn't risk her coming round and saving him.

The strength was beginning to return to Kershaw's body, but he was still dazed and he knew that he couldn't keep Ali at bay.

As Ali came nearer, he saw Kershaw's eyes register on a spot behind him.

As he turned, Angela swung the huge, cast iron wok, striking Ali on the back of the head.

It made a comical, cartoon like clanging noise and Ali grunted and bent over, cradling the back of his head with his free hand.

As he turned to face Angela again, she swung the utensil a second time, catching Ali a blow on the temple. He collapsed out cold, the knife sliding across the tiled floor.

Kershaw was struggling to get to his feet, as Angela reached him and helped him up.

She held his face in her hands and stared into his eyes.

"Are you okay?" she asked.

"Yeah, I'm fine. Thanks for that," he said, nodding to the wok that she had put down on the table.

"My pleasure," she replied and turned his head to one side to check the area where he had been kicked.

"That looked as though it hurt," she told him.

"No shit! It did hurt," he whined.

They both turned to look down at Ali, still unconscious on the floor.

"So who is he?" she asked.

Kershaw shrugged. "Search me. I've never seen him before."

"Well, he seems to know you."

Kershaw rubbed the side of his head. "Yes, that's a bit worrying."

"I've got a clothes line in the draw, I think we'd better tie him up," suggested Angela.

Kershaw had tied Ali's hands behind his back, had run the cord down and had just finished tying his ankles together when Ali's eyes flickered open.

Kershaw jumped up and stepped back. Even trussed up like a turkey, he got the impression that the man could still pose a threat.

Ali looked up at Angela. "You're a demon with that frying pan, girl."

"It's a wok," she replied, coldly.

"Whatever. So what happens now?"

"You tell me who you are and why you're looking for me," said Kershaw.

For a second, Ali looked confused. "You mean you don't know?"

"No, I don't know," said Kershaw, sharply.

Ali laughed. "Well, if you don't know, I'm fucked if I'm going to tell you."

Kershaw picked the knife up off of the table that Ali had tried to use on him, minutes earlier.

Ali stared at Kershaw, the derision all too evident in his eyes.

"What are you going to do with that, torture me?" he sneered. "You haven't got the bottle."

Kershaw knew that what he was saying was right. He could just hand the man over to the Police, but he wanted to know what was going on, what this was all about.

If he couldn't find a way to make him talk, he'd never know.

He had an idea. It might work, but if it didn't then he'd have no choice but to give him to the law.

He walked around Ali's outstretched legs and squatted down beside him.

"You're right. I couldn't do something like that, but I know someone who could," he said, smiling.

Kershaw turned to look at Angela. "Can you bring Russell in here?" he asked and using the arm that was hidden from Ali, Kershaw rubbed his nose, hoping that Angela would get the message.

She nodded and a smile played around her mouth, letting him know that she understood.

"So who's Russell, the lodger?" asked Ali, contemptuously.

Kershaw thought about that for a moment. "Yeah, I suppose you could call him a lodger."

Everyone has a fear, a room 101, personal to themselves. It can be something as straight forward as flying, or spiders, or it could be more obscure, such as open doors, or mirrors.

Either way, if you're smart, you keep it to yourself, to prevent other people from using it against you, even as a prank.

The moment Angela walked into the kitchen with Russell, Kershaw knew instantly what Ali's was.

It was more than Kershaw could have hoped for. At best, he thought that Ali might have been intimidated by the large animal, but for him to be petrified by it was nothing short of a miracle.

Even though sitting on the floor, with his back up against the kitchen cupboard, Ali tried to shuffle his body backwards, almost as if he were trying to get inside the cabinet itself.

The fear in his eyes was something Kershaw had never imagined he would see, not from a man like this.

Angela stroked the dog's snout. The animal shied away and revealed a very impressive set of teeth.

"Here's what's going to happen," said Kershaw, still crouching down next to Ali.

"Angela and myself are going into the next room, to watch some television, while you and Russell stay in here and...er...get to know each other."

As he stood up, the sudden rush of blood to his head made the spot where Ali had kicked him throb. "You two play nicely, now," he said, patting Ali on the shoulder.

He turned and as before, using the hand that was hidden from Ali, he stroked his nose again.

Angela followed suit and a low, menacing growl began to emanate from the dog's throat.

Kershaw walked to the door, his eyes half closed, in silent prayer.

He knew that he couldn't expect Angela to touch Russell's nose for a third time.

That could end up being dangerous for them all and if Ali was determined not to talk and was left alone with Russell, he would soon discover that he had nothing to fear from the animal.

Ali had to cave in before Kershaw got to the kitchen door, or else the game would be up.

"Alright! Just get rid of the fucking dog!" Ali shouted, as Kershaw was about to grip the door handle.

Kershaw smiled and nodded to Angela, who led Russell back to the lounge and to the comfort of his basket.

Kershaw stood in front of Ali, staring down at him.

"So, what's the story?" he asked, his heart beating slightly faster at the prospect of finally learning what this was all about.

Ali recounted the whole story, as French had recounted it to him, of how Penny had picked him up that night, how she had strung him along for the weeks that they had been seeing each other and then convincing him to help her to steal her Father's diamonds.

Kershaw pulled out a chair and sat down. Angela had, by this time, come back into the kitchen, minus the dog and was listening, along with him.

Kershaw was feeling such a fool at having been taken in by just a pretty face... and a pretty body.

It was almost as if Ali was reading his mind. "She was a looker, alright. The sort of girl that could make a man do crazy things."

Kershaw shot an embarrassed glance at Angela, but it didn't seem as though she was making any judgements.

Ali explained how Penny had taken the diamonds before he even got to the house and that she had woken her Father, who should have recognised him.

The Police were to be waiting for him at his flat when he returned, assuming that he had stashed the diamonds somewhere, en route, but Penny's Father had been unable to give them his name.

Kershaw was staring down at Ali, dumbfounded by all these revelations, which made everything begin to fall into place and make perfect sense.

Ali continued by telling him that French wanted him out of the way, in case he went to the Police, in effort to clear his name, once he found out, as he undoubtedly would, of what he was suspected of having done.

Kershaw realised that if he had gone to the Police, he wouldn't be in the mess that he was in now, that Andy and Penny might both still be alive.

"So who shot Andy, you?" asked Kershaw, getting up out of his chair.

Ali shrugged. "Hey, we all make mist…"

Kershaw kicked him in the mouth, splitting his lip, the blood splattering over his chin.

"That's for Andy," snarled Kershaw.

"Who's responsible for Penny?"

Ali ran his tongue over his already swollen lip. "Oh, that was French. When the girl knew I was coming down, she got all unnecessary. I think, deep down she had the hots for you and French didn't like it."

Kershaw sat back down. He couldn't believe what he was hearing, that Penny had been murdered, because of some scumbag's jealousy.

"So where's French now?" asked Kershaw, getting up out of his seat again.

"Why?"

"Because I'd like to meet him," said Kershaw.

CHAPTER TWENTY-NINE

It was Ali's turn to look dumbfounded. "You want to me...," he began to laugh, but stopped, when the movement hurt his lip.

"You want to meet French, what like a one on one, you mean?"

Kershaw nodded.

"That I'd want to see," said Ali. The tone in his voice made Kershaw feel that he was missing something, that there was something that Ali wasn't telling him, but he put it out of his mind.

French had murdered Penny and although he hadn't actually pulled the trigger, he was ultimately responsible for Andy's death as well.

Kershaw felt more hatred for the man than for anyone that he'd ever known.

"You know where he is, you can take me to him."

Ali looked doubtful. "He's in one of his hideaways that no one knows about. I'll tell you what I'll do. You let me go and I'll give him your message and then come back here. How's that?"

Kershaw caught Angela's movement out of the corner of his eye, as she stepped forward.

"You're not thinking of letting him go, after what he tried to do to you, to us?" she asked, incredulously.

"Hey, don't sweat it, I'll be back. I wouldn't miss this for the world."

Angela stared at Kershaw, wide eyed, hardly believing that he could even be considering turning the killer loose.

Kershaw walked over to her, took her by the arm and led her out into the hall.

"He knows where French is, he can bring him to me. If he doesn't come back, the Police will pick him up. I just need to meet this asshole."

"You heard what he said in there. This man French is obviously dangerous."

"So am I," said Kershaw.

Back in the kitchen, Kershaw knelt down beside Ali.

"If you don't come back, you better pray that the Police find you before I do, because if I find you first, I'll feed you to the fucking dog."

The mere mention of the word made Ali stiffen.

"I'll be back, you can bet on it and French is going to be only too pleased to meet you."

Angela walked into the kitchen with Russell, who was becoming a little disgruntled at dragged out of his basket, for no apparent reason, then sent back, then tugged out again.

Ali eyed the dog nervously, as Kershaw began to untie the cord.

"You so much as blink out of place and that dog will have you by the throat faster than you can say winalot."

Ali stood up, clenching and unclenching his fists, allowing the blood to recirculate.

He put his finger to his lip and smiled at Kershaw. He was about to say something, then glanced at the dog and thought better of it.

"I'll be back within an hour," he said and headed for the door, giving Russell a wide berth.

Angela stood there, staring at Kershaw. "Why are you doing this?" she asked.

"Two people are dead already, you almost died tonight. Hasn't there been enough violence?"

"This isn't violence," said Kershaw, an angry tone to his voice. "This is retribution. Okay, so I hand French over to the Police. What happens then? He ends up in a prison somewhere, with all his mates, being treated like royalty and for how long? Ten years? And then what? He comes out and carries on as if nothing's happened. Before he gets tucked up in his cosy little cell, I want a piece of him first. I'm owed that."

Angela didn't speak. "Anyway, what about you? You're ex-boyfriend wasn't going anywhere after I hit him, so why did you kick him in the ribs?"

"That's not the same and you know it," said Angela, defensively.

"I'm going upstairs for a bath," she told him and began to climb the stairs.

Kershaw wanted to call after her, to try and explain how he felt, but he guessed that he'd be wasting his time. He gave a heavy sigh and thrust his hands deep into the pockets of his jeans. Feeling a piece of paper in one of them, he pulled it out and unfolded it.

It was Clive's mobile number that Eddie had given him on Monday, at work.

If he ever needed someone's help, it was now and he couldn't think of a better person to ask.

Using the telephone in the lounge, he dialled the number. It rung four times and then was answered.

At first, all Kershaw could hear was people talking and the sound of music in the background. Kershaw's first thought was that Clive was working in a nightclub somewhere, which wouldn't have been any use to him.

"Hello?" It was Clive.

"Yeah, it's Bob, Bob Kershaw."

"Hello Boy, how are you?" asked Clive, sounding genuinely pleased to be hearing from him.

"Not too good, at the moment. I'm in a spot of bother and I was hoping that you could help me out."

"Spot of bother, eh? Sounds interesting. Tell me where you are and I'll be right over, after I've finished my pint, that is."

Kershaw was sitting in the kitchen, when he heard Angela coming down the stairs. As she reached the bottom, the doorbell sounded.

Kershaw came out of the kitchen at the same time as Angela came out of the lounge, hanging onto Russell's collar.

"Just in case," she told him, and she seemed to be a little more relaxed.

She opened the door and stood back when she saw Clive standing there.

He grinned when he caught sight of Kershaw. "Thought I had the wrong place for a moment there," he said, smiling at Angela.

She looked across at Kershaw, a question in her eyes.

"He's a friend," he told her.

French slammed the phone down. "Damn! No flights out until tomorrow morning. I was hoping to get out tonight."

The huge Errol was sitting on the other side of the room, watching television.

French picked up the phone and dialled a number.

"Hello Sammy? Yeah, it's French. I need you round here now, I've got some stuff I want you to price for me." French listened to the voice on the other end of the line.

"I said now. If you're not here in fifteen minutes, I'll send someone to get you.

Understand? I'm at Errol's."

French put the phone down and smiled at Errol. "I like Sammy, he makes me laugh, the snivelling little weasel."

Under the threat of being dragged out onto the street, within fifteen minutes the doorbell rang and Errol showed Sammy into the lounge.

He was about five foot six, in his late fifties and bald. He wore a checked jacket with leather patches on the elbows. Sammy appeared even more nervous than usual, what with the giant Errol behind him and the violent French in front.

"Sammy, glad you could make it," said French, making it sound as though he'd actually had a choice in the matter.

"Mr. French," greeted Sammy, nervously shifting from one foot to the other.

French pulled the velvet pouch out from behind him and emptied the contents out onto the coffee table.

"Give me a price for these, a good price," added French, a hint of menace to his voice.

Sammy leant over the table and peered down at the diamonds. He picked one up between this thumb and forefinger and held it up to the light, French looking on.

The jeweller put the diamond back down on the table and opened his bag.

Taking out an eyepiece, he screwed it into place and picked up the diamond again.

He examined it, then putting it back with the others, he picked up a second and then a third. He did this five or six times, French tapping his fingers on the edge of the table, clearly eager for an appraisal.

Sammy put his eyepiece away and when he stood up, there were beads of perspiration breaking out on his forehead.

He swallowed hard. "I can't give you anything for these, I'm afraid, Mr. French," he said, a slight tremor in his voice. "Well I could, but it would only be five hundred pounds."

French's ice blue eyes bored into the terrified little man.

"What's that, a fucking joke?"

Sammy shook his head, clearly having difficulty finding the words to say.

"They're paste," he managed to blurt out and moved back ever so slightly, the expression shooting the messenger, springing instantly to mind.

French stared at the costume jewellery in front of him, then up at Sammy then back to the table. For a moment, he was speechless, then the enormity of what he had just been told hit home.

"That fucking bitch!" he screamed and kicked out at the coffee table, knocking it over, the cheap imitation jewellery flying around the room.

Even the giant Errol appeared a little nervous at French's furious outburst and Sammy looked as though he was going to drop dead, there on the spot.

"Get out," ordered French to Sammy, who was only too pleased to be leaving with all his limbs intact.

"Oi!" called out French as Sammy was scuttling towards the door.

The terrified little man turned to look at French.

"If anyone gets to hear about this, I'll cut your fucking tongue out."

Sammy looked up at Errol, who nodded his huge head as if to say that French was more than capable of carrying out his threat. Five minutes after Sammy had left Ali turned up at the house. He walked into the lounge and looked at what he assumed to be diamonds, strewn all over the floor.

French was standing in the centre of the room, still seething. Errol had thought it wise to leave the man alone with his grief and had disappeared.

"What's up?" asked Ali.

"Paste. That cheating little tart gave me paste."

"So where are the real ones?"

French glared at him. "Who am I, Mystic Meg? How the fuck should I know? I'm not likely to either, unless you happen to have a Ouija board handy."

"Well, it's not all bad news. I found Kershaw."

"At least he's out the way, that's something I suppose," said French, moodily.

"Um, not exactly."

French stared at Ali in disbelief. "What's that supposed to mean?"

"He wants to meet you, you know one on one, mano-a-mano. I think he wants to kick your ass."

French stood there staring and then a grin began to spread across his face.

"Does he now? This whole thing might not turn out to be a complete waste of fucking time after all."

Kershaw and Clive walked in to the kitchen, while Angela, after leading Russell back into the lounge, went upstairs.

"So, is she you're...?"

Kershaw made a so-so gesture with his hand. "I'm not sure yet."

Clive nodded. "Oh, right, I see...I think. Anyway, what's this spot of bother that you're in?"

They both sat down at the table and Kershaw went through the whole story, for what he hoped would be the last time.

He told Clive about his meeting Penny, the break in, Andy being shot and killed by mistake, by a man that French had hired.

When Clive heard the name French, he held up his hands.

"Whoa, back up there, boy. Did you say French?"

Kershaw nodded.

"Peter French?"

"That's what I think his name is, why, do you know him?"

Clive looked surprised. "Don't you?"

Kershaw shook his head. "No, who is he?"

"Who is he? What is he, more like. He's only the biggest gangster since the Krays. He runs half of London and there a rumour that he's got shares in the other half."

Kershaw couldn't help but smile, despite everything.

No wonder the intruder that he and Angela had caught earlier had been so keen to see French and himself meet up.

"So what do you know about French?" asked Kershaw.

"He started off as a prize fighter, you know, a bare knuckle boxer."

Instantly, Kershaw's heart sank. This wasn't what he wanted to hear.

"I saw him once," continued Clive. "It was in a barn, out in the middle of Essex, somewhere, I think. Those things were illegal back then, in fact, as far as I know, they still are.

Anyway, I've seen some wicked fighters in my time, but French, he was out there in a league of his own. Vicious doesn't begin to describe what I saw that night.

I'll tell you boy, there aren't many men in this world that I'd step aside for, but if I had to make a list, French would definitely be on it."

By now, Kershaw's heart had sank down around his knees, somewhere. With every word that Clive uttered,

Kershaw was becoming less and less certain that he could, or even should go through with this.

"Anyway, French progressed from beating the shit out of people for money, to... well, beating the shit out of people for money, I guess, only on a much grander scale. Pretty soon, he'd..." Clive stared across the table and Kershaw felt that he was reading his thoughts.

"Why do you want to know about French?"

"Because I'm going to meet him, just the two of us."

For a moment, Clive was speechless, but only for a moment.

"Boy, that's not a very good idea," he said, shaking his head.

After all he'd heard, Kershaw was coming to the same conclusion, but when he thought of Penny, having the life choked out of her by this bastard French, his resolve found its backbone again.

"He strangled Penny, killed her and left her in his flat," he said, as if that were motive enough for meeting French.

Clive looked at him, sternly. "Don't do this, leave it alone. Good as you think you are, you'll never be in French's league. If you've crossed him and it sounds as though you have, he's not going to be content with giving you a beating, he's gonna want to kill you with his bare hands and believe me, he can do it."

Kershaw's stomach was turning over and over. He knew, after what Clive had told him, that if he backed out now, nobody would think less of him for it, least of all Clive, but for some strange, unfathomable reason, he felt he owed it to Penny, even after all she done, or had tried to do him.

Kershaw looked equally as stern. "I would have thought that you, of all people, would have understood, that this is something I have to do."

Clive nodded. "I do, but there's one thing you have to understand. You go up against French, you're gonna lose."

Just at that moment, Angela walked in. She looked at both of them and when she spoke, her voice was dripping with sarcasm.

"So what are you two doing, drawing up a battle plan, comparing testosterone levels?"

Clive looked at her calmly. "Actually, I'm trying to talk him out of it." He looked across the table at Kershaw.

"Without much luck, it seems."

Clive rubbed his chin, thoughtfully. "Okay, here's what I'll do. If you're dead set on meeting French, I'll come along. Alright, you might get in a lucky punch, but at the end of the day, you're going to get a beating. I'll make sure that that's all you get. If it looks like going to go any further, I'll put a stop to it."

He glanced at Angela, as if he were waiting for her approval.

She wasn't looking too convinced.

"What makes you so sure that you can stop it?" she asked.

Clive smiled, knowingly. "Oh, I can stop it alright, don't you worry about that."

CHAPTER THIRTY

Angela was about to ask Clive, that if he was so sure that he could stop it, why he just didn't stop it now, before it had even started, when the doorbell sounded.

"That'll be him," she said, coldly and walked out of the kitchen, yet again, dragging poor Russell from his warm basket.

Ali was smiling when she opened the door, but the smile soon vanished, when he saw the dog.

Angela stood to one side to allow him to enter, neither of them speaking.

When Ali walked into the kitchen and spotted Clive, a huge grin spread over his face.

"Hello, Westie, how are you, mate?" he asked.

Clive clearly wasn't as pleased to see Ali, as Ali was to see him.

"Alistair," said Clive, he voice flat.

Kershaw, with a surprised expression, looked from Clive to Ali and back to Clive again.

"At the risk of appearing thick, do you two know each other?"

"Oh yeah," said Ali, gleefully, "We served together, didn't we mucker?"

"Until they threw you out," said Clive.

Ali made a face. "Ah, politics, that's all that was."

"I heard a rumour that you were running with French. It doesn't surprise me, you two deserve each other."

Clive's tone wiped the grin off of Ali's face and he looked down at Kershaw.

"You know the pumping station at Hampton Court?" he asked.

Kershaw nodded.

"There's an empty warehouse behind. Seven o'clock tomorrow morning. Don't be late.

You going to be there, Westie?"

"I might be," replied Clive, his voice still cold.

"Ah, it'll be great! Just like old times, eh?"

Clive just stared at Ali and their eyes met for a moment.

"The old times were the times when you were someone to be relied on. Now, you're just another scumbag, like French."

Ali's eyes lost all their warmth and his face turned to stone. "See you tomorrow," he said, icily.

"What's the story with him?" asked Kershaw, after he'd heard the front door close.

"Alistair? He used to be a good soldier, one of the best, then he was involved in a rather nasty incident. In fact, I'm surprised he came into this house, what with there being a dog here."

"Oh yeah, what is it with him and dogs?"

"We were in Londonderry, back in the eighties. We were on our way to bust one of their top boys. We got into the house, around two o'clock in the morning.

I went up, he stayed down. It was bad Intel," said Clive, shaking his head.

"The guy wasn't even there. Alistair went into one of the rooms. There were two Rhodesian ridgebacks in there."

"What's that, a dog?"

Clive nodded. "Yeah, South African hunting dogs, specially bred, with no bark."

"The first I knew about it, was when he shouted out, or at least tried to. They were chewing his face off at the time."

Kershaw grimaced.

"Yes, it was a bit of a mess. I had to shoot both of the dogs, it was the only way I could get them off. They got him back home and he had reconstructive surgery.

It wasn't perfect, hence the beard. It hides the scars. Anyway, after that, he changed, in the worst possible way."

There was a question in Kershaw's eyes, as he waited for Clive to continue.

"Everyone knows that the S.A.S. are the best. They send us to places where no one else can go, or wants to. If the job requires us to kill, that's what we do, but it doesn't mean that we enjoy it.

Alistair did; a little too much. He never used to be like that before. It was almost as if he was getting off on it. Eventually, it got to the stage where he was becoming a liability. When the top brass wanted him to take a psychiatric evaluation, he went berserk. They had no choice but to kick him out.

I'd heard through the grapevine that he was hiring himself out. Sadly, he's the best man for the job."

They both fell silent and then Clive pushed his chair back and stood up.

"So I'll pick you up tomorrow at six."

He stared down at Kershaw, waiting, hoping, that he was going to have a change of heart.

When it was obvious that it wasn't forthcoming, Clive let out a breath.

"Don't be late," he said and started for the kitchen door, Kershaw following.

Angela came out from the lounge, when she heard the kitchen door open.

She looked at them both, expectantly.

"Don't worry, I'll bring him back in one piece," said Clive, in an attempt to reassure her.

"Make sure you do," she told him, sternly.

Clive had almost reached the front door, when he turned around.

"One thing I can't understand. Alistair told you everything you wanted to know, yeah?"

Kershaw nodded.

"Because you threatened him with the dog, right?"

Kershaw nodded again.

"So why didn't he just make a run for it?"

"He couldn't. He was tied up," said Kershaw.

Clive looked amazed. "Blimey, Boy! You're better than I thought."

Kershaw laughed. "It was nothing to do with me. I was out for the count. It was Angela. She laid him out with a frying pan."

"It was a wok, actually," said Angela.

Clive looked impressed.

He opened the front door and stepped out onto the porch.

"That list," said Kershaw.

"List?"

"Yeah, the list of men that you'd step aside for. Is Alistair on it?"

Clive smiled and nodded. "Oh yeah. He's number one."

When Kershaw shut the door and turned around, Angela was sitting on the stairs.

"Do you want me to leave?" he asked.

When she stood up and moved under the hall light, he could see that her eyes were moist.

"Please don't do this."

"This time tomorrow, this will all be over and you heard Clive. He's going to bring me back in one piece and I believe him. So should you."

He took hold of both her hands. "Anyway, I have to come back, to see you again."

Angela smiled weakly and squeezed his hands.

"I'll run you a bath," she said.

Kershaw lay in bed with his hands behind his head, staring up at the ceiling. Angela was next to him, fast asleep.

What had gone through their minds earlier that evening, before Ali had burst in on them had never materialized. It hadn't felt right, so they had just fallen asleep in each other's arms.

Kershaw had been dreaming. He had walked into a room, to face a semi-circle of chairs, occupied by everyone that had been involved in the last two weeks.

Penny, Andy, Clive, Eddie, the two that had come to his flat, Sylvia. Even Johnny the Skinhead and his pal were there. He looked at them and suddenly they all started laughing and pointing behind him.

When he turned around, there was a man standing behind him - a man with no face.

Kershaw knew that this had to be French, the man he'd never seen.

The laughing grew louder and louder, until finally, he awoke, sweating.

Lying, staring up at the ceiling, he felt scared. The emotions began to come in waves.

First fear, then anger, then fear again.

He remembered what Clive had told him about harnessing that fear, making it work for you. That was what he had to do tomorrow, but could he?

He could get up now, call the Police, tell them everything and have them pick up French.

Clive would be pleased, Angela would be over the moon, but how would he feel?

He could feel his whole body begin to tense. He wanted to slam his fist into French's face, whatever it looked like just the once and then he'd be content.

It might cost him a beating, he might not even get a single punch in, but he wanted to do it, even though the thought of it scared him to death.

He looked at the clock on the bedside table. It was almost three o'clock.

He didn't think that he'd be able to get back to sleep, but eventually, he drifted off.

Dunn had no such problem. He was fast asleep, when the telephone rang.

As he picked it up, he glanced at the clock on the bedside table. It was five minutes to six.

"Hello," said Dunn, sleepily.

"It's Moreton, Sir. We've got the girl's address."

The Inspector was wide awake in an instant. "Right, I want all the exits covered, but no one's to go in until I get there. Is that understood?"

"Yes Sir," replied Moreton.

"Come and get me," said Dunn, putting the phone down and leaping out of bed.

Kershaw had set Angela's alarm for a quarter to six. He woke at twenty to and turned it off, preferring for her not to wake up.

Slipping out of bed, he gathered up his clothes and left the room, closing the door quietly behind him.

He got dressed in the kitchen. He felt weak, his legs were like jelly and he had to keep telling himself that he was doing the right thing.

Closing the front door, he walked out onto the street. It was still dark, but the dawn was coming.

At a quarter to six, Clive picked up Eddie, who was waiting at the top of his road.

Clive was fairly certain that Ali wouldn't be the only person that French would be bringing with him this morning. He didn't want to arrive mob handed, but at the same time, he didn't want themselves to be heavily outnumbered.

Eddie, when Clive had spoken to him the previous evening, had agreed to come along, initially, to help out, if he was needed, but when Clive mentioned that the person responsible for the shooting of his workmate was going to be there, Eddie's eagerness to tag along took on a new dimension. As he so succinctly put it, he wanted to tear Ali a new asshole.

Clive had tried to explain that Ali wasn't to be taken lightly, but much like Kershaw, Eddie wasn't to be put off.

When Clive's huge vehicle turned into the road, Kershaw could make out another body in the front with him, but it wasn't until the truck pulled up alongside, that he realised who it was.

"Alright, Eddie," said Kershaw, as he clambered up into the cab.

He felt a little uneasy, not sure whether the giant blamed him for Andy's death, although in all honesty, Kershaw wouldn't condemn him if he did.

"Bob," greeted the big man. "Thought I'd come along, might get a chance to have a word with the bastard who shot Andy," he rumbled.

"That was a bad business," said Kershaw, mournfully.

"If I hadn't have got myself mixed up in all of this, Andy would still be alive."

Eddie nudged him. "Don't sweat it. I'll give him one for you."

The ride over was quiet, all three of them caught up in their own thoughts.

Kershaw felt slightly more comfortable, knowing that he had these two with him, but he also knew that at the end of the day, he was still going to have to face French on his own, which caused his stomach to begin performing cartwheels again.

Clive turned down the track that ran along the side of the pumping station just before six thirty.

"You two walk on down, I'm going to hide this beast. I'd prefer it if they thought that I wasn't here." Reaching into the back, he pulled out a large black holdall.

"What's in there?" asked Kershaw, indicating the bag.

Clive winked at him. "My little bag of tricks. Never leave home without it."

Out of the back of the truck, he also pulled out a four foot, wooden pole.

"You know what this is?" he asked Kershaw.

"Er, a stick?"

Clive smiled. "Yes... and no." "It's a jo, a martial arts weapon. In the right hands it can be devastatingly effective, but for you, it could help keep French at arm's length, if he decides to fight dirty."

"Fight dirty?" repeated Kershaw, a note of panic in his voice.

Clive nodded. "He could be carrying." He held the jo out to Kershaw.

"This could save your life, if I can't get to you quick enough."

Kershaw didn't like the direction this conversation was taking and it showed in his eyes.

"You haven't come here for an arm wrestling match," said Clive, seriously.

"This is the real thing. French is the real thing. If you don't want to do this, say now and we'll go."

Kershaw knew that it would be the easiest thing in the world for him to say yes and then they'd climb back into the truck and that would be it, over.

Kershaw took the jo off of Clive, felt the weight of it in his hand and imagined using it to strike French with.

"You go and hide your truck, me and Eddie will walk down," said Kershaw, by way of a reply.

When Dunn and Moreton pulled into Angela's road, there was a marked patrol car at the top, another further down.

Moreton pulled up outside the address that had been given him by the man whose hip Ali had shattered. There was a uniformed Sergeant waiting at the gate.

"There's two in the back garden and one at either end of the fence that runs down the side of the house. There's nowhere for him to go, Sir," said the Sergeant, confidently.

Dunn nodded and strode up the path to the front door.

Angela stretched her arm out, to find the space next to her, warm, but empty.

She stared at the wall for a moment, then grabbed the still warm pillow and held it tightly.

She had almost drifted back off to sleep, when she was woken by what sounded like someone knocking on her front door with a hammer.

Getting out of bed, she walked across the room. As she reached the window, the hammering was repeated.

Pulling back the curtain, she looked down onto the street below. She saw the two patrol cars, the car parked outside her door and the two men, looking up.

She opened the window. "I'm coming down!" she called out. When she opened the door, Dunn was about to introduce himself as a Police officer, when he recognised her.

"You were at Andrew Parkin's house the night he was shot."

Angela nodded.

"Is Kershaw here?" asked the Inspector.

"He was, but you've just missed him."

"What do you mean, missed him? Where's he gone?"

"He's gone to have a fight with that French, the man who's responsible for all of this."

Dunn looked horrified. "He's gone to meet with French, on his own?"

"No, he went with someone else."

"Who?"

"I don't know his full name. Bobby only introduced him as Clive. He's a big man, quite old, with white hair."

Dunn massaged his temples. "This is going from bad to worse."

"Do you know him, Sir?" asked Moreton.

"Oh, I know him alright. His name's Clive Weston and if he's gone along with Kershaw, then there's a very real possibility that the body count's going to go through the roof."

CHAPTER THIRTY-ONE

"Where's this taking place?" asked Dunn.

Angela turned back to the stairs from where she had just appeared.

"Let me get dressed and I'll tell you on the way."

Dunn stifled a laugh. "You're not coming," he told her.

Angela turned back and stared at him. "Then you won't know where it is, will you?"

The Inspector gawped at her. "Have you any idea of the danger that Kershaw's in right now?"

"Yes, of course I do, that's why I want to be there."

"Just fell me where this is happening and I'll make sure that you're kept informed," said Dunn.

Angela folded her arms across her chest and glared at the Policeman, defiantly. "Am I coming?" she asked.

"I could have you arrested for obstruction, you do realise that, don't you?"

It was if Angela could tell that it was a bluff. She continued to glare at Dunn, her arms still folded.

They continued to stare at each other and just when it looked as though it was going to be a stale mate, Dunn's shoulders sagged ever so slightly and he broke eye contact.

He looked away and then back at her. He pointed a finger.

"Alright, but when we get there, you stay in the car, understand?"

Angela grinned. "Righto. I'll be two minutes," she said and shot off upstairs to put some clothes on.

"So who's this Weston chap, Sir?" asked Moreton.

The young detective was all too aware of Dunn's overwhelming desire to put French behind bars and he also knew that wherever the Inspector went, he would have to follow. He didn't relish the prospect of coming face to face with both French and Simmonds, but as if that weren't bad enough, it now appeared, judging by Dunn's reaction on learning of Weston's involvement, that there was yet another, equally as dangerous player to contend with.

"Is he one of the good guys?" asked Moreton, optimistically.

Dunn made a so-so gesture with his hand.

"He used to be in the Special Air Service. Now he's into security, all kinds. Driver, bodyguard and on any Saturday night, you'll always find him on a door, somewhere. I had him in a couple of years ago, not for questioning just to make a statement. We had a long, interesting chat. He told me a few stories, but I got the impression that there was a lot he was keeping to himself.

He's a one man army and Kershaw's damned lucky to have him on his side."

Moreton was about to ask the Inspector if they had Weston on their side as well, when Dunn took a step into the hall and peered up the stairs.

"What time are they supposed to be meeting?" he called up.

Angela appeared at the top of the stairs, wearing a grey tracksuit.

"Seven o'clock," she said, as she began to walk down.

Dunn looked at his watch. It was ten to. "Shit!" he cursed.

He strode outside, to the uniformed sergeant, still standing on the pavement.

"Get them all in their cars and ready to move," he barked.

When he turned around, Angela was in the hall. She had just put on a green anorak and was saying goodbye to Russell.

Just then another patrol car pulled up and Sergeant Ryder got out.

"Heard that there might be some action going down," he said, walking up to Dunn.

The Inspector smiled. "You could say that. French, Alistair Simmonds and Clive Weston, all in the one place, getting ready for a punch up."

Ryder let out a short whistle. "Wow! I know people who'd pay good money to see that. I reckon you're going to need all the help you can get."

He sounded eager to be involved, which suited Moreton just fine. The more the merrier and safer, as far as he was concerned.

Angela walked out of the house, closing the door behind her.

"So, where are we going?" asked Dunn.

He noticed that she wasn't looking quite so determined as she had a few minutes ago, in fact, she appeared a little frightened.

Dunn could guess why. She was afraid that once she told them where to go, they would leave her behind. She really was desperate to come. He could only assume that she and Kershaw had struck up some kind of relationship and that she wanted to be by his side. His heart went out to her.

"Get in the car," he told her.

She smiled, weakly. "There's a deserted warehouse behind the pumping station at Hampton court," she said, opening the back door of the Inspector's car.

Dunn glanced at Ryder and the other uniformed Sergeant, standing next to him.

"You'd best get a move on. They're supposed to be meeting there at seven."

He checked his watch once more, as did the other two officers.

All four cars sped off in convoy, their lights flashing and their sirens wailing.

At five minutes to seven, Clive came jogging around the comer of the warehouse, his mysterious black holdall hanging by his side.

He looked at Eddie. "Me and the boy are going inside. You wait out here, but keep out of sight. Once you know that they're in there, come and wait by the door. I'll call you if I need you."

Eddie opened his mouth to speak, but Clive already knew what he was going to say.

"If you still want a crack at Alistair, you can have it when this is over."

The big man nodded and smiled, as if the wait would only serve to whet his appetite for what was to come.

The door to the warehouse had at some time been padlocked, but that had long since disappeared, as had all of the glass in the numerous windows, both upstairs and down.

Inside the building was empty, except for newspapers strewn around, along with drinks cans and various other pieces of discarded rubbish.

There were six, square concrete pillars, in pairs, down the centre of the building and Clive nodded at the jo that Kershaw was holding in his hand.

"Stand that up behind one of the pillars, out of sight and away from the door, so you can get to it, should you need to."

Kershaw nodded. His throat felt so parched, he felt that he'd lost the power to speak. At the far end was a flight of metal stairs that led up to a walkway that ran the length of the building.

Looking up, Clive spotted what appeared to be a large piece of tarpaulin.

"I'm going up there. You alright?"

As well as his throat feeling as dry as sandpaper, his felt as if his bladder was about to burst. He nodded again.

"One piece of advice," said Clive. "Always maintain eye contact. Never look down, never look away. Don't look at his hands, or his feet just his eyes. Got it?"

When Kershaw failed to answer, Clive clapped a large hand on his shoulder, making him jump.

"Got it?" repeated Clive.

Kershaw swallowed in an effort to lubricate his throat. "Yeah, I got it."

Clive squeezed his shoulder. "Remember, no guts, no glory."

With that he walked to the stairs and his footsteps echoed around the empty building as he climbed the metal steps.

Leaning the staff up against one of the pillars, Kershaw noticed that his hand was shaking, along, it seemed with the rest of his body.

Ali had taken French's Aston, as he wanted to get there early, to have a scout around, whilst French and Errol, who would never have fitted into the Aston Martin anyway, followed on behind in Ali's Mercedes.

Eddie was around the back of the building, about halfway down, when he heard a noise behind him.

When he turned around, he found himself staring at the man Clive had described to him and knew that he was looking at Andy's killer.

Ali was leaning up against the side of the building, his arms hanging casually down by his side.

"My, you're a big one, aren't you?"

Most people, when they first set eyes on Eddie, were immediately struck by his size, intimidated by his huge presence.

The fact that Ali didn't appear to be in the least bit concerned, set off warning bells in the big man's brain. He guessed that the man must be supremely confident in his ability, which was obviously why Clive had tried to warn him off.

It didn't make any difference to Eddie, he was still going to crush the murdering bastard anyway.

By the same token, Ali was well aware that one punch from the Giant, or to get caught in his huge arms, would mean the end. He was going to have to be on his toes with this one.

As the two men approached each other, Eddie swung a massive fist at Ali's head. Ali waited and waited, until he could almost feel the air being displaced as the punch headed his way. At the last moment, he ducked underneath and gracefully stepped around and behind Eddie, grabbing hold of his collar, while at the same time stamping down on the back of the giant's knee, forcing him to buckle.

Ali brought up his knee and cracked Eddie around the side of the head.

Although dazed, Eddie wasn't out of it completely and reached around behind him, in an attempt to grab hold of some part, any part of Ali's body, only to find he'd already stepped back out of distance.

As Eddie moved around on his knees and began to get back to his feet, Ali stepped in and whipping around, delivered a back kick, which struck Eddie full in the face, breaking his nose, the blood spraying everywhere.

Fury enabled Eddie to blot out the pain and despite blurred vision from his watering eyes, he stood up, towering over Ali.

Seeing the outline in front of him, Eddie reached out with both hands. If he could just get a hold of him, he'd tear the little shit apart!

Fighting Ali was like fighting a ghost. One second he was there, and then he was gone. Ali swooped down like a swallow, striking Eddie in the kidney with his elbow as he passed by. The big man coughed, spitting out blood that had trickled into his mouth and as he turned to follow the spectre, Ali brought up his right leg and hit him with a roundhouse kick, in exactly the same spot.

The pain was shooting across Eddie's stomach and around his back from the first strike, when the second hit.

His nose was throbbing, he couldn't see a whole lot now and his body was racked with pain. Unable to stop himself, Eddie doubled over.

Like all fighters, trained in martial arts, Ali didn't lash out wildly. Every attack was aimed at a specific area of the body, designed to cause the maximum amount of pain and damage. With the same leg, Ali delivered another roundhouse kick, the toe of his trainer catching Eddie on the temple.

The big man was out on his feet, so much so, that Ali considered it safe to move in within arm's length of the giant.

Placing his right leg behind, Ali stretched his right arm across Eddie's massive chest and pushed. Without any resistance, Eddie fell backwards and crashed to the floor.

Ali was about to finish it, by stamping down on his throat, crushing his windpipe, when he heard his Mercedes pull up on the other side of the building.

He smiled down at Eddie lying on the floor." Looks like your luck's in, pal," he said, even though he knew that the big man couldn't hear him.

"You may get to fight another day."

Clive walked up to the tarpaulin. It was filthy and probably had any number of things living on it and in it, not that he was unduly bothered. He'd lain in ambush in far worse places and for far longer.

Crawling underneath, he opened his holdall and taking out a small knife, cut an oblong out of the material. Peering through, he was happy with his arcs, being able to see most of the floor down below.

Dipping into his bag once more, he pulled out a small briefcase. It contained an air pistol, bit this was no ordinary weapon. He'd had it specially made for him by an armourer in Egypt.

Air pistols were ideal for removing someone temporarily, but were notoriously inaccurate and clumsy to load. If you missed with your round, the chances were, by the time you had reloaded, your mark would either have moved out of range, or was now in a position where a decent shot was impossible.

Clive had solved that problem by having an air pistol with two chambers. With both barrels loaded, if he missed the mark with his first shot, which it had to be said, didn't happen that often, he simply made the necessary adjustments and fired again. He'd used the pistol on numerous occasions and knew that it was the perfect weapon for the task ahead.

Inside the box, along with the pistol, was a small metal case. In this were six feathered darts. Rather than the usual gaudy colours, the flights on these were grey and the tips were red, having been coated in a toxin capable of knocking out a rhino. Slipping a dart into each chamber, he cocked the weapon and laid it down by his side. Peering through the hole in the tarpaulin, he looked at Kershaw down below.

Kershaw had never felt so alone in all his life, even though he knew that Clive and Eddie were with him. His heart was racing and his legs were trembling and for one brief moment, he found himself hoping that French couldn't be bothered with all of this and wasn't going to show. That thought evaporated the second he heard a car door slam outside. He let out a long breath and waited for the warehouse door to open.

He sucked that breath straight back in, when Errol squeezed through the doorway. Kershaw had thought that Eddie was big, but this guy was gigantic.

Even up on the walkway, concealed under the filthy tarpaulin, Clive's eyebrows rose when he caught sight of the huge black man.

Errol stepped to one side and Kershaw found himself staring at a man a good deal shorter than himself, with sandy coloured hair, piercing blue eyes and a hard, chiselled face.

This was the man who had turned his life upside down, who had choked the life out of Penny and who was ultimately responsible for Andy's death.

This was the man that he wanted to beat the living daylights out of and now that he was face to face with him, Kershaw found himself daring to believe that he could do it.

By the same token, French found himself looking at a tall, fresh faced kid, who looked as if he were about to piss his pants. This mummy's boy was the reason he was fleeing the country a couple of million pounds worse off. He was going to enjoy this!

French had only taken a couple of steps inside the building, when Ali appeared at the door. He nodded at Kershaw. "He brought a friend with him, almost as big as Errol here, but he won't be joining us."

Up on the walkway, Clive closed his eyes. Damn! He'd tried to warn Eddie off, but the big galoot wouldn't listen.

"Any sign of the other one?" asked French. Ali shook his head.

Kershaw could feel his new found confidence sinking down to his boots as French glared at him. "Where's Weston?"

Scared as he knew Kershaw must be, Clive prayed that he wouldn't look up. If he did, they would know where he was and the element of surprise would be lost.

Kershaw didn't trust himself to answer, in case his voice came out as a squeak, so he simply shrugged his shoulders.

French glanced across at Ali, who shook his head once more. "He's here," said Ali, looking around the empty building. "I know it."

French continued to glower at Kershaw. "Errol, rip this lying prick's arms off'.

Grabbing hold of the pistol, Clive shifted his position. Okay, he thought to himself, it's time to level the playing field.

CHAPTER THIRTY-TWO

This wasn't the way it was supposed to be, Kershaw thought to himself.

It was supposed to be just him and French, but now there was Ali the assassin and Errol, son of Kong. How the Hell was Clive going to bring him through this, he thought to himself, as the giant black man walked towards him, looking only too pleased to carry out French's request.

Up on the walkway, as huge as Errol was, Clive still regarded Ali as the biggest threat.

Sliding the pistol through the hole he'd cut in the tarpaulin, he took aim, drew a breath, held it and squeezed the first trigger.

Down below, all four men heard the noise, which sounded as if someone, somewhere, were cracking a walnut.

Standing next to French, Ali slapped the side of his neck, sank to his knees and then fell forward onto the floor, motionless.

French stared down at him, a startled expression on his face.

"What the fuck's the matter with him?" he asked, directing the question at Errol.

Suddenly, there was another walnut cracking noise and as French looked to his right, the monstrous black man's eyes rolled up into his head and he fell backwards onto the floor.

French looked nonplussed, as he glanced from one lifeless body to the other.

Catching the movement out of the corner of his eye, he looked up as Clive threw the tarpaulin off of himself and stood up.

French's confusion instantly turned to anger. "You must be Weston!" he snarled.

Clive smiled down. "You must be that asshole French."

French glared up at him, his eyes flickered over to Kershaw and then back to Clive.

"When I've finished with this wanker, I'm coming for you," he threatened.

As French turned to face him, Kershaw felt all the confidence that he had experienced only a few minutes ago, sink down to his boots and his stomach felt hollow once more.

French leered at him, when he saw the fear in his eyes.

Kershaw forgot Clive's words of wisdom and looked down at French's clenched fists.

They were large and calloused around the knuckles and, as he found out to his cost, very fast.

He missed the first one, which slammed into his mouth. As he staggered back, Kershaw could feel his top lip beginning to swell and it was while he was off balance that French hit him again, knocking him off his feet.

Kershaw landed on the floor, the concrete scraping the skin off of his right elbow, as he used it to steady himself. His eye was already beginning to close as a result of the second punch and he could taste the blood in his mouth from the first.

He was expecting French to launch an attack on him with his feet, while he was on the ground, but it never came.

Instead, French stood back and waited for Kershaw to get to his feet. He wanted this to be slow, slow and painful. He intended to demolish Kershaw a piece at a time and he wanted him to get up so that he could knock him back down.

Kershaw slowly climbed to his feet.

French was circling, like a vulture, ready to come swooping in.

Kershaw guessed that Clive must have had a reason for telling him to maintain eye contact and as French moved in and Kershaw stared into his ice blue pits, he realised what that reason was.

It was almost as if he could tell when French was going to make his move and as a fist came swinging towards him, Kershaw raised his right arm, blocking it.

Feeling quite pleased with himself, Kershaw brought up his left hand and was about to aim a punch at his opponent's head, when French slipped both hands inside, grabbed hold of Kershaw's jacket and head-butted him.

For a second, everything went black and the pain was so intense, Kershaw's knees almost buckled.

Stepping back, he put his hand up to his forehead and when he took it away it was covered in blood from an inch long cut between his eyebrows.

Kershaw knew that he was going to have to do something and quickly.

Up on the walkway, Clive was thinking the self-same thought.

The boy had only been down there for ninety seconds and with his lip split and swollen, his right eye almost closed and blood streaming down his face, Kershaw looked as though he'd already gone twelve rounds with Mike Tyson.

French stepped in once more with a punch, which Kershaw blocked and then he thrust both his hands into French's chest, knocking him off of his feet.

At one time, French had been a force to be reckoned with, not that he still wasn't, but even in his youth, he'd never had Kershaw's power and when he hit the floor, there was a genuine look of surprise on his face.

Kershaw wasn't playing a waiting game and as French began to scramble to his feet, he leapt in and kicked him in the ribs.

French grunted and sank down onto his hands and knees. He was used to pain, used to overcoming it and carrying on, so as Kershaw stepped in to kick him again, French had already recovered sufficiently to grab hold of his foot and push him backwards, giving himself time to get to his feet.

Kershaw could see that French was favouring his left side, where he had been kicked, so he knew that was going to have to be his target, from now on.

French threw a punch, but Kershaw stepped out of the way and as French turned to face him, Kershaw hit him in the ribs.

He heard the air whoosh out of French's mouth and the sight of his enemy in pain helped to fuel his confidence.

Blood had begun to trickle into the corner of Kershaw's eye, the one that wasn't closed and he had to wipe it away.

He caught the movement in front of him and swung wildly. His lucky punch collided with French's jaw as he was stepping in and as his fist connected, Kershaw felt an overwhelming sense of satisfaction.

He stepped back, to put some space between them and when he looked at French, he could see the man's chest heaving.

French was ring rusty and it was beginning to tell. He had the experience, but Kershaw was fitter and stronger and now he had the will to win.

French could tell this, so he reached into his inside jacket pocket and brought out a cut throat razor. If he couldn't beat this boy with his fists, he'd cut him to pieces, instead.

The end result would be the same.

Kershaw caught the glint of steel as French whipped the lethal razor out, but unfortunately, he was blocking Clive's view and when French lashed out, from up on the walkway, it just looked like a wild punch from a tired man.

The sight of the weapon made Kershaw's blood run cold and he knew that he had to get to the staff that Clive had given him, which he had stood up behind one of the pillars.

He bent his body backwards in an attempt to avoid French's slash with the razor and he thought that he had, until he felt a stinging in his shoulder.

Glancing down, he saw that his shirt had been torn and there was a deep, two inch gash across his shoulder.

He turned and ran for the pillar, a couple of yards away, where he had hidden his weapon.

That was when Clive spotted the razor in French's hand and when Kershaw grabbed hold of the staff and turned to face him, Clive was shocked to see that nearly all of Kershaw's right sleeve was stained crimson.

French was about to leap in and strike at Kershaw again, but he stopped dead when he saw the staff.

He began to move more cautiously now, looking for an opening, while at the same time avoiding the pole.

Kershaw swung the jo wildly, in an effort to keep him at bay, but it was clear that he wasn't an expert, which came as a relief to French.

As the staff swung harmlessly past him, French stepped in and slashed with the razor again, which struck the jo inches above Kershaw's hand, taking a chunk out of the wood.

Kershaw glanced down to where the razor had made contact and was shocked to realise that if it had been a fraction lower, he could well have lost most of his hand.

In more luck than judgement, as French stepped in once more, Kershaw swung the jo, catching him on the wrist. The weapon was solid and Kershaw understood why Clive had said it could be devastating in the hands of an expert.

He hadn't put that much strength behind the strike, but even so, he caused French to yelp and the razor dropped out of his hand and clattered to the floor.

Already, French's wrist had swollen up like a balloon, the bone obviously broken, the hand hanging lifeless by his side.

As Kershaw watched the deadly razor spin away, he caught a movement out of the corner of his eye and glancing down, he saw that it was his own blood, dripping off of the end of the jo and splashing onto the floor.

The action of swinging the staff had caused the wound to open, his lifeblood pumping out at an alarming rate. He couldn't be sure how much he had lost, but he knew that if it carried on for much longer, he could be in trouble.

Clive was thinking the same thing as he came clambering down the stairs.

He knew that Kershaw could begin to flag at any time and French, even with a broken wrist and most likely a couple of broken ribs as well could still be dangerous.

If French saw Kershaw start to weaken, he'd jump in and finish it, for good.

It had been a long time since French had been on the receiving end of anything and he didn't like it. It wasn't that the kid was good, but more because he was getting on and had lost the edge. His hand was worse than useless and his ribs hurt like Hell with every breath he took, but he knew that if he allowed this pretty boy to beat him, he'd be a laughing stock, all washed up.

He had to end it now.

With an almighty war cry, he rushed at Kershaw, who was still staring at his sleeve and hand, both drenched in blood. It was like a wakeup call and he instinctively thrust the jo out at French, catching him in the face. The end of the jo caught

French on the cheek, splitting the skin under the eye and knocking him clean off of his feet.

French lay on the floor, unable to get up. As Kershaw walked up to him, he thought of Penny and Andy. He wanted to shove the staff through to the back of French's head.

Standing over him, it was an effort, because of the burning pain in his shoulder, but Kershaw raised the weapon up in the air, looking for all the world like a whaler about to harpoon his catch.

French looked up at him, unable to defend himself any longer, but with a defiant look in his eyes. Kershaw would have done it, but the jo wouldn't move.

When he looked over his shoulder, he saw that Clive had a hold of it.

The big man shook his head.

"That's enough, son. Believe me, he's not worth it, not worth going to jail for."

Clive gently took the jo away from Kershaw and laid it on the ground behind him.

As he turned back, Kershaw's legs gave way beneath him and Clive managed to grab him before he collapsed on the floor.

"It's alright, boy, I've got you," said Clive, as he lowered Kershaw to the floor, propping him up against one of the pillars. Kershaw's pupils were dilated and his skin was pale.

Clive placed two fingers on the side of his neck. His pulse was strong, but Clive knew that it wouldn't stay that way for long if he didn't stem the bleeding.

"Hang on in there. I've got something in my bag that'll fix you up," Clive reassured him.

Kershaw's stomach felt empty and his chest was burning, almost as badly as his shoulder. He could hear what Clive was saying, but the man's voice seemed to be coming from a long way away.

Clive shot a glance over at French. He was still lying prostrate on the floor. He wasn't getting up and if he did, it wouldn't take much for Clive to put him back down.

French was a beaten man, which was more than could be said for Ali.

"Isn't that sweet."

Clive whipped his head round when he heard the voice behind him and saw Ali there, with the jo in his hands.

When Clive had fired the pistol for the first time, Ali was the only one of the four men below who recognised the sound for what it was. He'd heard it plenty of times in the past and he also knew, when Clive used his all singing, all dancing air pistol, where the preferred target was.

Ali had slapped his hand to his neck, in an effort to stop the toxin from entering his bloodstream. The tip of the dart had punctured his neck through a gap in his fingers and Ali pulled it out by moving his hand away from his neck a fraction.

So strong was the toxin that even that minute scratch made him feel slightly woozy.

He dropped to his knees and then onto his stomach. As long as he remained motionless, he knew he'd make a full recovery within a few minutes. His plan was to wait until the time was right and spring a little surprise of his own.

He heard the second crack of the pistol and then the sound of Errol's giant body hitting the floor. He still didn't know where Clive was hiding, but he knew that he would show himself, eventually.

Through half closed eyes, he watched Clive take the staff away from Kershaw and lay it on the ground. When Clive grabbed hold of Kershaw and sat him down, Ali felt that the moment had come for his awakening.

"The boy needs to get to hospital," said Clive, appealing to Ali's better nature, although he doubted very much that he had one.

He was right.

Ali screwed his face up and shook his head. "Nah, I don't think so. Besides, you've got more important things to worry about." He smiled and banged the jo on the concrete floor, the sound echoing around the empty building.

"Me."

Ali had spent almost half a lifetime perfecting his martial arts skills. Unarmed, he was a force to be reckoned with, but with a weapon, especially his favourite weapon, which just happened to be the jo, Clive knew that he was virtually invincible.

It was a scenario that he'd hoped he would never have to face, but now it was here, Clive felt scared.

He could tell by the glint in Ali's eye that he was in no mood to be reasoned with.

This was going to happen and there was nothing he could do or say to avoid it.

He looked over at Kershaw. His skin had taken on a waxy appearance and his chest was hardly rising at all.

"I wouldn't bother about him," said Ali. "He's going to live a lot longer than you.

Your time's come, big man."

Clive knew that to be able to save Kershaw, he was going to have to deal with Ali first.

As he got to his feet, Ali stepped back and flipped the jo into the air, catching it with both hands, the weapon looking for all the world as if it were a part of him, an extension of his own body.

The way Ali moved was an art in itself.

Front foot followed by the back foot, front then back, always perfectly balanced, moving with all the stealth of a big cat, stalking its prey. All the time he was moving, he was covering his body, ensuring that there was never a gap for Clive to try and leap in to disarm him.

With every step that Ali took towards him, Clive had no choice but to move back.

He knew what Ali's strategy was; to get him up against a wall or in a corner and then finish it. Clive's only chance was to get the weapon away from him before it reached that stage. He knew he was going to be hurt, but there was no other way.

Kershaw was slipping in and out of consciousness, when he caught sight of the two figures a few yards away from him. It took a moment or two for what he was seeing to sink in, but when it did finally register, he could see that Clive was in trouble.

If Ali was as good as Clive said he was, then there was a very real possibility that neither of them would be leaving, unless he helped out.

He spotted the razor that had caused him so much damage, no more than a yard away from where he was sitting. He felt so weak, that even the simple act of leaning over and picking it up with his good arm was a struggle.

With the razor in his hand, all he had to do now was to crawl over to where the outcome of this whole mess was being contested.

CHAPTER THIRTY-THREE

Ali moved the jo to his left, leaving the right side of his body exposed. Seizing his opportunity, Clive stepped in, realising too late that it was a feint.

Very nearly as fast as a speeding bullet, Ali brought the staff around behind him and struck Clive on his right arm just above the elbow.

The pain was excruciating and Clive knew, without having to look down, that his arm was broken. Determined not to give Ali the satisfaction of knowing how much pain he was in, Clive remained silent, but Ali could see it in his eyes.

Smiling cruelly, he moved forward, Clive moving back, his right arm hanging useless by his side.

Knowing Ali as he did, Clive guessed that evil streak in him would guide him towards his left arm; he'd like to break that one as well. If that happened, Clive knew he'd be finished. It was no use running and besides, that wasn't his style.

He had a plan. He'd offer up his left arm and then use his shoulder to protect himself.

When Ali attacked, he'd be close enough to grab him. He just had to hope that his one good arm would be enough.

For Kershaw, every movement he made sent shockwaves of pain through his arm.

He had to make sure that he kept the razor away from the floor. If Ali heard it scraping on the concrete, it would be curtains for both of them.

He had to hold the razor in his left hand, using his damaged right arm to support himself. Every time he placed his hand on the floor, he left a bloody palm print behind, but he was getting closer all the time.

He would have loved to have been able to stand, but he didn't think that he had the strength and anyway, there was less chance of Ali spotting him, the lower down he was.

He saw Ali's first strike and he too, could tell from the position of Clive's arm, that the limb was broken. He was going to have to get a move on, before Ali broke any more of the big man's bones.

Clive reached out with his left hand, as if making a grab for the jo. He couldn't move in any closer, without risking a blow to the head, which would undoubtedly prove fatal.

Ali repeated his previous move, but in reverse, bringing the staff around behind him and attacking from his right side. He was aiming for Clive's left arm, but at the last moment, Clive turned, dipping down slightly and the jo struck him across the back.

The pain took his breath away, but the weapon was within his grasp. He made a grab for it, but Ali was too fast for him, stepping back and raising the staff above his head, out of Clive's reach.

Taking a backward step put him within range of Kershaw and putting all his weight on his injured arm, which very nearly caused him to black out, Kershaw lashed out.

He was surprised at how easily the razor cut through the thick denim material of Ali's jeans and sliced through his calf muscle.

Jumping in the air, Ali cried out and turned towards Kershaw, fury in his eyes.

At the same time, Clive leapt in and swung his left fist with all his might, catching Ali on the side of the head. He was out cold before he hit the floor.

Kershaw collapsed onto the floor, completely exhausted and Clive knelt down by his side. He wasn't feeling too dapper himself, but Kershaw looked like a ghost.

Clive checked his pulse. It was still there, but it was very weak. Ripping the dry sleeve off of Kershaw's shirt, he bundled it up and placed it over the wound, then placed Kershaw's other hand on top of it, for more pressure.

"You stay with me, boy. Do you hear? These scumbags can take care of themselves," he said, looking around him. "We've got to get you to hospital."

Clive had his foot on the first step, on his way to collecting his belongings, when he heard sirens in the distance. If they were coming here, Angela must have told them, he thought to himself. Good girl! He just hoped that there was an ambulance on its way as well.

Dunn had had the foresight to call for an ambulance en route, although it didn't take a brain surgeon to deduce that if there was a fight and French was involved, first aid would undoubtedly be on the agenda.

Clive had just reached the bottom of the stairs with his holdall when the door burst open and two uniformed officers rushed in, Dunn and Moreton, hot on their heels.

The Inspector was trying to make sense of the sight that greeted him, when he was bundled aside by Angela, who ran over to Kershaw.

"Where's that ambulance?" she called out, after checking Kershaw's vital signs.

There was more than a hint of panic in her voice.

"Don't worry, it's right behind us," Dunn reassured her.

As the Inspector walked across the floor towards French, who was now sitting up, two more uniformed officers entered the building, followed by Sergeant Ryder.

Dunn stood in front of French and smiled down at him. His cheek was cut and swollen, as was his jaw and he was cradling his broken wrist.

"Had a bad day, have we?" asked the Inspector, sounding extremely pleased.

French glared up at him. Even if he hadn't have been in such a sorry state, with seven Police officers inside the warehouse, he wouldn't have gotten very far, anyway.

"Fuck you!" he snapped.

Just then, two paramedics ran into the building. Dunn nodded across at Kershaw.

"Get him to the hospital," he told them. "The rest are coming with us. And take her with you," he shouted.

He looked back down at French.

"Peter French, I'm arresting you for the murder of Penny Marshall. You do not have to say anything, but what you do say can and will be used against you in a court of law."

"Oh, joy," he muttered to himself, as he wandered away, leaving French to the uniformed officers.

Ali was sitting on the floor, having recovered from Clive's monstrous left hook and was using his belt to manufacture a tourniquet, in an effort to stem the bleeding from his calf.

"Alistair Simmonds, I'm arresting you for the murder of Andrew Parkin and for the murder of Alex Macarthy, who, in case you're interested was the name of the man whose neck you broke in the car park of the swan."

Ali didn't seem in the least bit concerned in what Dunn was saying, he only had eyes for Clive, who was walking across the floor of the building, his holdall in his left hand, having used his jacket as a sling for his broken right arm.

"You think this is over, big man? Believe me, it's only just begun," he promised.

The Inspector watched as the two paramedics carried Kershaw out of the building on a stretcher, followed by a very concerned looking Angela.

"I thought I told you to stay in the car," he said, reproachfully, as she passed by.

Angela didn't speak, she just stuck her tongue out at him.

"Kids, eh, Sir?" said Moreton, grinning. He was much more relaxed now, happy in the knowledge that he wouldn't be mixing it with French the gangster, or Simmonds the assassin.

Dunn glared at him. "Shut up!" he snapped. He turned to Clive, standing a couple of feet away. "Looks like you've had a fun morning."

Clive smiled. "Yeah, but all things considered, I'd rather have been somewhere else."

Dunn glanced across at the beached Errol, still out cold.

"What the Hell is that?" he asked.

"He certainly is a big one, isn't he?" said Clive, watching as Dunn knelt down and put his hand to Errol's neck.

The Inspector stood up and held out the dart. "This something to do with you, is it?"

Clive smiled, sheepishly and took the dart from off of him.

"There's another one outside, Jack," said Ryder, from behind.

Clive suddenly remembered Eddie. "He's with me. I'll get him out of here."

Dunn's voice took on a more serious note. "I'm going to need to know what went on here."

Clive nodded and indicated his broken arm. "Let me get this seen to and I'll get back to you, okay?"

That seemed to satisfy Dunn, who turned round to watch French and Ali being escorted out of the building.

"Just out of interest," he called out, as Clive was nearing the door. "Who did all the damage to French, you or the kid?"

"The boy's a fighter," said Clive, as if that answered the Inspector's question.

Dunn's expression was grave. "As he's the reason that French is going to prison, he'll need to be."

Moreton looked horrified. "Are you letting him go, Sir?" he asked, referring to Clive.

Dunn stared at the young detective and was about to remind him who was in charge, when he spotted French, handcuffed, being marched out of the building.

He smiled sweetly at Moreton. "I've got what I want. My day's complete."

Outside, Clive squatted down next to Eddie. The giant had blood splattered all over his shirt and there was bruising around both his eyes, from his broken nose.

He was looking very sorry for himself. Clive patted him gently on the shoulder.

"Don't take it to heart," he said, in an effort to console him.

"You were beaten by one of the best. In fact, you'd probably have had more success fighting the invisible man."

He helped Eddie to his feet. "We'd best go and get ourselves patched up," suggested Clive.

Eddie stopped. "What about Bobby?" he asked, looking concerned.

"He's in a bad way," replied Clive, deciding not to sugar coat things. "But I'm sure he'll pull through. He put French away though. There's more to that boy than meets the eye."

The following morning, Clive was at the hospital, when he bumped into Angela, on duty, in the corridor.

"I just tried to get into see Bob, but he's not receiving visitors."

"He needs rest," said Angela, in her capacity as an angel of mercy. "Give him a day or two and he'll be fine. You can see him then."

He smiled down at her. "Are we friends now?" he asked.

Angela stood on tiptoe and kissed him on the cheek. "Thank you."

Clive tapped the cast over his right arm, that he'd had put on yesterday.

"I've got some thanking of my own to do. If it wasn't for Bob, I might not be here now."

"Well, you can pop in tomorrow. I'm sure he'll be glad to see you."

Clive looked thoughtful for a moment. "I wonder if you could do me a favour.

Could you give him a message?"

Kershaw opened his eyes, to find himself staring up at a white ceiling. To his left was a green, metal chair and to his right, another chair, but with Angela sitting on it, reading a magazine.

"Hi there," he said, his voice croaky.

Angela looked up from her magazine and smiled at him. "Hello, nice to have you back."

"Where have I been?" he asked, surprised at how husky his voice sounded.

"I don't know, but wherever it was, you've been there for almost twenty four hours."

Kershaw looked surprised.

"You were very lucky. If we hadn't have got you here when we did, you might not be talking to me now. You lost an awful lot of blood."

"Whose we?"

"The Police brought you here." Angela saw him tense at the mention of the word Police.

"Don't worry," she said, calming him down. "They know the whole story. Who's responsible for what and who did what to whom. They know that you're innocent."

Kershaw lay his head back on the pillow and let out a heavy sigh of relief, glad that it was over.

"I'm going to have to pop out in a minute. They asked me to let them know when you came round. They said that they had a couple of questions to ask you."

"I thought they might," he said, a resigned tone to his voice.

"When can I get out of here?" he asked.

"The doctor says that you need a couple more days rest, then you can go home, if you are going home, that is." Angela looked at him expectantly.

"What come back with you, you mean?"

"Well, you'll need looking after, have you're dressing changed, a sensible diet."

"Bed bath?" he asked, hopefully.

"If you're a good boy," said Angela, grinning wickedly.

Kershaw tried to smile, but his split lip prevented him. Looking down, he could see his swollen cheek and now that he was onto the subject of pain, his shoulder felt sore and a little tight.

"Did I have any stitches?"

Angela nodded. "Twenty. You're going to have a very impressive scar."

She leant over and kissed him on the forehead. "I'd better go and do my duty and let the Police know that you're awake."

She was almost at the door, when she turned around. "I saw Clive earlier. He tried to get in to see you, but you weren't allowed any visitors. He said he'd pop in tomorrow, but he asked me to give you a message. It sounds a little cryptic, but he said that you'd understand."

Kershaw sat up, waiting.

"He said that he's added your name to his list. Does that make any sense to you?"

When he realised that Clive was referring to the list of men that he'd stand aside for, Kershaw felt a lump of pride in his throat. For a moment, he was unable to speak, so he just nodded.

"Yes, it does," he said, finally finding his voice.

Angela smiled. In her uniform, with her red hair, green eyes and baby freckles Kershaw was looking forward to going home with her.

He wasn't fully asleep, but dozing, when he heard the door open. He found himself looking at two men, one short and thickset, the other tall and thin, which he guessed were the Police.

"Hello son, how are you feeling?" asked the Inspector pleasantly

"Yeah, I'm fine," replied Kershaw, guardedly.

Dunn held out his warrant card. "I'm Chief Inspector Dunn and this is Detective Moreton. Seems like you've had a hectic couple of days, although credit where credit's due you managed to stay one step ahead of us, even though we had half the Met out looking for you."

Dunn held up his palms, when he saw the worried look in Kershaw's eyes

"We know the whole story, so you haven't got too much to sweat about. There is one thing that we need to know. Where are the diamonds'?"

Kershaw was mystified as to why the Policeman should be asking him that question.

"French has got them, hasn't he?"

Dunn shook his head, a look of disappointment on his face. "I'm afraid not. What Penny Marshall gave to him was paste. The real diamonds haven't surfaced yet."

CHAPTER THIRTY-FOUR

Nobody spoke for a few moments, then Dunn pulled an envelope out of his inside pocket.

"Penny slipped this under the door of your flat, obviously under the impression that you were still staying there."

He handed it to Kershaw, who opened it and began reading.

He knew from what Ali had said, that Penny had grown fond of him, but in the letter, she'd opened up her heart to him. He felt choked. Choked that he hadn't found this letter sooner; choked that he hadn't got to her before French.

The Inspector interrupted his train of thought.

"As you can see, she said that she'd made arrangements. You wouldn't happen to know what those arrangements were, I suppose?"

Kershaw shook his head. The Inspector's stern expression didn't change.

"Honestly," pleaded Kershaw. "I haven't seen Penny since I was in her house that night and I've never set eyes on the diamonds and I don't want to.

It's because of them that I've lost two people who I care about and my life has been turned upside down."

Dunn wasn't looking best pleased. "That means there's nigh on three million pounds worth of diamonds floating around somewhere and George Marshall's going apeshit. He wants them back, understandable, under the circumstances, I suppose."

"What's going to happen to me?" asked Kershaw, dreading the Inspector's reply.

"Well, seeing as you're partly responsible for French spending the rest of his life behind bars, we owe you. Of course, there's the assault on a Police officer that took place outside his flat."

Kershaw knew that was a serious offence and his heart began to sink.

"Did he identify himself as a Police officer, before the assault took place?" asked Dunn.

"Well, actually, he was waving his warrant card in my face, at the time," admitted Kershaw.

"No, you're not hearing me," said Dunn. "He didn't identify himself as a Police officer, did he?"

Kershaw realised what the Inspector was saying.

"Thinking back, no, he didn't."

Dunn nodded. "We'll gloss over that one, then. As for the robbery, you didn't actually take anything and as Penny Marshall invited you to the house and left she door unlocked, technically, it's not breaking and entering, more like trespass.

George Marshall still has a sore nose and his French doors have been reduced to firewood, but unfortunately, that's out of our hands. If he wants to make a complaint, there's not a lot we can do to stop him. However, with a few words in the right ears, you'll probably end up with a suspended sentence.

I don't think that you've got too much to worry about."

Kershaw felt his heart beginning to resurface.

"I'm just glad that it's all over," he said, sounding relieved.

"We will need to take a full statement, but until then..." The Inspector held out his hand.

Kershaw was a little taken aback. After all that had happened, the last thing he expected was to be shaking the hand of a Policeman.

The Inspector's grip was firm and he wasn't letting go.

"I'm not going to see you in a couple of weeks, riding around in a Rolls Royce, after having just got back from a holiday in the Bahamas, am I?" asked Dunn.

Kershaw guessed that this was a reference to the diamonds.

"Not unless I win the lottery," he replied.

After the two Policemen had left, Kershaw lay back and closed his eyes.

He thought of Andy and knew that he was going to miss his chubby, smiling face.

Then he thought of Penny and how different things could have been, if only...

Angela suddenly appeared in his mind's eye and he knew that he was coming out of all of this with more than he deserved.

Two days later he was sitting on the sofa in Angela's lounge, enjoying a bowl of chicken soup that she had made for him. Russell was perched at his feet, hoping to be given the bowl to lick out.

Walking in, Angela shooed him away and sat in the armchair.

"So what are you going to do now?" she asked, as he finished his soup and placed the bowl on the tray next to him, much to Russell's disgust, who snorted and curled up in his basket.

Kershaw thought about for a second. "I suppose the first thing to do would be to go down to the warehouse and see if I still have a job."

"I don't see why not," said Angela, getting out of the armchair and picking up his tray.

"You've only been away a week and it's not as if you've been found guilty of anything."

"Only a week? It seems a lot longer than that."

Angela stood by the door and nodded to indicate his shoulder. "We should change that dressing."

"Didn't you mention something about a bed bath?"

"Have you been a good boy?" asked Angela, a mischievous twinkle in her eye.

"You bet!" replied Kershaw.

The following morning, Kershaw walked into the warehouse to find that he had become something of a minor celebrity. It seemed that everyone wanted to shake his hand and on more than one occasion, someone tried to clap him on the shoulder, but he managed to stop them in time, explaining that he was still a little sore.

After being told by the umpteenth person, how glad they were to see him, he turned and almost bumped into Eddie.

He had a dressing across his nose and all around his eyes was the colour of aubergines.

"Eddie, how are you?"

"I'm okay," he boomed and pointed to his nose. "Except for this."

"Yeah, Clive popped in to see me in hospital. He said that you had a run in with Simmonds."

The big man looked embarrassed. "I wanted to rip his head off and shit down his neck, for what he did to Andy. Clive warned me, but I wasn't listening. I never got anywhere near him. I hear you did a job on French, though. That took some doing."

Kershaw wasn't quite sure what to say. He wasn't used to playing the hero.

He smiled. "I was lucky to get out of there alive, in fact, I should never have gone in there in the first place. Clive tried to warn me, but I guess I wasn't listening, either."

Kershaw walked into the office and was greeted by the manager, Simon James.

He wasn't much older than Kershaw, but by his own admission, was destined for bigger and better things, the warehouse merely a stepping stone on his route to the top.

"Bob, good to see you," he said, with genuine warmth in his voice. "Sit down."

Simon sat on the edge of the desk, facing Kershaw.

"Everyone was really cut up about Andy, although it couldn't have been a picnic for you either."

"Yeah, well, I've had better days. What I really need to know is, do I still have a job here?" asked Kershaw, getting straight to the point. He was desperate to put the previous week's events behind him, going over them all again was the last thing he wanted.

Simon beamed. "Of course you do. You can start back tomorrow, if you want."

Kershaw pointed to his shoulder. "It's still a bit tender. How about next Monday?"

Simon nodded, enthusiastically. "Sure, no problem. Just glad to have you back."

They shook hands and Kershaw headed for the door, relived that his life was slowly beginning to return to normal.

"Oh, this came for you," said Simon.

Turning around, Kershaw saw that he was holding out a registered letter.

Sitting in Andy's car, Kershaw studied the envelope. It was hand written and addressed to him, but he didn't recognise the handwriting.

Tearing it open, he took out a single sheet of paper. As he unfolded it, a small key fell out onto his lap. Holding the key in one hand, he looked at the open sheet of paper.

What was written on it didn't make a lot of sense. P.M. R.K.BONJOUR.

It took him a couple of seconds to recognise his own initials and then those of Penny and finally, that the last word was French, but he still didn't understand what it meant.

He looked at the key. Engraved on one side was a number and on the other, the word U store. He'd seen it somewhere before and then he remembered that it was a storage warehouse on the other side of the estate.

Five minutes later, he was standing at a counter, across from an elderly man in blue overalls, with the U store logo on his chest pocket.

"Yes Sir, what can I do for you?" asked the assistant, politely.

"I've got a key," Kershaw replied, simply. He was unsure of the procedure and was hoping that the old man would take the lead.

"Number?" asked the assistant.

"Four one seven zero," said Kershaw, reading off of the key.

The assistant punched the digits into the computer on the counter and stared at the screen. After a few moments, the information that he was waiting for came up.

"The person who took out this box, left specific instructions that it was only to be opened upon receipt of a certain phrase."

The old man stared at Kershaw, expectantly.

"P.M. R.K. BONJOUR," said Kershaw, praying that was what the assistant was waiting to hear.

He checked the screen and nodded. "If you'd like to follow me."

He walked to the end of the counter and lifted a flap.

Kershaw was led down a corridor and into a room which contained a table and chair. "If you wait here, I'll bring you your box," said the assistant.

Waiting in the sparsely furnished room, Kershaw had an inkling as to what he would find in the box and his heart began to beat faster.

A few minutes later, the old man returned, carrying a metal container, about the size of a shoe box.

"Just give me a shout when you're finished," he told Kershaw and with that, he left, closing the door behind him.

Kershaw's fingers were trembling as he inserted the key and opened the box.

Inside was a plain brown envelope and small velvet pouch.

The moment he saw the bag, he knew what it contained. Even so, he still held his breath as he pulled the drawstring and tipped the pouch upside down on the table.

The diamonds scattered out onto the surface, twinkling and sparkling in the single light from above.

He stared at the jewels for a few moments, trying to get his head around the fact that he was staring at three million pounds. These were what had cost Penny and Andy their lives and had very nearly cost him his.

He opened the envelope and took out the note inside.

Bobby,

If you are reading this, then it means that something has happened to me.

I hope that you can forgive me for what I tried to do to you. I made a mistake, but I realised that mistake too late.

These diamonds are what all this was about. What you do with them is up to you. If you want to return them to my Father, watch out for Billy, he's not a very nice person. If you decide to keep them, I hope that they make you happy. I only wish that I could be there with you.

Please be careful. Do not underestimate Peter,
He is extremely dangerous.
I love you,
Penny.

Kershaw got the feeling that Penny knew something was going to happen to her, even while she was writing this letter. He could only imagine what she must have been feeling and the thought of her putting pen to paper, knowing what her fate was likely to be, brought a lump to his throat.

Regretfully, he put the letter back in the envelope, the diamonds back in the pouch and headed for the door.

Clive, Kershaw and Angela were sitting around her kitchen table, staring at the diamonds that Kershaw had just tipped out onto it.

He had experienced this moment earlier, so he wasn't mesmerized by the sparkling jewels, as were the other two.

Strange as it seemed, Kershaw was feeling a little disheartened.

Just when it appeared that his life was beginning to return to something resembling normality, these diamonds had turned it on its head once more.

Clive looked up, for all the world as if he'd just come out of a hypnotic trance.

"So what was the question again?" he asked.

"Should I keep them, or should I give them back?"

Kershaw was in need of some serious guidance.

"The Police told me that these had disappeared and Penny left me a note saying that she had made arrangements. I guess this was what she meant."

Clive was pondering Kershaw's question.

"Well, from what you've said, these diamonds would never have been found and even when the rental on the box ran out and it was opened, they still wouldn't know where they came from, or who they belonged to.

For all intents and purposes, these diamonds no longer exist."

Clive stared at Kershaw for a second. "But if I were you, I'd give them back, earn yourself a few brownie points."

Kershaw looked across at Angela. "What do you think?" he asked, looking for a second opinion.

Angela moved the diamonds around the table, singling one out with her index finger.

"I think this one would look nice in a ring."

CHAPTER THIRTY-FIVE

"When I say give them back, I mean most of them," said Clive.

Kershaw's eyebrows rose. Most?"

"Keep one for yourself. I'd say you've earnt it."

Kershaw picked up one of the diamonds and held it in his palm.

"How much would this be worth, then?" he asked.

"Going on what you've told me, about a hundred grand."

Kershaw gawped at the small fortune nestling in the centre of his hand.

"But won't Marshall notice that there's one missing?"

"I dare say he will, but I'm betting he'll only be too pleased to get nearly all of them back, rather than none at all."

Clive shrugged his shoulders. "If anyone asks, you don't know where it went."

Kershaw looked at Angela, a question in his eyes.

"If it wasn't for you, Marshall would never see those again," she said, clearly in agreement with Clive. "After all that's happened, I can't see him offering you a reward. You didn't steal them. Call it a finder's fee, if you like."

"I have to be honest, my reason for suggesting that you keep one, is purely mercenary," said Clive.

"I'm thinking of starting up my own company. I've got some capital to put into it and so have you now, if you're interested, that is."

"What sort of company?"

"Security. The sort of stuff that I'm doing at the moment, but instead of working for someone else, I, we, will be working for ourselves. What do you think?"

Kershaw felt privileged that Clive would want to consider him as a partner.

"I don't know the first thing about that sort of work."

"That's alright. You'll learn as you go."

All Kershaw wanted was to get his life back to normal, but did he really want to spend the rest of it unloading cans of baked beans and packets of washing powder? He found the idea of working with Clive alluring.

"What about you? You want to join us?" asked Clive, looking over the table at Angela.

"Me?"

"Why not? Anyone who can take Alistair out with a fr...a wok, is someone I'd want on my team and you're as much a part of all that's happened as we are, whether you like it or not."

Kershaw looked at her and gently nudged her elbow. "Go on," he urged, having made up his mind to agree to Clive's proposal.

"It'll be neat."

"Let me think about it," she replied.

Two weeks later, Kershaw was in the cemetery, standing in front of Penny's headstone.

He had read her obituary in the newspaper, but hadn't gone to her funeral, deciding that it would be wise to stay away.

He had attended Andy's though. With Angela by his side, it had gone as well as any funeral could. He'd bumped into Clare, who told him that she no longer held him directly responsible for Andy's death, but he could tell that she thought, had it not been for him, Andy would still be alive.

Kershaw didn't need her to tell him that and he was grateful that Angela was there with him. She held his hand tightly throughout the service, as if she were experiencing his sadness.

Back in the cemetery, try as he may, he was unable to conjure up in his mind's eye an image of Penny, which saddened him. He knew that he would never forget her.

She had altered his life forever, altered him, made him into a different person.

He silently paid his respects and walked away.

This whole sorry affair wasn't over yet and wouldn't be, for quite some time.

There was French's trial to attend, which he wasn't looking forward to.

Then there was his own trial, although, when he'd made a full statement, Inspector Dunn had again reassured him that he didn't have too much to worry about, even less so since he'd returned the diamonds.

As yet, he hadn't heard anything, but he was half expecting a visit from George Marshall and his tame chimp, Billy, demanding to know where the missing jewel was, but he wasn't unduly concerned about that.

His main concern now was in getting the business up and running, Clive had acquired them their first assignment, a private party at a hotel in the West End.

With his contacts, Clive had assured Kershaw that there would be no shortage of work and tonight should be the beginning of a lucrative career, for all three of them.

Angela had agreed to come along. She still wasn't absolutely sure that she wanted to give up nursing, but she was prepared to give it a go.

Walking out of the cemetery gates, Kershaw made his way to Andy's Mazda, which was parked a little way down the road.

Coming towards him were two lads, each with a can of beer in their hands and it was pretty evident that it wasn't their first.

A month ago, if he had seen these two coming towards him, he would have crossed over to the other side of the road and kept his head down and his eyes averted.

Things were different now. As the gap closed and they could see that he was staring straight at them, they stopped laughing.

Kershaw felt sure that they were going to try something, in fact, part of him hoped that they would.

At the last moment, one stepped off of the pavement and into the gutter.

Kershaw's shoulder collided with the other one, knocking him into the hedge, the half full can of beer falling out of his hand and onto the floor.

Kershaw stopped and looked back at him. The youth appeared to be about to say something, then thought better of it.

Disentangling himself from out of the hedge, he caught up with his pal and they carried on walking. Something had told them that this was someone that they shouldn't be messing with.

On this occasion they were right.